Juha
LAST OF THE
ERRANT KNIGHTS

Written by
Mustapha Kamal
Translated by
Jack Briggs
Illustrated by
Farwaz Arnawut

Previously published with the
support and encouragement of

EPPCO

MOTIVATE
PUBLISHING

Foreword

I have been attracted to the Arabic language throughout my 50 years in the Middle East, but to arrive at a level of ability where I could read and enjoy Arabic literature, whether classical or modern, has been a long, slow process. So when I read Mustapha Kamal's *Juha, Last of the Errant Knights*, I was quite fascinated by this mythical story which previously had only been known to me as orally transmitted tales. I enjoyed it so much when it first appeared as a serialised story in *Al Bayan* newspaper that I wanted to make it available to people who couldn't read the Arabic.

Mustapha Kamal, a writer and journalist of considerable standing, kindly agreed for me to translate it, and I very much hope that Juha gives as much pleasure to those who read about him here, as he has given to me.

I would like to dedicate this book to the memory of Jack Humphreys, a person, like Juha, of great understanding and tolerance.

Jack Briggs

Published by **Motivate Publishing**
PO Box 2331, Dubai, UAE, Tel 824060, Fax 824436
PO Box 43072, Abu Dhabi, UAE, Tel 271666, Fax 271888
Macmillan House, 96 Kensington High Street, London W8 4SG
Tel 071 937 7733, Fax 071 937 7293.

Directors: Obaid Humaid Al Tayer & Ian Fairservice. Editor: Julia Roles.

Introduction

I do not claim that I am the author of this story, for it is an episode from the tales of my grandmother, which were told to me many years ago, and which became so entangled in my imagination that I am unable to tell whether it was my imagination which was affected by the tales or the tales which were affected by my imagination.

I used to ask her to repeat them, and every time she retold her stories she would add to them or change them, insisting each time that that was how she had heard them from her grandmother, in the days when the world was different from this world and people were other than today's people.

It may even be that I, in my turn, have gone along the same lines as my grandmother, and added things and omitted others. But the honour of having composed them remains hers, and the memory of her charm will never leave me.

Mustapha Kamal

First published in Arabic by Al Bayan Press 1990
Reprinted 1999

ISBN 1 873544 09 X

Printed by Rashid Printers & Stationers L.L.C., Ajman, UAE

4

Chapter 1

There is probably no need to introduce Juha to whoever reads this book, for Juha is a well-known and famous name in most corners of the Islamic world as the hero of numerous adventures, humorous stories and fables. People have passed on the droll tales of him from generation to generation but rarely has anyone written about him. Countries have vied with each other on the subject of his name with each trying to associate him with its own soil. For there are those who say that he was born and lived in Syria and those who affirm that he was a Yemeni or a Hadhrami from the south. In Iraq, Turkey, Iran and Bukhara they say that he is indeed the same Khuja Nasruddin whose life story has been passed on for generations, whilst the Egyptians persist in ascribing him to their country and insist that he is an Egyptian, father to son and that it is possible that he can be traced right back to Khufu, who built the big pyramid.

In Afghanistan, near the Khyber Pass, there is a long established stream known as 'The Stream of Juha', whilst close to it there is an old, abandoned garden named 'Juha's Garden', and nearby is a mountain track which leads behind the frontier and which is still known as 'Juha's Path'. It's generally thought that Juha lived in all these countries, spending part of his life in each of them. But on each occasion he was forced to move away, either pursued and leaving against his will, or continuously seeking the unknown, looking for yet another adventure to drive away the boredom and dullness of life. For Juha Nasruddin was a great traveller and explorer. He would no sooner settle in a place than he would migrate again. But he was also a fine agitator, unable to remain silent about any injustice, whatever the station in life of the tyrant might be. And the tyrants in those days, whether the Mamluks of Egypt or the Khans, lords of Khurasan, had tremendous ability in tyranny and oppression, as a result of which Juha lived a life of continuous pursuit and his head was wanted in at least seven capitals of that period.

Then, in an insane adventure, in which the other party was the Khan of Samarkand, Juha won the heart of Julshan, the most beautiful slave-girl of the Khan himself — or perhaps it was Julshan who captured his heart. Whichever way it was, Juha married her and fled with her from Samarkand, pursued by a full regiment of troops and dozens of spies along the whole length of the way.

The days passed, whilst Juha was still at his familiar game, never ceasing from travel or looking for things to do. Julshan, on the other hand, was prolific in child bearing and in less than ten years she had produced seven sons and daughters. And with every son or daughter came a new worry for Juha. But even more than these worries was the burden which was placed by the restriction on his movements. Also, Julshan's tongue became sharper as the burden of the children increased, especially when she began to press for her husband to settle and remain at peace.

* * * * * *

Finally, the day came when time allied itself to Julshan and Juha's legs became too heavy to answer his permanent, perpetual and burning demand for revolution. His heart had become too delicate to refuse Julshan's pleas when one day he surprised her whilst they were at a crossroads where one road led to Jazawand and the other to Nahawand.

"Julshan, my dear, the time has come for us to end the days of travel and exploration, whilst only a little remains, my flower, of life, and I wish to spend this little time in reflection and consideration of the secrets of existence itself."

Julshan cried out, unbelievingly, with pleasure: "Praise be to God, can I take it that you have come to your senses?"

Juha said: "My donkey has got old and he is no longer capable..."

But she interrupted him smartly as if her sharp tongue did not want to let an opportunity slip: "Indeed, you say that you have got old — what has your donkey got to do with it?"

Juha smiled, preferring peace: "Let it be that I have grown old, my bride, but you, you will never grow old, you are still just as you were when I saw you for the first time in the palace of the Khan, with the same youthfulness, the same vigour."

6

A bright smile clothed the face of Julshan. She stretched out her hand, gently touching the locks of her hair as if in reproval of the white hairs which it contained. Then the tension in her voice was lowered and she asked, whispering, as if she was afraid that the children might hear her: "But where do you want us to take up residence?"

"In Jazawand, naturally."

But the words were hardly out of his mouth before he was regretting his haste. He ought really, if he wanted to go to Jazawand, to have suggested the other road to give free rein to her customary obstinacy when she would choose, entirely of her own will, Jazawand, and he would submit to her wishes. She would be very happy with her victory and he would also be happy in obtaining exactly what he wanted. For thus had his experience with Julshan taught him over the years, but it was too late, and Juha upbraided himself, silently saying: "Woe to that tongue when it precedes your thoughts, one of these days it will lead you to your grave".

And the voice of Julshan raised sharply, like that of a wounded bird: "What sort of a place is that which you wish to settle down in. I could not possibly stand the clamour and the din of the mad life which the people of Jazawand live".

Juha had no inclination to enter into a long argument. Whatever reasons he might put forward, they would never satisfy Julshan. Also Juha believed in the proverb which says, "Whoever argues with his wife about empty and full will expire before his time."

Thus did Juha raise the flag of surrender and set off, with his wife and seven children, on the backs of the three donkeys, towards Nahawand, as he said with a sigh: "I know Nahawand well, it's a very quiet place, surrounded by streams and vineyards, whilst the bulk of the population are old people, well on in years, who have no concern except to wait for death in a beautiful place."

* * * * * *

Nahawand was not, in those days, the great city which was known in the days of the first Abassid State. Then one of the most important centres of commerce, a meeting point for the great caravans and a market of constant movement and clamour, it had dwindled in size and its status had decreased so that today it was a sleepy little town by day as well as by night. In it there were only nine or ten shops, well scattered on all sides, whilst its streets, gliding through the vineyards, were practically empty of passers-by. It was surrounded by high mountains from the slopes of which descended hundreds of small streams, which watered the ground and quenched the thirst of the people.

Indeed, Nahawand was a small paradise, a retreat to which hundreds of retired judges, learned men of religion and retired servants of the state were drawn in the hope that they could spend what was left of their lives in the arms of that peaceful residence. Certainly the number of old people in Nahawand was extraordinarily great, so much so that a man might believe that it was — by today's standards — an open refuge for those with bent backs and white beards. And the people of Nahawand were extremely happy in the grace of God's blessings upon them and spent their time in prayer in praise of God for his graces and asking for his peace and goodwill.

Only one person in Nahawand thought differently from the others. If he prayed he praised God, but only because no one other than He could be praised for a reprehensible matter and he was always depressed and despondent. His mouth never loosened to a smile, unless it be to a smile of bitterness, he never mixed with anyone nor did he permit anyone to mix with him. His face was obscured by a large thick beard through which scarcely anything of his features appeared, whilst the ends of his turban were hanging down so that they practically covered his eyes. He became, by his strange appearance, an object of ridicule to the small number of youths of Nahawand. Many times he used to hear them, on his way to and from the 'masjid', describing him as 'the owl, herald of ill-omen'. Then he would shake his head in bitterness and keep moving, looking down at the ground between his feet as if he were reading the pages of a book. It had been the custom of the people of Nahawand for many years to check the past of a person when he came to live there amongst them and finally they came to know that he was previously a tax-collector who had come there to live after he had retired and that his name was Al Haj Abdussabur. But it never crossed the mind of a single one of them that the eccentric old man was Juha himself whose feats had long been discussed amongst them — round the fire during the winter evenings and on top of the mountains in the summer.

There was no end to Juha's misery and his anguish from his lot where he had ended up. Many times did he look at his white donkey, so favoured by him, and which had, for so long, accompanied him on his journeys and adventures, to note that he had become fat, pot-bellied and dull-witted from too much idleness. The pain and sorrow at his situation increased with the deadly boredom, practically making him take leave of his senses. He would lift his eyes to the heavens, praying for something to happen in which would be his salvation.

As for Julshan, well, she was alarmed, at first, by his squirming and dejection at being settled down, but it wasn't long before she became satisfied that the spark of rebellion had disappeared, indeed, had been extinguished under the pressure of time and seven children.

Every evening Juha would leave the mosque after the dinner prayers, but he did not go home. Instead, he turned his face towards the eastern gate of the town, overlooking the old caravan route, where he would spend his evening in a coffee-shop which was by far the smallest coffee-shop in the length of the track which crossed Asia from East to West. Nobody frequented it except robbers, highwaymen and beggars and he would sit there, facing the faraway, eastern star, whilst every shred of his emotions would be begging for some unforeseen happening to release him from stagnation. Perhaps one of the caravans would bring news of an event which would cause a wave on the still waters. But every day passed, as the previous one, with nothing new.

And Juha remained sitting in his isolated spot, some distance from the other customers of the coffee-shop, and his eyes never moved from the eastern star until the coffee-shop had emptied and only he remained. Then he would rise heavily to his feet, pay for the cup of coffee he had had and turned away to return to his home.

However, he never forgot to put out his hand with some small change as alms and drop them into the lap of the deaf, dumb and blind beggar who had made his station on the threshold of an old, abandoned mosque, most of which had been in ruins for hundreds of years.

* * * * * *

Until one day ...

Juha drew his gown around him, after the coffee-shop had emptied of all but its owner, and paid for his coffee. And he walked with a heavy step in the empty street, moving along discontentedly and without hope. As usual, he did not forget the deaf, dumb and blind beggar, and he automatically put his hand in the pocket of his gown, brought out the usual small coin and threw it into the lap of the beggar as he had done a thousand times before. But he had hardly taken another step after he had tossed the coin when he heard a voice whisper, in a clear tone, as if it were in his very ear: "Do not worry oh Juha, do not worry, God's release from suffering is at hand, should He so will."

Juha whipped round in fear, as if he had been bitten by a snake. For to be called here, by his true name, was the disaster of all disasters, especially as the spies of the Khan were everywhere. The town-criers of the seven states were still passing through the market-places, calling for his head, valued at ten thousand dirhams, in full. But he couldn't see anyone. There was nobody there in the moonlight except the deaf, dumb and blind beggar. He stopped for a moment while his eyes passed all around him. Not even the closed windows were missed by his troubled eyes. Finally he realised that there was no one there who was speaking to him or calling his name and that the voice undoubtedly came from within himself, expressing a dear hope which he had long craved but which had not been realised. But, before he could carry on his passage, the voice came again, this time with even more apprehension and in words which practically shed tears: "I entreat you, oh Master, hear me — allow me to talk to you."

Juha almost lost his senses with astonishment. For the person who had spoken was the deaf, dumb and blind beggar and he went towards him with hesitant steps whilst hardly able to believe himself. Indeed, he had already poked his thigh with his finger to make certain that he wasn't dreaming. The fact that the dumb man had spoken was not what had alarmed him — for that was a trick which many beggars resorted to — the calamity was how did this man know his secret? Juha stood in front of the beggar, bewildered as to what he should say or do. And it was as if the beggar had realised what was going on in his mind and he began to talk quickly.

10

"There is no call to be distressed, oh Juha, for nobody here knows your secret except me. By the Lord, calm yourself and listen to me for I have need of you for an important matter."

"What is this important matter in which you wish to involve me? And why has this matter become serious tonight only? Why did you not take the matter up with me before now whilst I have been passing by you every evening for more than four years?"

The beggar tugged at the back of Juha's gown in order to stand upright, saying: "Come with me to a safer place — fear nothing — I shall answer every question which you ask, only I beg of you to calm yourself and be reassured." There was something in the man's voice which evoked all Juha's tendency to sympathy and there was something else, something that made him feel reassured about him.

* * * * * *

The beggar led his companion to the inside of the abandoned mosque — in the moonlight they passed through the courtyard to a passage and, at the end of the passage, the beggar put out his hand, feeling at the wall. Suddenly it opened like the cave of Ali Baba. They had hardly gone inside when Juha heard the wall close behind him. The two were enveloped in darkness so that Juha could barely see the sleeve of his gown. But Juha was not afraid; indeed, he could hardly restrain himself from excess of curiosity; whatever was this man up to?

The man struck a flint with which he lit an oil lamp, which produced more smoke than light, but it was enough for him to see the place wherein he was contained.

* * * * * *

The place was like a room but without a window or a door. It had a stone floor and where the coating of its walls had been eaten away, the old building stones appeared. Time had also worn them away and the cracks between them were so wide that a man could put his arm in them right to the armpit.

There was no furniture in the room — which Juha guessed had

11

probably been some kind of a prison for one of the enemies of the Sultan, the founder of the mosque — except the remains of a palm-frond mat, the colour of the earth; a covered cooking pot and another open cooking pot, half full of water, which the man most likely used to use for both drinking and the ritual ablution before prayer. There was also an old basket, hanging by a nail in the wall.

The beggar stretched out his hand and took a dry loaf of bread from the basket whilst indicating to Juha that he should take his place on the delapidated mat. He sat down whilst observing his comrade, waiting for him to begin the conversation.

But the man did not appear to be in any hurry. For, as soon as he was satisfied that Juha had seated himself, he sat himself down slowly beside him without uttering a word. He then began to break off the edges of the dry loaf into small pieces until he had a little pile of them in the palm of his hand. Then he threw them into a hole in the wall. Juha was surprised by a big rat coming out of the hole, followed by seven smaller rats which all surrounded the broken pieces of bread and devoured them in silence.

All this and the man was silent, not speaking at all. Indeed he was now watching the rats, wholly absorbed, until it appeared to Juha that he had forgotten him entirely. So he coughed lightly, so that perhaps he would become aware of his presence.

The man turned towards him and, for the first time, a smile appeared on his face.

"Will you look at those creatures, oh Juha, for God alone knows what sins they have committed through which they have descended to such a despicable form. Yet it is certain that the crime which I committed was of greater hideousness and was more abominable in the eyes of God. For this reason I believe that I shall return to this life the next time in the shape of a cockroach or even a worm. Nevertheless, it is within your power alone, oh Juha, to save me — by thy Lord oh Juha — oh you who have lived the whole of your life bringing justice to the oppressed against the oppressors — save me, I implore you."

And he dropped at the foot of Juha, attempting to kiss it in supplication, but the other pulled it away sharply, drew the wasted body of the beggar to him and said: "Indeed, it is I who implore you, my honest fellow, to get me out of this labyrinth into which you have thrown me. I promise you that I shall do all that is within my power in order to assist you. Only please, answer my questions, and tell me your story from the beginning, then put your trust in God."

＊ ＊ ＊ ＊ ＊ ＊

The man sighed sharply with his head bowed, then he began to speak in a strange voice and in words which Juha could almost see written on the wall of the closed room, in the shade of the small oil lamp.

"Know this, oh Juha, I belong to the Patience and Silence group and one of the traditions of this group is that the faithful of its members refrain from speaking for 364 days each year and are permitted to speak on one day only, from midnight until the cock crows." Juha knew quite a lot about the Patience and Silence group which was an ancient secret society.

Nobody knew exactly what the actual aims of the society were but each member was committed to various kinds of unbelievable ascetic and abstemious life. He also knew that this society believed in the reincarnation of souls and that a creature which devoted its life to the service of God and performed good deeds in its life would be promoted, on reincarnation, or being born again, to a higher rank amongst God's creatures. That scorpions, snakes and flies — for example — had been, in previous stages of their existence, human beings who committed such grievous sins as warranted their reduction to the lowest form of life, just as the human beings whom we see today have been, in previous lives, dogs or lions which had performed good deeds and deserved to be promoted to the human form, and so on. But this was the first time Juha had actually met one of the members of this strange society face to face.

The man continued with his story: "For more than ten years I have been following you like your shadow, waiting for the opportunity to speak to you, after a brother in the fraternity told me that my salvation would be through your hands. And after you settled here in Nahawand I observed you until I learned that you visited the coffee-shop every evening. When I took my stand along your path, awaiting the suitable moment. And all these years my ill-fated luck stood in the way of my being able to speak to you. Either something would prevent your daily visit to the coffee-shop or you would leave early before the appointed time for speech. Then last year, I was on the very point of speaking, but spotted the head-guard hiding behind a nearby pillar. He was watching some of the customers of the coffee-shop. But now, I praise God who made my patience worth while."

Juha said: "Hold fast, dear sir. Perhaps, if time allowed I would ask you more questions but I see that the night is moving fast and the cock will not be long before he crows. So permit me to suggest to you that you begin to tell me your story so that I may absorb it before the permitted time for speech passes when you will be compelled to silence for yet another full year."

The man replied, and in his voice was a ring of joy: "You are, then, longing to hear my story ... although I really wanted to explain to you the principle and objects of our society. Your true place is with us, oh Juha. You have lived your life, seeking redemption, you are already advanced in years, coming near to the end and you have not yet found the way to salvation. Your redemption, oh Juha, is in our hands."

In vain did Juha attempt to bring the man down to earth after he had begun what he had to say on the heavens and then went on to explain the order of the universe with great enthusiasm to Juha and how the life of mankind in the end, is nothing but a transient stage to a form of greater perfection and that the righteous man who has performed good deeds will be elevated in his following birth to the rank of diviner and later to the rank of cosmic man until he becomes one of the elite surrounding the highest throne.

But Juha was not prepared to listen to all these sermons from the old and undoubtedly pious man so he turned off the valves of his mind and tuned in to another station until when the man had finished his narrative, he said to him, very calmly: "I shall consider all that you have said and I will let you have my opinion by some gesture one day, but is this the important mission which you wanted me for? Then, how would it be within my power to rescue you from your decline to the level of the cockroaches and worms?"

The man said quickly: "That you should repair what I have corrupted. I have committed a grievous crime in respect of my people for I caused suffering and distress to descend upon them which was beyond the capacity of anyone to bear. It is up to you Juha to put matters to right. None other than you is capable of this. For I have studied the movements of the stars and meditated on the paths of the constellations and I found that..."

But Juha did not allow the man to go on to describe what he had discovered from the science of astronomy, and he hurriedly cut him off whilst still keeping his patience.

"I earnestly entreat you, by God, oh my dear sir, illustrious savant, that you should first tell me about your affair — what is the crime which you have committed and how can I, personally, correct it?"

The man bowed his head to the ground and sighed and when he raised it and his sunken eyes met the questioning eyes of Juha his beard was wet with tears and he said: "That is my problem — within me is a touch of the devil which pushes me towards my own destruction. Indeed, I know that time passes quickly and nevertheless I try to escape from relating details of my crime by proselytisation on behalf of the Society of Patience and Silence and talking about the constellations and the orbits of the stars."

Juha muttered in sympathy whilst patting the shoulder of the man; he could almost feel his bones: "Do not worry — do not worry — speak — my ears are wide open."

"This destructive touch inside me, that is what has brought me to this state. I was born to one of the richest of men — he was head of the merchant's guild in his state and he possessed unending and unlimited wealth. When God took him to be by his side to be reincarnated to a higher level, no doubt, I was about twenty years of age. He bequeathed me enormous sums from his wealth which I began to spend, indeed I threw it away without care and I was surrounded by a handful of evil people who swept me to the world of pleasure and lust. I became addicted to strong drink, women and a life of deceit and debauchery. In addition, I became addicted to gambling. I did not yet know my path to truth and, naturally, I knew nothing of the Patience and Silence Group. I was totally immersed in my pleasures, up to my ears, totally unaware of the fate which awaited me. Nor did I have any fears of exhausting my wealth for it was far too extensive to meet with a shortage. Whilst on the subject ..."

He rose from his position, and the two eyes of Juha never left him. Then he put out his hand to the basket which was hanging on the wall, and took from it an old leather bag and threw it in Juha's lap. "That is the money which you used to give me as alms every day — take it".

Juha said, refusing: "That is impossible, my friend, I will not take back alms which have been given by my own hand but you are able, in any case, to give it away, in your turn, to any person in need or even consider it a contribution, from me, to the Patience and Silence Group."

The man adjusted himself where he was sitting, put out his hand and began stroking his beard, saying: "I, personally, have a view about alms. For alms, I am certain, are of three kinds. The first kind ..."

Juha shouted out loud for he had almost lost his patience: "I beg of you, my venerable savant, leave the discussion about alms until later, until next year if you wish and if Allah allows us to live that long, but you have not yet told me exactly what it is that you want me to do."

"Indeed, indeed, this is true, here I go again, surrendering to that accursed folly, but I will now deal with the subject directly."

* * * * * *

"I told you that I had become addicted to gambling. I used to gamble in all its forms, backgammon, tossing stones, tossing shells and betting on anything. On that blackest of days, undoubtedly the darkest days of my entire life, I made an ill-fated bet with a man called Haji Agha. Amongst my properties was a sweet water spring in the mountains of Farghana with some hundreds of simple farmers living by the water of the well. Without making a long story of it, in one game of backgammon I lost the well to Haji Agha to whom I made out a bill of sale. But Haji Agha was a snake in the form of a man, for he began to sell the water to the farmers, drop by drop at the highest of prices until their condition was reduced to poverty and starvation and the extensive land which was irrigated by the spring, which had been like a part of heaven, became as a part of hell.

"Every year, with the advent of spring, the wails of the farmers reach my ears as they complain of the oppressive cost of the water which Haji Agha raises one year after the other until the price of the water almost equals the produce of the land. I wail and weep and my days become darker. I know well that God will answer the prayers of the oppressed and that he will surely punish Haji Agha and will reduce him to either a fly or a wall lizard. But he will also punish me. He will probably forgive me for all the sins that I have committed in respect of myself but he will never, ever forgive me for this terrible sin which I have committed in respect of my own people and reduced them by one toss of the dice, in one futile, mad moment, from prosperity to poverty, from free-born farmers to slaves of an accursed speckled snake by the name of Haji Agha".

Juha said: "And exactly what is required of me?"

"That you remove this snake from the spring, that you recover it from him, that the water should be returned to the farmers of the land at no cost."

The face of the man shone with tears and his voice trembled whilst he seized Juha by the collar, imploring him: "I ask you to swear oh Juha, by all that is dear to you, by your seven children, by your wife Julshan, by all the persons whom you have loved and by every pleasant moment which you have ever spent, that you will save me oh Juha, indeed, save my people, my subjects whom I have betrayed, sold their happiness for one game of backgammon."

Juha, who was moved by the words of the man, replied: "I swear that I will, at least I swear that I will try, but first tell me, where can I find him?"

But the lips of the recluse were sealed, as if a bar of molten iron had been placed across them and he began to look at the face of Juha from two eyes from which the light had disappeared, and all the shaking and shouting of Juha were without success in trying to make the man speak. From a distance the sound of a cock crowing came to the ears of Juha, greeting the dawn of a new day and Juha jumped up, infuriated with anger.

"And so, sir, my learned and pious man, my distinguished savant, your time was long enough for you to speak on every subject and to comment on the stars and to explain the principles and thoughts of the Patience and Silence group, but it was not enough for you to say one word on the single matter which was of any use amongst all which you have mentioned. Where can I find Haji Agha? How can I deliver you from your torment, and rescue you from the fate of a cockroach or a worm if I know not the place of the snake of whom you speak."

* * * * * *

It was all to no avail for the man had been converted to a statue. The tears flowed likes streams in his beard and dropped on the remains of his gown and the bare parts of his lower legs.

Juha looked around himself in the small, sealed room and then spoke, and this time there was a note of concern in his voice.

"I believe that you can at least get me out of this place for you come out of it every day as far as I know, otherwise how could I meet you every evening?"

But the man, it appeared, had also become deaf. However, the flow of his tears had already increased to such an extent that they had created a little pool below him on the stone floor.

Juha said in a gentle voice: "Do not despair for I shall find him and I shall take from him the spring, only show me the way out of here. I do not believe that you are deprived of movement."

At this point, only, did the man move, as if he were a machine. Juha approached him in order to grab hold of his gown to assist him in getting to his feet. The man then stretched out his arm like a blind man, feeling around the wall until he reached the basket and then from the basket his fingers slipped to the nail on which it was hanging. His fingers had hardiy touched the nail when the wall opened, revealing in front of him the passage and the courtyard of the abandoned mosque. The moon had gone but the first light of dawn was appearing.

Juha said farewell to his friend, assuring him that he would undoubtedly save him and went off in the first rays of morning to his house, finding himself light-footed and sprightly as if the days of his youth had returned. Yes indeed, he knew nothing about this Haji Agha except his name and he did not know about the mountain spring except that it was somewhere in Farghana. But that was no problem. He would find them both even if he had to go around the world twice. But the big problem was how he was going to persuade Julshan to let him journey off without a big fuss which he could not put up with at this stage of his life. But before he stepped inside the door which he opened with great caution so that none would awake, the idea had been born in his mind.

So, for the first time for many years, Juha stretched himself out on his bed alongside Julshan without sighing regretfully and when after a little while he slept, he was smiling.

* * * * * *

Chapter 2

Juha completed his prayers, stretching out his hand for his prayer beads and praying for the forgiveness of God several times before he raised his voice, directing what he had to say towards his wife, Julshan, but without turning in her direction.

"I met a man yesterday from Samarkand, one of the caravan returning from Peshawar. He told me that he had seen your mother, Ratiba, three months ago, before his caravan moved off, and she gave him, for us, a host of greetings with fondest love."

Then Juha stopped. For he had sown the seed, deep in the earth — it was now up to him to be patient for a time, until the green shoot sprouted.

He turned his head just a little, whilst moving his sitting position, as he praised God, in order to see his wife, bent over the gown which she was braiding by hand, and noted that she was now even more bowed over, and more silent. She didn't want to say a word.

He said to himself: "The green shoot is now struggling to reach the light." Then he asked for God's pardon twenty times more before he raised his voice, saying: "I would have liked to have invited him to have lunch with us today but he asked to be excused because his caravan moves off again at dawn.

Julshan still gave the appearance of being concerned totally with the gown in her hands. However, a quick glance from the corner of his eye allowed him to realise that she was 'all ears', listening to him. And he had hardly heard her sigh again when he followed up her sighs by saying: "Aye, may God's curse be upon that Khan 'of black face' — if he were no longer there we could have set off for Samarkand and presented to your mother her grandchildren, whom fate has decreed she shall never see. This time he saw, out of the corner of his eye, a great big tear rolling down Julshan's cheek as she reverted to sighing, whilst her hand speeded up the movements of the needle in the gown.

He said to himself: "May God forgive me for this white lie, and you too, Julshan, pardon me." Then he also sighed, deeply, saying: "After only ten days the caravan will arrive at Samarkand. It will go through the South Gate and your mother Ratiba, at that moment, will probably be on the roof of her house. She will see it, and my friend Ma'mun will go to her and will tell her that he has given us her greetings. He will reassure her about our situation and will say that we are here, living in Nahawand, at a distance of only ten days from her home. He will also tell her that God has blessed her with seven grandchildren like flowers and they have all heard about their grandmother, that they love her and they all send their fondest greetings and kisses, even if they have never met her nor are ever likely to do so."

Julshan's sighs became longer and deeper whilst the great big tear had become a flood. Now the time had come for the shoot to appear on the surface. He said: "How I had hoped that the children should not be prevented from knowing their grandmother. How I had hoped that my dear mother-in-law would see her grandchildren. It could be that seeing them would cause her recovery from what she is suffering." And at this very moment Julshan called out anxiously — and the green shoot appeared on the surface of the ground in full bloom.

"What? Is she ill? Did the man tell you that she was sick?"

Juha answered quickly, as if he had realised that he had made a slip to the tongue.

"Sick? Who said that? Indeed, no — she is not sick — but it is natural that old age, the longing to see her daughter and nobody there to care for her. Naturally, you understand these things."

"Certainly, there is no doubt but that she is sick — you are hiding the truth from me — very definitely, she is sick. Who knows? She may, even now, be on the point of dying." Her wailing rose.

"Oh light of my eye, oh my mother, oh my darling mother, how can you die without me seeing you? Without you seeing your seven grandchildren?" God is greatest — indeed the shoot grows strongly.

Said Juha: "My dearest, no creature on earth would accept that a grandmother should be prevented from seeing her grandchildren during her last days, but these are our circumstances and you know well that I am unable to enter Samarkand, they want my head there, as you know."

Julshan said, whilst still choking on her tears: "No, you cannot, but

I can!! There is no one demanding my head and there is nothing to stop me from going to Samarkand to see my mother and to show the children to their grandmother Ratiba. There are no judgements against me there, and nobody will know me as I have got older and my appearance has changed completely."

Said Juha to himself: "Yes, who would believe that this corpulent, flabby woman with heavy limbs and a tongue as sharp as a whip is the same, captivating Julshan — the most beautiful of the girls of Samarkand only twenty years ago? But what is important is that the green shoot has risen and has begun to flower and bear fruit as well."

Said Juha, knowing full well that if he surrendered quickly it would only arouse the suspicions of Julshan: "I would have loved for you to go and give joy to my mother-in-law, Ratiba. How long have I wished to kiss her hands and receive her blessing. But you know, my dear, that a trip such as this will cost a lot of money whilst we, as you well know, have no wealth, neither plenty nor little..."

And Julshan jeered in a voice resounding like thunder: "What? You say we have not sufficient money for the trip? And that bag which you have got hidden away in the box — do you think that I do not know anything about it? There is a full eight hundred dirhams in it, exactly. Will the trip cost one quarter of that sum?"

Nothing now remained before Juha except simply to stretch out his hand and pluck the fruit. For the conversation with his wife had now reached the point where he understood perfectly what was to follow, just as the ship with its captain arrives at a point in the ocean which he, the captain, knows well, and knows the details of each sea-lane from there on. Then he also raised his voice sharply.

"Undoubtedly, no. No one should lay a hand on this money. It is put away for one purpose only and I will not allow it to be spent on anything else."

"So? And what purpose is this which is more important than that I should see my mother — and that my children should see their grandmother whilst she is on her death bed?"

Juha replied calmly this time, realising that his calmness would stir up Julshan even more. "First, I want to build a small pool in the garden in order that the children can swim in it in the summer."

Julshan's voice raised several scales as she said, sarcastically: "Naturally, who would say that we are not in need of a pool whilst the whole river is only footsteps away? Probably you also want to surround it with a wall of polished limestone and create marble statues around it."

But Juha paid no attention to her screaming, and carried on in the same calm voice. "The pool will cost two hundred dirhams and the sitting room which will be built at the side of it will also cost two hundred and after that there will be the carpets and the curtains ..."

Julshan cut him off. "Let us say two hundred so the total will be six hundred dirhams. That will be it — the remaining two hundred will be more than enough for me."

"But that is also set aside for the gate and the ornamental work of the stonemason."

"What gate and what ornamental stonework?"

Juha said, in the same calm tones which he knew would arouse all the obstinacy of his wife: "I shall put up a big gate at the entrance to the garden and I shall repaint the house in a seablue colour whilst I have already agreed with the stonemason, in fact, that he should decorate it with silver and gold stars." The idea of the stars had evolved just at that moment. It had occurred to him at the moment in which he noticed the beginnings of the storm which was about to blow up. And sure enough it was sufficient for the storm to erupt with all its force.

* * * * * *

And from before noon until after dinner the storm raged over the head of Juha. Julshan did not stop for one moment from screaming and crying, raining down all possible curses upon Juha and the black day when she met him. She had sacrificed every thing for him and here he was now, that ungrateful, ignorant, wicked wastrel, denying her the right to visit her mother after all this long time and for what?

For decorating the walls of the house with gold and silver stars, whilst all these stars would disappear after the first rains. In the end there was no alternative for Juha except to surrender. And two days had not passed before there was a horse-drawn cart standing in front of the house whilst Juha was carrying to it fruit picking implements, garbage containers and sacks of all sizes. Sometimes the cart driver would help him but more often than not he would appear to be looking after the horse or the baggage. Until, finally when Julshan had mounted the cart and behind her were the seven children, in order of age, the driver called out: "God is greatest. In the name of God the Merciful, the Compassionate, we have placed our trust in God."

And Juha cried out: "Go, in the safe keeping of God."

The driver cracked his whip and the horse leaped forward, pulling the cart with its heavy load behind it, and by the side of it was Juha, running in order to hear the final instructions of Julshan.

"I shall not be gone more than three months," said Julshan. "Do not forget what I have recommended you to do."

"I shall not forget a thing, oh love of my life — sixteen dirhams for the butcher — I shall repair the gap in the wall — I shall get the tea-cooler fixed at the blacksmith's shop and I will plant the green peppers in the back garden."

"I hope that you will not forget," said Julshan, "and if you intend to run alongside us for the whole of the trip saying goodbye to us why don't you just get in with us?"

Juha, having caught her meaning, stopped, waving his hand and calling out: "Go, in the safe keeping of God. Go, in the safe keeping of God."

* * * * * *

"Be of good heart oh venerable and pious man. I am off now to Faraghana and I shall not return until I have regained the water spring from the ill-fated Agha."

The answer of the man was two, large tears which ran down his cheeks and a knowing look on his face which was more eloquent than any words. So Juha went off on his way and it was as if he was flying on the wing of a fabulous great Rukh above the clouds instead of being on the saddle of his donkey, Masoud. And it was not many moments before Juha and his donkey were on the wide road at the meeting-place of the caravans coming from both the south and the north, where there were hundreds of camels, goats, cows, vendors, vagrants, fortune tellers and slaves of all nationalities and colour, with conversations in every tongue, known and unknown.

Juha took his place in the middle of the caravan which was going to the north whilst the sun was roasting the ground as if with sharp tongues of heat and the heat and sweat were lashing Juha's face, head and body. Then the tail of a great bull swept off Juha's turban and he hastened to pick it up and wrap its ends in the middle of the throng. But, in spite of all this, he was lively and light-hearted as if, suddenly, all the enthusiasm of youth had returned to him. Then, as if he had, at that moment, realised the weight of his turban as he was trying to steady it on his head, he threw it into his haversack, leaving a small skull-cap to protect him from the burning heat of the sun.

And off he went in front, always to the front, whilst the memories of earlier days began to return — his adventures with the chief judge in Cairo, how he escaped from the prison of the army commander in Mosul, then his story of Damascus when he returned the abducted son of an old widow to her, then of his mad adventure with the Khan of Bukhara and finally, the great love affair in Tashkent which ended with his marriage to Julshan. Was this the end? A wife, a house and seven children, with decaying but secure tranquillity, in exile in the vineyards of Nahawand, whilst oppression, skullduggery, deception and embezzlement of the wealth of people was still rife everywhere? What have you done, oh Juha, all these years? Rescued some tens of people, yes; ridiculed the arrogance of the sultans and khans, yes; but the world has not changed. Can you, Juha, change the world on your own?

Juha began to repeat to himself, as if playing tunes on a snake charmer's horn. "Ayeee, if only I had my time over again, I would follow a different path. I would not be on my own but with all the people — yes, with all the people — for people together are able to change the world and remove tyranny from the face of the earth, but one person cannot, even if he be Juha."

But now he was on his way to Farghana. All he knew was that the well that he was seeking was somewhere in the mountainous area of Farghana and that its present owner was a greedy man whose name was Haji Agha. But despite that he would find him — yes, he would find him — and he would have a bone to pick with him and what a bone...

* * * * * *

Suddenly, Juha became aware that silence surrounded him and that he no longer heard the din of the caravan which he had sneaked into. He became aware that his donkey had wandered far away from the caravan and the main road to a little track amongst the fields. It appeared that this had happened a long time ago whilst Juha was completely absorbed in his thoughts because he was unable to make out where he was. The sun had set and the stars were hidden behind thick cloud and he was unable to hear the noise of the main road. But Masoud was off with Juha and his baggage as if he was an expert on the road and knew where he was going. Juha's eyes caught a light, hidden at the end of the solitary track and he began to move towards it, congratulating himself that he might be able to find someone whom he could ask about the main road.

Suddenly, he found himself at an isolated roadhouse, which appeared to be near nowhere at all, although he thought that it was inevitable that there would be a village beyond the mountain. He got off his donkey and entered the roadhouse saying: "Peace be upon you."

But the reply was an inaudible muttering which was nearer to scolding than it was to talking and ten eyes were all looking at him, first of all in astonishment and then with suspicion.

Juha said to himself: "The stranger to these people is always a tax collector who meets nothing but hatred and repugnance from them. For the strangers who visit them are always either spies for the Sultan or collectors of taxes — and the latter are even worse than the former." He sat down meekly and signed to the owner of the place to bring him a cup of tea. He began to look at the other four men. The first was a man getting on in years whose face was covered with an old style beard in which the grey hairs were more numerous than the black ones. Jutting out below his eyes was a protruding nose like the beak of a hawk, whilst above them were two curved eyebrows. He was most likely a peasant from the village, whilst the second and the third men appeared to be younger and were wearing the clothes of shepherds.

But Juha concluded from his appearance, that the fourth worked at the dyeing of clothes for his hands were painted a dark blue colour which no oil or pumice stone would ever succeed in removing. The four men were huddled together around a tea flask and four cups and were whispering to each other. Juha realised immediately that the subject about which they were whispering was without doubt concerned with certain matters which were taboo to him. He turned his face to the wall in order not to upset them and did not see the exchange of looks between the owner of the roadhouse and the four companions whilst he sat and drank his tea.

* * * * * *

The whispered conversation went on for quite some time behind Juha's back and Juha could sense the whispers getting more heated and the eyes of the five men almost piercing his back. Suddenly the older peasant jumped to his feet and came over to Juha: "Peace be upon you, oh stranger — welcome to our village which is isolated from the whole world. We have noticed the yellow dust covering your clothes which indicates that you have come from afar, beyond this valley in which is to be found neither desert nor sand."

Juha replied, looking at the man's face in all innocence: "Just so my friend, I have indeed come from a faraway place — my donkey led me to here without me even noticing that I had left the main road behind me."

The man muttered a few sounds beyond understanding whilst sitting down next to Juha, then he said: "So, tell us, oh stranger, how are things there, beyond the valley? Has a rebellion broken out amongst the slaves? Have the peasants refused to pay the taxes? Has the governor killed his brother? Or has the brother killed the governor?"

Juha replied, amazed by these questions: "Not at all — nothing such as you have mentioned has happened. Everything there is first-rate. Peace is well-established whilst order is maintained and is as good as it has ever been. The people, as they walk along, keep close to the wall and they almost chew their food with their noses in order not to have to open their mouths."

Whilst exchanging a knowing look with his companions and the owner of the roadhouse the man said: "You mean that you have not heard any news of this nature?"

"Never, I haven't heard a thing."

Said the man: "Nor us here, we've heard nothing. We, here, as I told you, are isolated from the world. It was for this reason, only, that I wished to ask you. We don't know anything, we don't hear anything and we don't see anything, that's the lot."

Juha realised what the man was thinking about, what they were all thinking about and it pricked his conscience that he should be the reason for such worry and trouble to these poor people. He put out his hand to touch, gently, the shoulder of the person to whom he was speaking, saying: "Take a good look at my face, oh venerable old man. Do I look like a spy?"

The peasant looked at him for a moment before he said: "It's just as if you had read what was in my mind, oh stranger. To tell the truth, we have been doubtful about you from the moment you entered the place. We do have a question and we are still hesitating as to whether we should ask you about it. These days one can't trust his own brother. What would you think about a man, a stranger, dropping in on us in this remote place, far away from any road and at this time of the evening?"

"So just take it easy. If you are still doubtful about me then keep your question to yourself. But if you find that I prompt your trust then ask what you will and, hopefully, God will grant me the ability to answer."

The man hesitated again for a moment before he said: "There is something about you that makes me trust you and therefore I shall ask you the question which we are burning with desire to know the answer to." And the tone of his voice dropped to a whisper as he said: "Have you heard anything about the appearance of Juha in these parts recently?"

Now Juha had been prepared to hear anything except his own name. It took him so much by surprise that the cup of tea almost fell out of his hand. And before he could say a word the younger of the two herdsmen leaped enthusiastically in front of him, whispering, but in a sharper voice: "Oh yes, Juha has appeared. My friend Umran saw him with his own two eyes whilst on his donkey, Masoud, in the middle of a caravan on the main road."

And the second herdsman exclaimed: "Umran lived for a long time in Samarkand and knows Juha very well and he noticed him when his turban fell off." What a calamity, thought Juha. So more than one person must have seen him. If the news of his whereabouts could have reached this isolated village then no doubt it would also have reached the sultans and the khans, the guards and the spies in every place.

Juha said quickly: "This is impossible, my friends. No doubt it is some other person of similar appearance that these people saw."

The old peasant said: "How can you say with certainty that this is impossible."

Juha replied: "Because Juha now lives in a place very far away from these parts."

The older of the herdsmen said: "That is of no importance, for Juha, as you well know, is a person of great standing."

Juha continued determinedly: "Oh my good friends, you must understand that the Juha you knew is finished, he is no longer able to travel about. He married, has produced seven children and has taken to himself a house and another name. He has become a decrepit, old man whilst his donkey, Masoud, is fat and heavy of movement. He, himself, has become idle and dull-witted and hardly leaves his house out of fear of his wife's sharp tongue."

The dyer said, in a very significant tone: "You are probably also going to say that he has become a coward. All the world knows that Juha fears not a creature on earth."

Juha snorted, derisively: "Most of the stories which you have heard about Juha were lies, fabrications of someone's imagination."

The young herdsman then cried out: "Fabrications of imagination! Who, then, was the champion who brought fear to the hearts of all the tyrants, who burst the gates of the black prison of Al Taneen and released all those innocent persons who were imprisoned there? Who?"

Juha cut him short, sharply: "I don't know. All I know is that Juha now shakes timidly in front of his wife, Julshan, and never disobeys any of her instructions."

Juha was talking excitedly and he never even noticed the doubtful looks which were being exchanged between the owner of the road-house and the other four men until after these exchanges bore fruit. For he had hardly said his last world when he suddenly felt as if a mountain had fallen on the back of his neck and he fell down on the ground. Before he could even pull himself together they all set upon him with punches and kicks as their anger exploded like a number of volcanoes, all at the same time.

"You claim that Juha is no longer Juha, you miserable spy. We know the tricks of your lot very well, you pigs. You want to distort the prestige of Juha and to deceive the people that he is not able to help them any more."

In vain did Juha Nasruddin attempt to defend himself. He was al-most ready to announce that he was Juha, flesh and blood, but he pulled back in the belief that one word would be sufficient to ruin everything and would cause the mobilisation of seven complete armies to be on his tail.

Anyway, it was more than likely that they would now be complete-ly unprepared to accept such a claim. Finally, the end of his thrashing was an enormous kick from the owner of the roadhouse which threw him outside whilst the owner screamed: "Don't let us ever see your filthy face around here again you spy."

* * * * * *

Juha ran, with his donkey Masoud running behind him, for a long way before he fell to the ground from exhaustion; it was as if all his bones were groaning but, praise be to God, none of them were broken. After he had recovered his senses he mounted his donkey again, but the ex-cruciating pain was still attacking his limbs. However, he was happy, in spite of this, with the enthusiasm of the people for him; or rather for his name. But, although he had owned his name in the past, now it ap-peared as if his name owned him.

Daylight had gone, and the scent of jasmine filled the place. His donkey was running along without being directed when, suddenly, he stopped, raising his head in the air as if he sniffed the odour of devil himself. Juha looked around him, seeking whatever it was that had provoked Masoud, when he saw a bundle of clothes in the middle of the road. When he approached it he discovered that it was a person, piled up on the road, moaning in pain. He walked up to him and asked: "What ails you, my son, why are you moaning in this fashion as if your soul was on the point of departing from you?"

The man exposed his face and, suddenly, there was the face of a young man at the peak of his youth. In spite of the contractions from the frightful excruciating pain, Juha was able to note in his features signs of strength and determination, as well as something else which made him feel uneasy. Nevertheless, asking the pardon of God, he asked: "What can I do to help you, my son?"

"Indeed, my suffering is unbearable oh venerable old man. Death would be a thousand times better."

"Have you been in this state for a long time?"

"Every year for five years, at this time, this accursed pain, which no human being could stand, attacks me. I cannot recover from it except by a special medicine which I myself must prepare. But here I am, struck down like a dog. I cannot prepare the necessary medicine. I can't even lift my hand to it."

Juha said: "Never mind. Come, mount my donkey, and I will go with you to the nearest village. Perhaps there you will be able to prepare your medicine."

The sick man mounted Masoud and behind them came Juha. The moans of the man never ceased, indeed they got louder until, at last, they reached the outskirts of a village and set down at the door of an old roadhouse. There, Juha asked the owner for something to cover the ailing youth. He also asked for a cup of tea for him and for himself, and then lay himself down beside him. It wasn't many moments before the sick youth went into a deep sleep, punctuated by heart-breaking moans whilst Juha busied himself asking the people he met in the roadhouse about Haji Agha and the mountain water well but he met no one who had ever heard the name. And as he was busy talking to the people he became aware of a hand touching his shoulder.

He turned to find the sick, young man, standing like a huge, towering mountain, safe and sound, with a great big smile, and before Juha could get over his astonishment the other one said: "Let us be off oh venerable sir. I have prepared my medicine and I am cured, praise be to God. However, we must leave here immediately or the sickness will return to me anew. For the first thing which I must do, after I have taken my medicine, is to leave the place in which I have prepared it. So let us be off." And without awaiting a reply from Juha he rushed to Masoud and started to saddle him and load the baggage.

Juha said, to himself: "Indeed, he's a nice lad, after he has regained his health he now wants to return the favour." He moved quickly towards him to assist him in preparing the donkey, saying: "I am on my way to Sandashah, the capital of Farghana."

The youth said, showing his bright, white teeth: "Me too."

And before Juha realised what was happening, the youth had jumped on the back of Masoud whilst signalling for Juha to follow him.

Said Juha, reprovingly: "Do you not wish, also, to mount me on the donkey after you have regained your health?"

The youth jumped down from the donkey, his face red with shame, saying that he only wanted to assure himself that Masoud was safely saddled. Juha remarked to himself: "At least he can feel ashamed."

But they had hardly started to draw away before they became aware of the sound of horses' hooves behind them. Juha turned to look behind him to find the owner of the roadhouse and some of his comrades racing towards them with the roadhouse owner crying out: "Stop thieves; stop thieves." And the man leaped off his horse right on top of Juha, throwing him to the ground and grabbing him by his collar whilst the others were holding down his companion.

"Where is the silver goblet with the inlaid gold, you thief?"

"What are you talking about!" Juha exclaimed.

"What is this goblet you are talking about and what gold? By what right, you so-and-so, do you search my baggage? Has your goblet jumped to here like a monkey?"

"By the right of this, oh you thief," said one of the companions of the roadhouse owner as he took a beautiful goblet, made from silver, decorated with gold, from Juha's baggage.

And then the group set about beating up Juha and his companion, whilst cursing them most fully and saying angrily: "All that talk about Haji Agha, keeping us busy whilst his mate there steals the flagon. And the other one here, claiming to be sick whilst he's as strong as an ox."

Inevitably, the beating came to an end, and Juha managed to open his eyes as he heard the beat of the hooves of the horses as they rode away. He looked around him and found the donkey, standing with his long ears hanging down towards the ground as if he were seeking forgiveness because it was he who had led his friend to this end.

And there, to the left of the donkey, was the strange youth, stretched out on the ground as if all life had left him.

Juha approached him hesitantly when he suddenly opened his eyes and leapt to his feet: "Have they gone? Praise be to God. By good luck they were all barefoot."

"And where is the good luck in the fact that they were all barefoot?"

"As far as we were concerned of course. Do you not realise that if they had all been wearing boots our ribs would, by now, all be smashed up? Why don't you laugh? Do you not get the joke?"

"Listen, lad," said Juha firmly, his patience exhausted, "I do not want to hear a thing from you nor do I wish to see your face again after today. For you deceived me, stole from people who had been kind to us and caused me to be beaten, a bitter reward to me for my help to you. That is enough for me from one person."

Then Juha leaped onto the back of his donkey but the youth suddenly knelt down on the ground in his path, lifting his hands in the air in supplication with his face wet with tears.

"I entreat you, in the name of God sir, hear me, be merciful to me and hear my story before you judge me. Then you can leave me, if you wish, but after you have heard me."

Juha's heart was touched and he sensed the truth in the tone of the youth and he said to him: "Come along, by my side, and let me hear your story."

So off they went, Juha on the donkey Masoud and the youth quickening his pace beside him, panting, saying: "Yes, sir, I am a thief. Indeed, I am the most contemptible thief in existence. For I began to steal from the age of five years. I would steal from my father, my mother and my neighbours. I could hardly see anything but that I would be possessed of an irresistible desire to steal it. My father would curse me and curse the day on which I was conceived, whilst my mother could not look at my face without wailing. I practised every form of theft: pickpocketing, bag-snatching, breaking open strongboxes; indeed, I even broke open the strong-room of the Sultan one day. I became, no great glory, the greatest thief on the face of the earth until this very day."

And Juha said, as he goaded on his donkey: "Don't say that, for you cannot be greater than the Thief of Baghdad."

"Of course not, because I am the Thief of Baghdad!!!"

* * * * * *

Chapter 3

Juha reined in his donkey, Masoud, as he said to his companion, with a mixture of surprise and revulsion: "I could not have imagined that the Thief of Baghdad would have sunk to such a low level as to have stolen from people who extended to him their hospitality and to have caused harm to a person who had treated him with kindness. I used to believe him to be a sort of knight who had lost his way in his quest for chivalry and had taken to stealing as a method of redistribution of wealth, or perhaps of lightening the rich of some of their burdens. For a long time I felt pity for him, despite the fact that I was jealous of his intelligence. How long had I hoped that I might meet him one day and give him some guidance towards the straight path. But what you have done today, my friend, has satisfied me that you are no more than a common thief, just like the rest. Get out of my sight; never let me set eyes on you again."

The thief collapsed, crying, under the hooves of the donkey and began to throw dirt on his head, slapping his cheeks as he implored: "I beg of you, in the name of God, oh my master, allow me to complete my story. Allow me to explain to you what happened to me."

Once again, Juha felt pity for him for he was never able to turn his back on a man crying, even though that man might be the most despicable thief.

"Verily, oh my master, I am the most wretched creature on this earth. Do you know why? Because the door of repentance has been shut in my face. Do not be astonished, yes, I wish to repent but I am unable to do so. For I decided on contrition more than five years ago and I came to the firm resolve to abandon stealing for ever..."

"Then why did you not do so? What power exists which can prevent a man from doing the right thing when he so wishes? Unless, of course, his soul is so evil by nature that the very seed of goodness can never, ever reach his heart?"

"That is what I wish to explain to you. For, as I have told you, I was completely satisfied with myself and my way of life, until the day when I chanced to meet a pious recluse who was blind, deaf and dumb and who did not speak, see nor hear except once each year. I still do not know whether it was good luck or bad luck that the night when I happened to meet him was the night during which it was permissible for him to speak and he talked from the middle of the night until the cock crowed, about one man only, who was — Juha."

Juha's heart nearly jumped out of his body when he heard his name and he was all ears. Indeed, even Masoud raised and shook his head when he heard the name of his owner. And Juha suppressed a cry of surprise before it even got out of his mouth and he said not a word. But now, he was much more attentive to what his companion had to say. He continued his story saying: "I don't want to make this too long for you, for everybody knows about Juha. No doubt you have heard about him. At the very beginning the recluse asked me if, during my many travels, I had come to know where life had finally taken Juha. I said, I hadn't but then I got carried away by enthusiasm and added that no doubt by now he had become old and flabby and the spark of fervour for helping people had become extinguished. However, the recluse rejected my idea but instead of leaving me to go and ask other people he began to talk to me about Juha. And the deeper he went into the conversation the more I began to despise myself, thinking, this is the sort of life that a man ought to live; to live for the benefit of all mankind; to give of yourself for the people; to feel the pain and the agony of those oppressed and to use yourself, your strength, your intelligence, your wealth and your efforts for the elimination of oppression and the reduction of hardship."

* * * * * *

"And so on until the man had nearly completed his talking — and I do think, as far as it appeared, that he would never have ended had not the cock crowed — and until I had made up my mind that I would abandon stealing for ever and I would search for this Juha. When I should find him I would make myself a disciple of his and become an apprentice to him so that when he became old, and time caused him to retire, then I would become his hand which would strike and his foot which travelled and his eye which would see behind the barriers. "

The eyes of Juha shone and he said, in a reproving manner: "And, in spite of this you continued stealing — why?"

And the Thief of Baghdad replied: "Patience, oh my master, for this is what I wanted to explain to you, even though I did not understand why. For a long time I have hoped that I might meet someone to whom I could pass on my problem. That is, I was possessed by such a strong desire to meet Juha that I was unable to think of anything else except such a meeting. And after a lot of thought I decided that the best method would be to open a roadhouse at the point where the caravans met near Sindashah for at this point all persons going and coming from both east and west meet. Here people gather from all colours, races and creeds and it would be inevitable that I would find news of Juha, one day, from one of them.

"Then I would gather together my belongings and I would go to him. But, as much as I was a thief, so also, was I a bigger wastrel. For, despite all the wealth which I had stolen I had nothing of value and I had decided that I would make the roadhouse into a place suitable for all classes of people to enter. But the lack of money had never been a problem and I said to myself that I would begin my penance tomorrow rather than today and that I would end a life of stealing by one big theft which would be sufficient to open the roadhouse and then I would repent for ever."

And the sobbing of the man reached such a pitch that Masoud himself began to bray in his turn, to join in with him, whilst Juha, patiently, longing to listen to the rest of the story, began to calm down the grief of the man and urged him to complete his tale: "Get hold of yourself, my son, for the door of repentance is open until the moment when the spirit leaves the throat. I don't really know whether in fact, the spirit leaves the body from the throat or from some other place. But, however, the door of penitence is the door of He who is most noble and is not closed in the face of any of God's servants."

And the Thief of Baghdad said, moaning gently: "Only in my face. It has been decreed against me that I shall never be able to repent. That I should be condemned to be a despicable thief who will commit only the most mean of thefts."

Juḥa then exclaimed: "How, how? How could this be decreed against you and who decreed it?"

The youth then sighed so deeply that it was almost as if his soul left his body with it. "Do you understand, oh my master, what it was that I stole on the night that I decided to repent my sins. I stole from the holy man of God, my lord, Abulayal Tahruddin."

* * * * * *

We will leave our two friends and Masoud for a moment, to talk a little about my lord, the holy man of God, Abulayal Tahruddin.

About two leagues from the city of Sindashah, on the road coming from Nahawand, the traveller will see an imposing, ancient tomb, surrounded by a wide courtyard and a low wall. This is the tomb of my lord, the holy man of God, Abulayal Tahruddin. No one knows, for certain, the period during which this holy man lived. But it is said that hundreds of years ago he was living in Sindashah. He became an orphan child, for his father had died in one of the wars of that time, even before he was born, and his mother died when he was five years old. He had no family to bring him up and he was brought up in the street. He tasted the bitterness of orphanhood, of deprivation and begging to its very dregs, until when he reached puberty, he disappeared from the city, suddenly, to reappear there after twenty years... It was said that he had spent all these years in Tibet where he studied medicine, philosophy and astronomy, together with the secrets of the universe, with the monks of the secluded monasteries which no human foot could ever reach.

It was also said that he was able, by a single laying on of his hand, whilst saying, "In the name of God", to heal the sick and restore sight to the blind and that he was one of those persons who can move from place to place in an instant. He would be moving along the streets of Sindashah and, in the same moment, he could move to pray the noon prayer with the pilgrims in Mecca and return in the twinkling of an eye, covering, in a split second, a distance over which the caravans would take four months. He was greatly loved by the children and the young. He could not pass along a road without being surrounded by dozens of boys and girls. For he was never constrained by their presence and would spend all the money that came to him buying games and presents, including clothes, for them, whilst on many occasions he would join in with them in their games, as if he were one of them.

And when fate finally decreed his death there was not a single child in Sindashah who did not cry for Tahruddin until its eyes were sore, whilst the mothers and fathers cried as much as their children. This tomb was built for him and his name became a legend, passed on from one generation to the next. If a mother wished to stop her child from doing something it would be sufficient for her to say that our lord, Abulayal Tahruddin, will be angry if you do that or, he will be pleased with you if you don't do it. The celebration of his date of birth became a great party for the children every year. They would go off to his tomb after the dawn prayer and each of them would receive from the caretaker of the tomb a sack on which would be the name or the special mark of the recipient and in which the child would find everything which would give pleasure and delight, like toys, clothes, presents and sweets.

Then years passed and Sindashah was raided by the Mogul Sultan and the law of the sword and fire became established in the pleasant city of Sindashah. One of the first things which was done was to cancel the children's party and the fathers were forbidden to keep the sacks of presents for their children in the tomb of Abulayal Tahruddin. Indeed, the very mention of his name, Abulayal, became an offence punishable by law.

However, the name, Abulayal, remained imprinted in the hearts of the people and every year, with the beginning of spring and on the very night of the birth of the holy man Abulayal, each child would hang his sack behind the garden door of his house, confident that when he would awake in the morning he would find it full of presents, new clothes and sweetmeats.

* * * * * *

We return to our two friends, Juha and the Thief of Baghdad. We left them both in conversation, Juha on his donkey, Masoud, and the Thief of Baghdad, who got up from the ground where he was rubbing his face in the dirt and began to run at the side of Masoud whilst weeping and beating his own cheek like a bereaved mother.

"That night was the night of the forbidden party on the birthday of the holy man Abulayal. I had thought, at first, of breaking into the Sultan's palace but the guard, that night, was unusually strong. Then I attempted to slip into the residence of the Head of the Merchants Guild but I was unable to do this, then suddenly, as I was sneaking through the dark streets, looking for a place in which I might find what would be suitable for the theft which I was intending to carry out, the thought leaped to my mind which the Devil himself must have put there.

"Behind every one of these doors a sack is hanging which contains the presents which the children of the house will find in the morning. Let these sacks be my final theft. And so, the malignant thought had hardly entered my head before I had begun to carry it out. Dawn did not arrive until I had collected all the children's presents and had taken them to my hiding place in ten separate trips and I began, when I had finished, to make an estimation of what I had collected and I said to myself: "This will be sufficient to open the biggest roadhouse in this whole area." Then I gave myself over to sleep and I was very happy. For I had successfully completed the first step towards repentance for my sins. But I had hardly closed my eyes when I saw the lord, Abulayal Tahruddin himself, standing like a giant above my head, his eyes emitting sparks whilst screaming at me in a voice like thunder: 'What have you done, oh you fool? How has depravity reached such a degree in you that you have stolen presents and toys from innocent children? How could you permit yourself to deprive them of happiness, wipe away their smiles and turn their holiday into a day of weeping and wailing?'

"Fear froze my tongue. I couldn't speak a word but I was aware of tears streaming down my face, as if they were begging for mercy. Then the holy man returned and said, in a fearful voice:

'Then listen to the punishment you have earned, a penalty commensurate with the crime which you have committed. You will remain, seeking repentance, until the end of time, but you will never receive it. You will remain a thief, stealing until the end. You will never cease to steal, ever. And on the anniversary of this day, every year, you will be visited by pain and torment to a degree which no man can bear and such torment shall not cease until you have stolen something, anything, and you shall remain, eternally, amongst the body of thieves until the day you die when you will meet God, bearing with you the consequences of all the sins which you have committed'."

* * * * * *

And the Thief of Baghdad began, again, slapping his face whilst continuing his story: "Abulayal then disappeared from before me whilst I was still dumbfounded, trembling with fear, incapable of speaking a single world, by which to ask for mercy. Suddenly, everything blew up around me, as if I were in the very mouth of a volcano. For the ground began to incline whilst the walls leaned over amidst a terrible roaring of both thunder and lightning, and the place began to collapse over my head. However, I managed to escape by the skin of my teeth, leaving behind me all the children's presents which disappeared in a second, below the ruins." At this point the voice of the youth was smothered by his tears so that he was incapable of continuing what he was saying.

In completion, Juha said: "I am able to realise what happened after that for since that time the attack of pain has come back to you on each anniversary of that day and today was the appointed day for it. Is that not so?"

The Thief of Baghdad replied, whilst still sobbing: "It is as you say, sir. Now you know my story. Will you hold out your hand? Will you help me?"

Said Juha, feeling very sympathetic towards the thief, deprived of repentance: "Alas, it is as if it has been decreed for me, after a long life, that I shall spend what remains to me of life in saving a hermit from turning into a worm and guiding a thief in the path of repentance. Take it easy, my son, how can I help you?"

The youth jumped to his feet where he was, forgetting his tears and crying: "That you permit me to accompany you, oh sir, that I become a disciple of yours."

Juha declared, in surprise: "And why should you want to become a follower of mine, specifically?"

The Thief of Baghdad answered, saying: "You are the person for whom I have spent all these years searching. You are the only person in this world who is capable of healing me." Then he continued, saying: "When you bent over me whilst I was lying on the ground by the side of the road, moaning in pain, and you asked me, 'What's wrong with you, son?' I became aware of an overwhelming wave of compassion, such as I have never felt before in my life. I can almost say that I heard the voice of Abulayal, crying to me from within myself, 'This man, oh Thief of Baghdad, is the man at whose hand could be your salvation'. "

Then Juha spoke in amazement: "So!! So!!"

The enthusiasm of the youth increased: "Then there was your forgiveness of me, after all that you had heard about me and after the abuse that you had suffered because of me. Then, your acceptance of my accompanying you will be an indication to me that the door of repentance is not closed in my face for ever and of a new hope that I may eventually return to be a whole man."

Juha said: "Will you accept my conditions?"

The youth replied even more enthusiastically: "I accept them without even knowing what they are."

Juha then said: "The first of these conditions is that you refrain from ... let me call it the treatment that you practice every time that the attack of pain comes to you."

The youth cried: "I promise that I will not do so, even though the pain cuts me to pieces."

"And the second and final condition is that your trust in me shall be total, even though something that I might do gives you cause for concern. For I am an eccentric sort of a man, in a way, and I may do some strange things from time to time but you must not allow doubt to creep into your mind at any time."

And the youth replied: "Indeed, sir, I shall surrender my soul to you and even though it may be on the very brink of disaster I shall not doubt for one single moment but that you will be able to restore it to a state of well-being."

Juha said: "Well, now, let us get on our way to Sindashah. Perhaps the heart of Abulayal will be touched by pity for you."

* * * * * *

Then Juha rubbed the head of his donkey in order to urge him on his way. "Get on, oh Masoud."

When the Thief of Baghdad heard the name of the donkey he said — for his happiness had loosened his tongue and this tears had dried up a little: "Is your donkey called Masoud then, sir?"

And Juha replied, with his thoughts miles away: "Yes, his name is Masoud."

The youth was quiet for a moment and then he said, in a tone of some significance: "The name of Juha's donkey is also Masoud."

Juha could have cursed himself, and his donkey. But he just said, in an attempt to change the course of the conversation: "Did you ever see Juha, at any time?"

The young man said: "I saw him only once, I shall never forget the time, ever. I was just a lad at the time, ten, or maybe a bit older. I had heard people talk about Juha, about his sharp wit and his amazing adventures with the sultans and the khans. Then, one day, as I was passing through the market in the city of Samarkand, I was surprised by a great clamour and voices calling, eagerly, as people pointed to a man buying a silk garment at one of the shops — 'Juha! Juha!'

"Then the devilish thought leaped to my mind — if I could steal the garment from Juha, I should have the right to boast in front of all the thieves, great and small, that I was the only man in the world to have made a fool of Juha. And I immediately began to execute my plan. For I moved closer to Juha; with a handful of hot pepper, until, when I had positioned myself right at the back of the donkey, I pushed the pepper under the top of the donkeys tail. He had hardly felt the fire scorching him when he brayed at the top of his voice and, wishing himself far away from Juha, kicking, and tossing his head and his legs in all directions, he slipped away from his hand and ran, for all he was worth, through the market with Juha running behind him, leaving the garment in my hand. Naturally, I took the garment in the flash of an eye."

Juha whispered: "So it was you, be damned, who did this to me. You."

* * * * * *

Juha realised, when it was too late, that he had made another slip of the tongue and he stopped speaking whilst the Thief of Baghdad was leaping about like an acrobat, then hugging the head of Masoud and pointing to Juha, shouting: "You are Juha! You are Juha!"

Juha, fearful that someone might hear him, looked around him and whispered: "Lower your voice, even if I am Juha, do you need to shout like that for someone to hear what he ought not to hear or to know something that he ought not to know."

The Thief of Baghdad answered, panting: "Indeed, no, but — you really are Juha. How was it that I did not come to realise that until now? All that compassion and love of people, the ability to forgive, these qualities can only be combined in one person, and he is Juha. All right, I'll drop my voice. My voice is very low as you can hear. But do not forbid me from saying to the road, 'Blessed are you, oh road, upon which passes Masoud, upon whom is his owner. Blessed are you, oh day, which has united me with he for whom I have been searching and in whose hands lies my deliverance'. "

Said Juha: "As you now know who I am there is yet a third condition for us to accompany each other."

The young man whispered. "A third, a fourth, a fifth, it is of no importance. For today, I am safe."

Juha continued to speak: "You should know me, only by the name, Al Haj Abdussabur. You should forget, entirely, that my name is Juha."

"I understand, I understand Ju.., I mean Haji Abdussabur."

* * * * * *

On the course of the way to Sindashah, Juha, his friend and Masoud stopped at the tomb of the holy man Abulayal Tahruddin. Juha tied the donkey to the wall and entered to pray but the Thief of Baghdad remained in his place, outside the wall, not daring to enter, but knelt on the ground, lifting his hands to the heavens. And when Juha had completed his prayers and turned to greet the man next to him he discovered him to be a venerable Sheikh, getting on in years, his white beard hanging down to his feet. The man came out with him for the two of them to find that the Thief of Baghdad was still kneeling in his place but with his head bent down, touching the ground.

The venerable old Sheikh, who it appeared was the caretaker of the mosque and tomb, said: "Every year this wretched man comes here and sets a seed in this place but it never, ever grows."

The voice of the Thief of Baghdad raised itself: "Forgive me, forgive me, I beg of you, oh Tahruddin, forgive me!"

Juha said: "Come on, let us be off — as long as you are sincere in your repentance, then he will forgive you."

The thief replied, bursting into tears: "I have undertaken to trust in you for as long as I shall live and as long as you say that then I shall believe what you say but I shall never be truly sure that he has forgiven me until the jasmine bush, which I plant here every year, and which he prevents from growing and blooming, grows."

Said Juha: "The jasmine bush will grow this year, you shall see."

They then set off until they entered the city of Samarkand as the voice of the mu'adhin was making the call to prayer: "God is Greatest, God is Greatest. I testify that there is no God but God."

* * * * * *

Chapter 4

The day that Juha and his friend entered the city of Sindashah was market day. Nobody noticed their entry as dozens of people entered at the same time as themselves through the west gate of the city. Some of them were on donkeys, the appearance of which did not differ from that of Masoud, whilst most of them were on foot with just one or two of the upper classes on horses.

The market was noisy, teeming with people, with the buyers, the sellers and the brokers all going and coming from this group to that group whilst the guards, in their black uniforms, were everywhere. There were a lot of boys, and people with nothing else to do, who were standing around one of the snake charmers. The shopkeepers were all calling out about their wares to attract customers, coming from the villages, both near and far, whilst in another corner was an Indian magician, playing his pipe to a cobra whose head was looking out from a big cooking pot and which was dancing to the tune of the pipe. There were the sounds of drums, beating regularly, from afar, with an overall clamour, to which there was no beginning and no end, and which was deafening to the ears. Everyone was talking and shouting and nobody was listening, whilst the braying of the donkeys in amongst the thick cloud of dust, which got thicker and thicker as the day went on, continued. Juha tied his donkey to a tree which had some low-hanging branches. Then he made his way, followed by his friend, to a nearby teashop, where they sat at a table overlooking the market square. Immediately opposite was a small shop, in the doorway of which were hanging dozens of little cages, each of which imprisoned a bird. The owner of the shop was a giant of a man who had an enormous frame and an evil appearance, just as if he were one of the myrmidons of hell who had just escaped and come to this place. At the moment when Juha and his friend turned to look at the shop of birds, the giant was bargaining with a customer about his goods. Between the two, was a metal cage in which was a shrivelled-up bird, trembling in fear of its unknown fate. At least, that is how it appeared to Juha and his friend, who were drawn by the argument between the vendor and the purchaser. And while these two were both pulling away at the cage the door flew open. The imprisoned bird did not miss the opportunity for it went off like an arrow, spreading out its wings and its breast to the wind. It went around the place two or three times with the cries of the two men and the eyes of Juha and his friend following it as it went higher and higher and then landed on the top branch of the tree underneath which Juha had tied his donkey, whilst singing, its trilling even rising above the clamour of the market.

The Thief of Baghdad cried out, as he almost leaped for joy where he was: "Did you see? Just how great is the joy of a prisoner with his freedom, even if it is only a bird. I felt as if my heart was flying with it as it escaped from the prisoner's cage. How happy I am at this moment as I hear him singing about his freedom."

Said Juha: "And what do you think about the other birds which are imprisoned in the cages?"

There was sadness in the voice of the Thief of Baghdad as he replied: "How miserable they are — indeed, how miserable am I about them whilst they are there, in their cages. For I swear that it is as if, in each cage, there is some part of myself, suffering the bitterness of imprisonment behind the bars."

Then Juha said: "Can I show you something which will make you very happy and which will, at the same time, bring to you the good will of our friend, Abulayal? Take this bag and go over to that fool of a giant and buy whatever birds that you can from him."

The Thief of Baghdad cried out in completion: "Then I let them all go, to fly freely in the skies? Allah — Allah."

* * * * * *

Hardly had the bag settled in the hand of the Thief of Baghdad when he was off, flying to the bird-shop, followed by Juha. Not a minute had passed before the door of one of the cages was open and the bird had set off flying and singing. Our friend was leaping with joy like the children, clapping and laughing and Juha was very pleased with himself as he had been able to make his friend happy and also, he had made the birds happy. Then, a few small coins were transferred to the pocket of the seller of the birds, the door of a second cage was opened and another bird was released from it. And after that, a third, then a fourth, and the Thief of Baghdad rejoiced whilst his heart sang from the excess of pleasure, and he cried: "Did you see? Did you hear? Truly, I hear its song and it is almost as if I can understand what it is saying."

Juha whispered in his ear, as he smiled: "And what do the birds say, my friend?"

The Thief of Baghdad replied, winking: "They say, our thanks to you, good man. We shall fly now, immediately, to the holy man of God, Abulayal, to tell him about you and your friend." And he turned to the owner of the shop, who was dumbfounded with amazement at what he was seeing, calling to him: "Give me this bird, and that one also, and that one as well, give me all the birds. Each bird for two fils, are we agreed?"

And the people in the market gathered round this lunatic who was buying the birds just to release them in the air, who clapped and sang to them as they slipped away to where no hand of a trapper could reach them. Then, suddenly, everybody's attention was drawn to the sharp sound of a drum, reverberating above their heads, and the yells of a man shouting in a voice above all the sounds: "Make way, you ruffians, for His Honour the Chief of Police, General Mahmar."

And the yell of the man was followed by the sound of the cracking of whips, both in the air and on the bodies of the people who separated in alarm with everyone trying to escape with his skin intact or to get close to the wall. Everyone dispersed and none remained except Juha, his friend and the giant of the shop who shrank into himself, bending so low that his turban was touching the ground. Juha looked in front of him and saw a troop of horsemen and men on foot, all wearing the clothing of patrolmen. The leader, at the front, was wearing a uniform of brilliant white, with silver and gold tassels hanging from the edges whilst his chest was decorated with more than twenty decorations and medals. This was the Chief of Police, General Mahmar, without doubt: neat, exceptionally neat. The saddle of his steed was embroidered with gold and silver. His face was red and taut, as if he had just leaped out of the bath, whilst his moustache pointed upwards at the ends as if it was the horns of an ox. On his head was a tall, silk turban, in the centre of which was a magnificent, sapphire stone. Springing out from the top of it was a long feather, a metre or more in length. And in his hand was a whip which was longer than the feather — and more dangerous.

* * * * * *

The troop of patrolmen halted at the front of the shop, led by His Honour, the Chief of Police, who cracked his whip with a great report which almost caused the heart of the Thief of Baghdad to leave his body, and which touched the edges of Juha's gown. He was boiling with rage with sparks almost flying from his eyes like those which were flying with his words, whilst his chest was blown up like a balloon about to burst and his lips were stretched in derision: "Where have you come from, you two rogues? And what are you doing?"

Oh, if only His Honour, the Chief of Police, had known who that man was who was standing before him, busy chewing mulberries and on whom appeared the signs of fear and foolishness. Oh, also, if he had known who his friend was. Juha swallowed the last of his food, with difficulty, whilst his eye gave a passing glance at the Chief of Police, brandishing his whip, and the troop of patrolmen behind him, waving about their swords and lances. Then he said, in a simple-minded fashion: "My friend and I are two poor peasants from a nearby village. We came to the market to buy two new axes after rust and time have eaten away all our axes. Then we saw the birds in the cages and we said, 'Let us set them free, that they might sing and bring the glory and praises of God upon our master, the greatest of all the Khans, of land and sea since the beginning of time, and as an expression of our love and respect for Your Honour. May God lengthen your life and keep us, always, of your good opinion'. " The Chief of Police twisted his lips, lifting, slightly, the degree of contempt in his expression, and reached out his hand to twirl the end of his moustache with disdain, whilst puffing himself up like a viper: "Can the two of you find only this stupid way of expressing your loyalty to the Khan and your respect for me? You have already committed two crimes, punishable by law. Firstly, you have assisted prisoners to escape. For the law, when it said prisoners, did not distinguish as to whether the prisoner was a man, or a mule, or a bird or even an ox — article 1989 of the Penal Code states: 'Whosoever assists a prisoner to escape shall be sentenced to life imprisonment' — that is one offence." Here the Chief of Police turned his head in a royalistic fashion towards his followers who were all standing in admiration of his genius and the extent of his knowledge. He twirled his moustache with even greater care as he continued: "And article 1990, as amended, states: 'Whosoever shall cause an assembly of persons and a gathering together, for any purpose other than for the performance of prayers, shall be sentenced to hard labour'."

Then he raised his voice, and his hands, in supplication to God, saying: "Oh Lord, assist us that we may rid our land of the likes of these."

Juha said: "Sir, we did not do anything. We did not call upon anyone to assemble. Now that magician, who was playing his pipe to the dancing cobra ..."

But his Honour, the Chief of Police, did not allow him to finish but waved his hand, disdainfully, as if he were driving away a fly, as he turned to his followers, saying: "Search these two ruffians."

* * * * * *

Like hunting dogs leaping upon their prey, the patrolmen fell upon Juha and the Thief of Baghdad and one of them wasn't very long before he took a heavy bag out of Juha's belt and handed it to His Honour, the Chief of Police, who cried out as soon as he had opened it: "So, this is just what I had expected. You have with you all this money and you buy birds just to set them free in the air instead of paying it in to the Tax Office. We shall confiscate this cash in order to place it in the State Treasury. And now, this will be sufficient to punish you. Get out of my sight before I change my mind." He said this as he was pushing the bag into the pocket of his baggy trousers which was as deep as a well.

Then he turned the head of his steed in preparation for setting off, without paying any attention to the Thief of Baghdad, who sprang forward towards him, hanging on by the side of his leg pleading: "I beg of you, my Master, this is the money with which we were going to buy the axes. If I go back without the axes my wife will beat me." But a cut from the whip of the Chief of Police sent the Thief of Baghdad away. Until this very moment Juha had not known that the real name of the Thief of Baghdad was 'The Skinner'.

However, General Mahmar had gone off on his steed, surrounded by the troop of horsemen, whilst he was still twirling his moustache, sending his haughty, piercing looks, left and right, with the people in the road fleeing away from in front of him, finding protection in the walls, columns and trees, just as if they were rats running away.

'Skinner' looked at Juha whilst they were both going in the direction towards where Masoud, the donkey, was tied up: "My fingers were itching with longing to get into the pocket of the Chief of Police which was as deep as a well, but unfortunately I had not asked you for permission."

Juha sighed, submissively, as he answered the comment of his friend, rebukingly: "It would have been better for you to have used your wit to know that there is a difference between putting your hand in someone else's pocket in order to take their wealth and in doing so in order to return something stolen to its rightful owner."

Said Skinner: "Then take your bag, perhaps your belief in my intelligence will now increase?"

And he threw the cash bag to Juha, who stuffed it quickly into his pocket, saying: "Thou hast done well."

* * * * * *

So they went off, carried away by joy, until, when they were half-way up the market street, they found a place behind a tree, luxuriant with shade, and they tied the donkey to it. Then Juha took some dates and a couple of coconuts from the saddle-bag. Skinner cracked the coconuts with a single blow of his hand and they drank the cold milk which was in them and which was sweet to the taste, celebrating the return of the bag from His Honour, the Chief of Police, General Mahmàr.

On the other side of the road, the shops were smarter. Here were magnificent Shiraz carpets, silver ornaments from the Khan Al Khalili market in Cairo, brass ornaments from Hyderabad, Damasene silks, Samarkand woollens, Chinese mirrors, manuscript copies of the Holy Quran, Verified Traditions by Al Bukhari, books of Ibn Al Haitham and Jabir bin Hayan. Here, also, were the trading premises of the Head of the Merchants' Guild. On top of the wide gate was a large notice board on which was written, in beautiful Kufi script, 'Sultan's Jewellery', whilst underneath was the name of the Head of the Merchants' Guild and his title. And at the door was the 'Shahbandar' himself, fat, with a large, white face and his crystalline, bright, bald pate. He was wearing a voluminous, silk gown, a successful advertisement for the great 'Shahbandar' himself. There was something, there, in the form of the Shahbandar, which attracted the attention of Juha. Perhaps it was in his narrow, slant eyes, and possibly it was his curved nose, like a beak above his lips, or even his rolling, pot-belly which would shake like a ball of mercury every time its owner moved his arm with the fly whisk in his hand, whilst he was busily engaged in counting the quantities of gold coins which were before him.

Then a woman appeard, enveloped in a heavy, black robe, just as if it were a tent enclosing her, with not even the tip of a toenail or a hair from her head appearing. The edge of the robe was embroidered with a dark, blue tape, from which Juha realised that the woman had been recently widowed. In this part of the market the noise was lower. Indeed, there was hardly any noise there at all as the sun was nearly setting and the market day was almost over. The voice of the woman reached the ears of Juha and his friend as she said, almost weeping: "May God lengthen your life and keep you amongst the living, oh my Master, the Shahbandar, I beg of you to help me."

The man replied, disdainfully, without lifting his eyes from his money: "May God provide for you, for I have been distributing alms today since the morning."

And the voice of the woman came back again, entreating: "I am not asking for alms, oh my Master, may God lengthen your life. It is just that I wish to sell something to you." Only now did the man lift his eyes and his curved nose, to look at the woman, dressed in black. She continued her interrupted story, whilst taking a rolled napkin from her breast: "Perhaps, my Master, you still remember my husband for he was your neighbour here in the market, Suhail bin Hassan?"

The Shahbandar said: "Yes, yes, of course I remember him. Sit down my lady, he was, may God have mercy on his soul, one who did many favours for all the people."

The lady seated herself, hesitantly, adding, as she sighed: "May the mercy of God be upon him. His favours were many, yes, so that when he passed on to the mercy of God, he did not leave me anything except this jewellery which I have kept for the day of need and the day of need has arrived, oh my Master. For my three children are sick and I have neither the fee of the doctor nor the price of the medicine. I have tried to sell this jewellery since early morning but I have not found a single merchant who is prepared to purchase it before it has been pro-duced before the official for weights and measures, and marked by his seal. You know better than anybody about the official, my Master. Just as soon as he sees the jewellery he will claim, inevitably, that it is stolen and he will issue a retention order in respect of it until an inves-tigation has been made and that means that it will be lost for ever. You are the only one who can help me."

The Shahbander compressed his lips and snored through his curved nose and said: "Let me have a look at this jewellery."

* * * * * *

The man put his hand out to unroll the napkin. The contents were a fortune of gold and silver jewellery, inlaid with diamonds, sapphires, emeralds and crystals and the man began to examine them, piece by piece, and the rays of light reflecting from them almost took away one's sight. Juha heard his friend moaning, as if there was something causing him pain, and he turned to him enquiringly and the other one said: "I am an expert on these things. This jewellery is worth forty thousand pieces of silver, at least."

Then came the cove of the Shahbander, saying: "How sorry I am, my lady, to have to tell you that most of this jewellery is imitation and is not worth anything. But, the deceased was my friend, yes, although the deceased was a wastrel and a big spendthrift he was my friend. And for that reason I shall give you a thousand pieces of silver for it, purely as assistance for you and out of mercy for the deceased."

Skinner raged with anger and he was digging Juha in his side: "Look at the thief? And I thought that I was the greatest thief of all!"

The lady groaned and almost fell full length. "What are you saying, my Master? My husband paid one thousand pieces of silver for this necklace alone."

"I do not want a lot of talk. You know, very well, that the purchase of this jewellery, without the seal of the official, is a matter which is illegal. Then, who knows whether they're not stolen? In any case, out of respect for the soul of the deceased, Suhail bin Hassan, I'll make the sum one thousand and two hundred."

The widow stood aghast and did not speak a word whilst Skinner was boiling and practically blowing up. "Did you see what this beast is doing? Are you going to let him deceive the widow in this way?"

Nasruddin said, calmly: "Wait, the tale is not finished yet."

And, indeed, the story was not yet completed. For when the widow counted the cash which the Shahbandar had given to her she cried out: "It would appear that you have made a mistake in the counting, my Master, may God lengthen your life. For this is six hundred and fifty pieces, only."

The Shahbandar exploded with a roar: "Have you gone mad, you evil woman, get out of my sight."

The woman screamed, without knowing what she was saying: "The thief — the thief — people — everyone — help me — to my rescue — this Shahbandar has robbed me — he has taken away the daily bread of my children."

Here, at this point, Skinner could not take it any longer and he leaped from where he was like a maniac. But Juha held on to his robe to hold him back. And the only thing that saved the situation was the sound of the drums of the Chief of Police being beaten and the call of the crier shouting: "Make way you scoundrels for His Honour the Hikimdar."

The few people who had run up at the screams of the widow hurried away to hide behind the columns and the doors, whilst the miserable widow ceased her screaming and rushed to run away in her black cloak and, when the retinue of the Hikimdar arrived, the poor widow was hidden from sight. Then the Shahbandar came out to the door of his shop, stroking his belly with satisfaction, to greet His Honour the Hikimdar, who acknowledged him with a lofty toss from the feather of his turban whilst his fingers went speedily to twirl his moustache.

"May God give you life, oh Shahbandar. What is all this noise? It seems to me that I heard a woman screaming?"

"True, sir, there was a low class woman here, it's generally thought that she is part of a plot against Your Honour, himself, because she began, for no reason, to scream and repeat talk about thieves and robberies, and phrases of that nature which threaten security and good order."

The Hikimdar turned to his followers and said, firmly: "Search for this woman and arrest her, immediately."

At that moment the woman was passing, walking slowly, to a track behind the tree where Juha and his friend were. Then Juha said: "Go quickly, behind her, and do not allow any of the patrolmen to catch up with her and seize her. And get to know where her residence is before you come back."

In the flash of an eye Skinner was gone. This was one of the many features by which the Thief of Baghdad could be distinguished. For he could disappear, suddenly, as if the ground had swallowed him up.

It was Juha's good luck that those who had begun to go speedily in every direction, like hunting dogs, were looking for a woman dressed in black, and not one of them paid any attention to the man sleeping peacefully in the shade of the tree, facing the trading house of the Shahbandar. And it never occurred to any one of them that this man could be the same man that they had found just a few hours before with the vendor of the birds, or, what was even more important, that this poor, old man, who looked more like a hermit or a beggar, was the Juha of great fame, himself.

But Juha was not sleeping. He was fully awake and alert, hearing and seeing all that was happening around him and, particularly, in the shop of the Shahbandar of the merchants.

The Hikimdar accepted the invitation of the Shabandar to drink a cup of tea with him at the entrance to his shop. He sat down, conceited and puffed up like a turkey cock. The conversation quickly got around to the horse-race, the date for which was getting close, in about seven or eight days' time; about how this race, which the Khan himself patronised, was the most important event, which everybody had been very interested in for months and which would remain their main interest, after it had taken place, for many months to come until the date approached for the next year's race.

The Hikimdar said: "I am confident of winning the prize this year, also, just as I won it last year. But I have to tell you the truth, I do not fear any of the challengers except one, and that is you, my friend the Shahbandar."

The Shahbandar said, flatteringly: "Whilst I, in my turn, am afraid of no one but you. But I am determined to grab the prize this year."

The Hikimdar then said: "I hear that you have bought two, pure Arabian horses specially for this race and that you paid forty-two thousand pieces of silver for them and you are hiding them in a secret place, which nobody else knows about, until their sudden appearance on the day of the race."

The Shahbandar said proudly: "Indeed, they cost me fifty four thousand, your Honour, the Hikimdar, fifty four."

"But that is a lot, the whole prize will not cover that amount."

"That is true, but I am not concerned with any expense just so long as the affair is connected with the pleasure of the Khan, my Lord, and of him being pleased with me." The merchant did not mention, naturally, that his success in winning the prize would double the value of the two horses, that he might be able to sell them for an unimaginable price, doubled and redoubled from what he had spent, to one of the sultans or khans who would be invited to watch the race.

The Hikimdar then said, as he lifted up his fingers to his twirled moustache: "But why all this secrecy. Are you afraid for their safety from jealousy?"

The Shahbandar quickly replied: "No, rather from sickness, oh Your Honour the Hikimdar. One of the strange sicknesses might find its way to my horses, such as happened to the two steeds of our friend, the Commander of the Army, last year, and they were unable to take part in the race." The Shahbandar of the merchants was silent for a moment, before he added, boldly: "Naturally, that was lucky for you, your honour the Hikimdar, for the Commander of the Army was your most dangerous challenger."

The Hikimdar realised what the Shahbandar was implying, but he preferred to let it pass, politely. Then he said: "Maintain secrecy about your two steeds and their site as you wish. It may help you to win the second prize. But the first prize, rest assured that it will be mine."

* * * * * *

Then the conversation became more and more boring and Juha was on the point of really going to sleep when it was as if the ground split open to reveal Skinner, just as if he had never left the place. There he was, standing in front of him, smiling peacefully: "The widow lives quite close to here. Her three children are two boys and a girl, the oldest of which is ten, and they are all sick. The doctor came and took all of the six hundred and fifty pieces of silver and gave her medicine which will not be sufficient for a week. God alone knows what she is going to do as it was quite clear to me that she does not possess anything that it is possible to sell."

Juha said, with his eye still on the shop of the Shahbandar of the merchants: "Do not worry. We shall find a solution. How much was that jewellery worth, in your opinion, which the merchant bought?"

"Not less than forty thousand pieces of silver."

Juha was quiet for a moment and then he went on: "This man is in debt to the widow for forty thousand pieces of silver and he will pay them." Skinner did not understand what it was that Juha was trying to say and before he could enquire, the place was suddenly filled with the fragrance of a bewitching scent and there was a woman, beautiful in step and shape, whose figure practically spoke of beauty under her wonderful, velvety cloak.

The Hikimdar, as she stepped to the door of the store, called out: "Welcome to the perfect, dear lady, wife of my great friend, the Shahbandar of the merchants."

The lady replied to the greeting of the Hikimdar with an elegant nod of her head and a few words which did not reach the hearing of Juha and his friend.

Then she took her place next to her husband without removing her veil and he said, gently: "Hello to my dear wife. What brings you here today?"

She replied, whilst making a signal with a slight movement of her hand which her husband did not notice but Juha did: "It is my good luck that brought me here today. Then, I ...," and she leant over to her husband to whisper whilst he gave her his ear and neither Juha nor his friend could hear what was being said but they both saw her foot come out slowly from under the table and rub up against the foot of the Hikimdar.

Juha and Skinner exchanged a meaningful look and the Shahbandar of the merchants jumped up, went to his safe, to take out from it one of the necklaces which he had taken from the widow and gave it as a present to his beautiful wife, saying: "This is for you, my dearest. I bought it today for three thousand pieces of silver."

The Hikimdar said: "Wear it now, my lady and allow the sapphires to feel the delight of touching your ivory neck. I beg of you, my dear sir, the Shahbandar, ask her to wear the necklace, now, to let us see how it lights up on her."

The pretty woman did not wait for the permission of her husband for she quickly raised her veil and placed the necklace around her neck as her eyes and the eyes of the Hikimdar embraced together, passionately, whilst the activity of their feet, under the table, increased. All this was going on whilst the Shahbandar was happy about his wife and the admiration of the Hikimdar for her, and the necklace which he had presented to her.

And Juha said to his friend, as they were moving away: "That is enough. For we now have all the elements of an attractive game so let us postpone the game until tomorrow."

* * * * * *

Chapter 5

The people in the city of Sindashah had no subject of conversation except the horse-race, before which there now only remained seven days. And as the appointed date grew nearer, enthusiasm, both public and personal, of those actually involved, increased. The rivalry was at its fiercest between two nominees for success in taking the first prize this year — the General Mahmar, and Al Mimari, the Shahbandar of the merchants — and the reason for the fury of the competition and struggle for supremacy was not solely the enormous prize but, much more important than the prize, was the fact that the winner would achieve grace and favour with the Khan.

For the Khan had no concern beyond the worship of God and staying up late at night over matters concerning the security of the State, except the horse-race. Our friend, General Mahmar, was very keen to maintain his authority and his position in the court of the Khan and was fully aware that if he lost the race his standing would fall and that he might never, ever, be able to reinstate himself.

As for our other friend, Al Mimari, the head of the merchants guild, he of the big, potbelly and the beautiful wife, he too was also longing to win so that he could succeed in getting a place in the court. He considered that the one thing which he lacked in order to be distinguished as a person of quality was his presence amongst the followers of the Khan. For proximity to the Khan, naturally, was an honour above all honour. However, the ambition towards this great honour was not the only thing in the mind of the inflated Mimari, for he had many great schemes in mind, which, if he could only have the opportunity to satisfy the Khan himself about them, would redouble his wealth several times over. Talk of the race excluded all other matters in the alleyways, passages and tracks, in the tea shops, the shops, the various corners of the market and the caravan termini. Even the Khan himself was unable to bear any other form of conversation. So that when the Chief of Police of the city came to see him in the evening, in an attempt to incite him against the Commander of the Army, the Khan refused to listen to him until he had spoken to him about the two horses which he had specially trained for the great race.

General Mahmar said: "All which I hope, my Lord, is that I bring pleasure to your eyes in seeing my two, grey steeds, flying like the wind, leaving the remainder of the field behind them like a flock of sheep. For, my Lord, I shall win yet again this year, and I shall present my win to you, 'inshallah' (if God so wills)."

The Khan yawned, fixing two, hawk-like eyes on the Chief of Police: "I hope that you are not over-confident about your two horses. For I have heard that a merchant in the market, I can't remember his name, has brought two, pure-bred, Arab steeds, especially for the race, and that he has spent on them, up to now, seventy thousand dirhams."

"Twenty thousand only, my Lord, actually. For I have carried out an investigation and came to know the correct figure."

The Khan waved his hand, languidly. "Twenty thousand or forty thousand, it is of no consequence. What is important is who is going to be the winner, of the prize and my favours."

The Hikimdar called out, excitedly; bending over the hand of the Khan and kissing it, with agitation and submission: "My fondest hope, my Lord, is that God will cause your approval of myself to continue."

The Khan pursed his lips and snorted: "Marvellous, marvellous, bravo! I desire that the race this year will be the talk of the people for generations to come. I do truly wish that you should be the winner. For, as you know, I do not wish that one of that rabble of merchants should join the retinue of the court."

"I shall not permit him to win, my Lord."

The Khan then said, in a very significant tone: "I pray that none will resort to open trickery or suspicious activity such as we had last year. I want a straight race and a true winner. Do you understand?"

And the sweat poured off the face of the Hikimdar until it wet the ends of his twirled moustache, whilst he tried his absolute best to make his voice sound natural as he answered: "I understand, I understand, my Lord."

* * * * * *

The Khan continued his torture of the Hikimdar, saying: "If anything happens this year of a suspicious nature, there will be a few heads dropping off some shoulders." Then the Khan was silent for a moment, considering the effect of his words on the Hikimdar, before he went on: "Now, what was it that you wanted to say to me about our friend the Commander of the Army."

The Hikimdar wasn't very pleased with the use of the words, 'our friend', but he had already made up his mind and arranged what he was going to say and he could not very well withdraw at this stage. So he coughed, lightly, clearing his throat before he spoke: "Indeed, what I have to say to you, now, my Lord, upsets me a great deal, and causes me unbearable pain. For my Lord knows that the Commander of the Army is my friend and that I am indebted to him for many favours. However, when friendship clashes with the call of duty, with my loyalty to my Lord, then there is no room for choice."

The Khan looked, with his two old eyes, into the face of the man who was talking to him and moved around in his seat. Something inside the General called out, warning him about this look, and the voice of the Khan was heard again, this time in a tone with not a lot of friendship in it.

"Talk on, without the preamble. What lies do you have which you wish to tell about the Commander of the Army?"

"Lies? God forbid, my Lord. What I have to say are proven facts, supported by witnesses. The Commander of the Army is plotting against you, my Lord. Do you remember, my Lord, when he asked you for permission to travel to Hindustan for medical treatment? He did not go to Hindustan. Indeed, he hid himself in the clothing of a merchant and went to Isfahan. And there he met, in secret, with the enemy of God the accursed idolator, the Khan Arqub. The meeting of the two was repeated three times, according to my investigations. I have not yet been able to learn the details of what went on at the three meetings but, I ask myself, my Lord, why did he lie and feign sickness and claim that he was going to Hindustan whilst, instead, he was arranging such suspicious meetings with the enemy of God and your enemy, my Lord?"

The General was speaking quickly whilst the Khan fixed his eyes upon him and they did not move away until, the man had completed what he was saying. Knowing the effect which the mention of the Khan Arqub would have on his Khan's spirit, the General, went silent, awaiting the comment of the Khan, whilst saying to himself, "The moment for the removal of the Commander of the Army from his position has arrived."

The gaze of the Khan to the Hikimdar went on for a long time until the man began to feel perturbed and, finally, he said: "This is dangerous talk, Hikimdar. You are directing your accusations at the most sincere and loyal of my men. The man in whom I have placed my trust and to whom I have entrusted responsibility for the defence of the country. I believe that you do not deny that he has undertaken this responsibility full well; at a time when someone else was, and still is, engaged in twirling his moustaches and flirting with beautiful women."

The world darkened before the eyes of the Hikimdar. What ill omen had suggested to him that he should choose this moment in which to begin the presentation of his plan to bring about the downfall of the Commander of the Army? Also, what did the Khan mean by the reference to the flirting with beautiful women? Did he know anything about his relationship with the lady, the wife of the Shahbandar? When he spoke after that his speech was based on his instinct: "How great is your wisdom, my Lord, how kind is your heart and how splendid is your concern for your men! I had, indeed, realised, my Lord, that it was not possible for such talk to be true. To even think such a thing is a sin. But then I accused myself, that my friendship and my faith in the Commander of the Army, they were the two things which were preventing me from believing such talk as this and I said to myself, my Lord, that the proper attitude would be to put up to you the result of the investigations. For you alone, my Lord, by the veracity of your discernment, purity of spirit and unique astuteness, would be capable of distinguishing between truth and falsehood. It is probably some slander, spread by a jealous person or a trick put about which is aiming at dimensions much wider than simply the removal of the Commander of the Army."

* * * * * *

The Khan then said, each syllable of his words plunging into the breast of the Hikimdar like the blade of a sword: "Who would be the slanderer but you? The most likely thought which I have is that you invented this story, totally, for some purpose of your own and that there have been neither investigations nor anything else."

"But no! But no! My Lord! This is not true. I have not invented anything. Do you not remember, my Lord, the two villains whom we arrested a month ago, who, in the beginning were refusing to talk. They talked yesterday, voluntarily, and confessed that they were working on behalf of Arqub, that they came here with a letter which they handed over to the Commander of the Army and they confessed to me, personally, about the meetings which took place between the Commander of the Army and Arqub in Isfahan. But now, I have realised, my Lord, that these confessions are false and that they only wish to cause an incident, the rogues! I shall hang them both immediately, as a suitable punishment for these lies; this instant, at once, with your permission, my Lord. Had it not been for your elevated wisdom I would not have realised the true facts so easily. Yes, I was wrong to believe this defamation without proper investigation but please accept my apology, my Lord, for I, with an excess of concern and my sensitivity with everything which affects the safety of my Lord and..."

The Hikimdar was speaking very quickly and backing away, taking steps to the rear, bowing low so that the feather in his headdress touched the ground with every step. But before he could reach the door, praising God as he did so, for his escape with his skin intact, the Khan called out, ordering: "Wait, I wish to interrogate these two villains myself so do not be in too much of a hurry to hang them. Where are they now?"

"In the vault prison, my Lord."

Said the Khan, as he pressed a brass button on the right of his throne, calling for the Head Guard: "You will remain here with me. But you, Head Guard, will take four of your men to the vault prison, and bring, immediately, the two villains who...." But the Khan did not complete what he had to say for he was suddenly seized by a choking epileptic fit which he used to take from time to time. He was hardly able to breathe and began to pull at his neck with one hand whilst throwing out the other as if he wanted to grab a handful of air. And before the Head of the Guard could understand what was happening, the Khan was on the ground unconscious whilst froth was foaming from his lips as he breathed heavily.

* * * * * *

The General was quite sure that the gods had saved him, at the last moment, and that if the series of misfortunes of that night had been completed and the two prisoners had appeared, then the case would have been ... If the Khan had realised that all the investigations which had been claimed by the Hikimdar were of his own authorship and fabrication, then the certain result would have been that his head would have been hanging from the gallows or he would have been impaled on a sharp pointed stake, the khazuq.

Probably, even the General himself never knew how he managed to find his way out of the palace. It was as if he was coming out of his grave. There was a storm raging outside but the Hikimdar paid no attention to it. For he was pushing his way towards the vault prison and one thought only had taken possession of him. Those two villains from Isfahan must be hidden away immediately. It was imperative that they should not be available when the Khan came round. He knew from his previous experience that the Khan would not come to before morning. Therefore, everything must be completed tonight.

The easiest way, and the quickest, would be to kill the two villains in the vault prison, but this would arouse the suspicions of the Khan. And the Khan, it would appear, had become close to being suspicious about everything. Then what was to be done?

The Hikimdar, General Mahmar kept asking himself about the solution as he rushed along to the vault prison with the storm raging around him and without a single one of the patrolmen, all of whom were hidden away in some kind of shelter from the storm, even sensing his departure. When he arrived at the vault prison, the plan had ripened in his mind. The solution at which he had arrived was that the two prisoners should escape, yes, escape. The two of them had taken advantage of the storm and had escaped the same night. Of course, it would be inevitable that the guards who had allowed them to escape would have to be punished. And it was likely the Khan would direct some pretty hard criticism towards him but the matter would not be a question of execution.

The two villains were nothing more that a couple of simple villagers from a faraway village whom ill-luck had led to the wicked city on an illfated day. And when they suddenly found the door of their dark cell being opened at night with the Hikimdar himself there and two of the guards behind him, and being ordered to follow them, they were quite sure that their end had come and that they were about to be hanged for a crime they knew nothing about. They began to plead and beg for mercy, but the Hikimdar had no time to waste in discussion and he ordered his followers to hit them both over the head and render them unconscious. The two villains were then put into sacks as if they were bits of baggage. And the two sacks were taken outside the wall of the city where they were thrown down, surrounded by darkness and the storm which was still raging. When the two men awoke and rid themselves of their sacks they found some money in their pockets. They assured themselves that they were outside the city, on their own without any guards, prison or bars. And they turned their backs on the wicked city and rushed to get away. No one knows where they went but one thing is for sure, they never went anywhere near the city of Sindashah from that day onwards.

* * * * * *

All this happened far away from Juha and his friend Skinner, the Thief of Baghdad. On that night they had taken themselves off to a road-house at the far end of the city where they slept the night. As for the Thief of Baghdad, he slept deeply, all night, like an innocent babe. But Juha, he lay awake on his back, thinking about how was he going to get back the wealth of the wretched widow which the Shahbandar of the merchants had extorted from her. When he finally surrendered to sleep, two hours later, the plan was complete in his mind, as clear as clear could be.

* * * * * *

And morning came at the Bridge of the Massacres, where around fifty fortune-tellers and astrologers had established a cluster of huts, made of straw, where they would receive their customers of all kinds and types — a woman who needs an amulet to preserve for her the love of her husband, and the barren woman who wishes to give birth, and the husband who is perplexed between the problems of his third and fourth wives, then the one who is seeking employment at the treasury and a merchant who wants to travel by caravan to the country around Damascus — everyone, who has a problem or prospect, who wishes to know what the unknown has in store for him.

The fortune-tellers had a master who was the chief or head of the guild. He had, instead of a hut, a tent which was bigger and more elegant. At the entrance was an old carpet which was practically without colour or shape, at the top of which was an ancient skull, thought, most likely, to have escaped from an excavation of a pre-historic site. There were also pieces of shell and carved stones in the shape of animals of strange forms. Some had one head whilst others had numerous heads. Then the entrance was concealed by a black sheet, covered by a drawing of a monster, with fire coming out of its mouths and other parts, whilst above it cooking pots were hanging, with the heads of snakes looking over the top of some of them.

As for the chief of the fortune-tellers himself, he was an old man, getting on in years. His light beard hung down in the shape of a fine rope until it reached his knees, and his single yellow, hollow eye was as if it was sunken into the sea of time. His turban of black and red, on the top of which was a glass ball, was the turban of the leadership and the badge of the head of the guild.

On that particular morning the man was nervous and of an ill-tempered disposition. For since the morning began, not a single customer had passed by the bridge, asking for knowledge of the unknown, so he had not received any commission from the fifty fortune-tellers who made up his kingdom.

Perhaps he was not at all prepared to receive the new arrival who came asking for his permission to become one of his flock and for him to appoint the place in which he would be able to set up his bed matting or his hut. For he looked at him, examining him slowly with his single sunken eye, and in his look was a mixture of disdain, mockery and derision. Finally he said to the round-shouldered man with the enormous turban which almost concealed half his face, and with the heavy sack which he was carrying on his shoulder: "In which branch of fortune-telling do you wish to work? You appear to be ignorant and stupid, knowing nothing of the secrets of sand, shells or the stars."

The man, who was none other than our friend Juha, said: "I, oh wise man of our time, did not come here to compete with anyone for a livelihood coming to him from above. For I specialise in one thing only, the Mandal." (This is a magic practice, in which a fortune-teller, or a medium, makes prophecies whilst contemplating a mirror-like surface.)

The old fortune-teller snorted through his nose, twisted his mouth in a sarcastic smile under which appeared a black cave with a door of two, widely-spaced fangs, and cried out, deeming that what he had heard was absurd: "What do you say? Whatever is this Mandal that you are talking about?" Then he raised his voice, directing what he was saying to his followers: "Has anyone of you ever heard of anything in the science of astrology called a Mandal? The shouts of them all were raised, loud and clear, in sharp denial, astonishment, confusion or just plain disapproval of the arrival of this new competitor.

Juha Nasruddin then said, apologetically: "It may have a different name in this pleasant country. However, the art of finding things, both lost and stolen, is an ancient art of a special kind, well-known amongst the disciplines of astrology and I claim that I am the most knowledgeable person on earth in this great science."

The head of the fortune-tellers, who by now had quietened down, said: "You say things which have been stolen? Then lay out your things in any place that you wish, nobody will ever come to you, 'inshallah'. Do you not know that Sindashah is a town which knows nothing of theft; that not a single thief has entered the town for more than four years?"

Whilst pointing to a place, suitable for laying out his matting and bedding, Juha said, in a tone of submission: "That's me and my luck. Have you any objection if I lay out my matting here?"

Said the head fortune-teller, disdainfully: "Put it wherever you like.

For I am confident that you will be away from here in two or three days."

* * * * * *

The fortune-tellers reception of their new comrade was not one of welcome. He set out his matting in a spot not far from the tent of the head of the guild, without paying any attention to the sarcastic and mocking comments coming from right and left. He took an unusually shaped, big, yellow book out of his sack, on the leather binding of which some very strange markings were engraved. Of course, nobody understood that the book was an old dictionary of the Chinese language.

A middle-aged woman, who appeared to be a widow, came to the man on his right. She threw the usual fee into his lap and a question in his ear: "Shall I be happy in my forthcoming marriage?"

The fortune-teller emptied a sack out on his matting and spread out a collection of various items from it, buttons, shells and pieces of metal. Then the man began to write with his finger, moving among the pieces whilst mumbling words of magic, which could not be understood, until inspiration came to him, and he said: "If a black eagle does not pass over your house, between the rising of the sun and the period immediately before noon then you will be the happiest of wives. But also, take care that a female mouse does not give birth in your house seven times."

And, at the same time, the fortune-teller on his left was telling a man, dressed like a merchant: "It is a profit-making deal, 'inshallah' but when you pay the price of the goods, take care if there is a bald-headed man at a distance of twenty paces from where you are."

* * * * * *

The first, second and third days passed without anyone stopping at the new fortune-teller and everyone expected that he would pack up in despair on the fourth day. But the city awoke on that day to an event which shook it from end to end. Even the fortune-tellers, who always preoccupy themselves with understanding the unknown more than with the facts of the day, reacted to the event. For the two steeds specially prepared by the Shahbandar of the merchants for the race had disappeared as if the ground had opened up beneath them. It was said that the owner had torn his clothes, thrown his turban on the ground and had been smitten, in fact, by a touch of madness, and also that all the patrolmen of the city were searching for the two horses, but to no effect.

A crier passed through the city until he reached the Bridge of the Massacres, announcing that a reward of five hundred silver dirhams awaited whoever could indicate where the two missing horses were to be found. The fortune-tellers and the astrologers then began winking at each other and ridiculing Juha, or the Haji Abdussabur as they knew him, saying: "Congratulations to you, master. Here, a theft has come to you from the very gates of heaven."

"Now then! You have nothing to do but read the Mandal and you will know the place of the two steeds and you will get five hundred silver dirhams!!!"

Even the sedate old man, head of the fortune-tellers guild, took part in the campaign of mocking: "Do not forget, oh Haji Abdussabur, that my commission is twenty per cent, ha... ha... ha..."

Then they all burst out laughing. But the situation in the palace of the Khan and the house of the Shahbandar of the merchants and most public places in the city of Sindashah, was a long way from being a laughing matter.

* * * * * *

The Khan, who was still abed, sent for the Hikimdar. He had not received him since the escape of the two prisoners had occurred. And the meeting was a one-sided conversation. From the other person came a bending of the head and the lower leg and even the knee, and movements of the body which the sons of Adam, the ordinary people, had learnt thousands of years ago to cause happiness to enter into the hearts of chiefs, rulers and other persons in authority. What mattered was that the Khan asked the Hikimdar to find the two steeds before the appointed day of the race. Otherwise, it would be within the right of the Khan to consider him personally responsible for their loss.

73

The Hikimdar came out from the terror of the meeting with the Khan to hold another meeting, of even greater terror, with his subordinates. He warned them, very clearly, that if the two stolen horses were not found in the course of two days, then ten heads, at least, would be hanging from the gallows. And those people in their turn, called a meeting with their subordinates, in which the language used was even more abusive and ended with the threat of the hanging of one hundred heads from the gallows if the two stolen horses were not recovered before the day of the race. Just before noon, the Bridge of the Massacres witnessed the arrival of His Honour, the Hikimdar, bursting with anger and irritation, astride his horse, and, behind him, the troop of his guard in their highly decorative clothing. When they stopped in front of the tent of the head of the astronomers' guild, the old man came to him in great fear, bending down like the Arabic figure eight ( ), whilst the flaming eye of the Hikimdar looked him over and the fifty fortunetellers looked who had all came out of their huts, in fear and trembling of what might be expected from such a visit.

The Hikimdar began directing his questions to the astrologers, one after the other, to see if they had heard anything from their visitors, persons seeking knowledge of the unknown. But their frightened answers were all in the negative. Then, exactly what Juha had been expecting, happened. Out came the voice of one of the astrologers saying: "But did you not say, precisely, that you were capable of finding out, through what you call the Mandal, the location of anything stolen?"

The Hikimdar whipped round like someone who had been stung, and there was Juha, standing there, not making a movement. He cried out to his guards: "Seize that idiot, tie him to one of those stakes, and give him a good thrashing with the whips until he discloses the location of the two stolen horses or confesses, in front of everyone, that he is a wicked liar, an impostor and trickster."

The guards fell upon Juha like a pack of hunting dogs and stripped him of his cloak and turban. The whips were lifted, ready to set about his almost naked body, whilst two of them went up to him with ropes, ready to tie him to the nearest stake. But Juha had not lost his self-possession and he raised his voice high, above all the clamour: "I en-

74

treat you, Your Majesty, listen first to what I have to say, then do with me what you will. Yes, I open the Mandal and I am able to recover anything which has been stolen, even though it be hidden on the moon. And no other fortune-teller on earth can compete with me in this matter."

The Hikimdar gave a majestic signal with his hand to his followers, in order that they should stop preparing for the beating, and then he said: "If what you say is true, then why did you not do just that? Why have you not found the stolen horses by now? Do you think that I am demented that I should believe such lies?"

Juha replied, in the same, clear, confident voice: "The reason is simple, Your Honour the Hikimdar. The Mandal will not disclose its secrets, except if the owner of the thing stolen is, himself, present, and requests this with his own tongue."

"And how much time do you require to recover the two horses?"

"One night, Your Honour the Hikimdar, and I shall return the two horses, even if they be in the land of Waq Al Waq, (according to the descriptions of the ancient Arab geographers, the name of one of two different groups of islands, one east of China and the other located in the Indian Ocean), on one condition, that their owner comes to me here, before the middle of the day."

The Hikimdar hesitated for a moment, turning his eyes to the fortune-teller standing in front of him, then he said: "You will remain here, under guard in this place, until I come back to you. And hear this: if you have deceived me I shall make you regret the very day in which your mother gave birth to you."

And he set off, on his horse, with his troop of men following him, repeating furiously, whilst cracking his whip in the air: "Dogs — rogues — by God, I will smash all your skulls, for sure."

* * * * * *

Chapter 6

The Shahbandar of the merchants came to the Bridge of the Massacres as if he was walking to his own funeral. The loss of the two Arabian steeds had so thrown his mind off balance that he could no longer be hypocritical in talking to the Hikimdar. For he refused, at first, to accompany him to the fortune-teller, the discloser of the contents of the Mandal, who claimed that he was able to find out the location of the two horses. He said that he could not believe in such humbug and wallowing in superstition. Indeed, he could even go so far as to accuse His Honour, the Hikimdar, of being quite happy about the loss of the two steeds, which were certainly going to have won the race this year, and of only being so determined to accompany him to the Bridge of Massacres to present him to the charlatans of fortune-tellers, in order to increase his own happiness at his suffering and to get more enjoyment from his revenge upon him.

What was going on in the head of the Shahbandar did not affect Juha. Also, he knew how to deal with this type of human jackal. For he left him standing before him, alongside the Hikimdar, for a long time, while he busied himself with a series of rituals, incantations and mumblings. These came out from inside him with a fearful ring, with a rhythm in harmony with the movements of his hand and head and the twitching of his fingers and his beard. His looks were like sparks at times, and like a gentle breeze at others. There was a halo of smoke from the burning incense around, which wafted over to all the fifty huts of the charlatans, extending on both sides of the Bridge of the Massacres.

After the Shahbandar had cleared his throat for the tenth time and the whip of the Hikimdar had cracked for the twentieth time, Juha raised his head, slowly, from the brass goblet which he had been observing. Then his mutterings began to be lower and lower until, finally, they were reduced to simply a light movement of his lips and a direct look from his eyes into the eyes of the merchant, in which, at that moment, there was nothing but a mixture of anger, derision and disbelief. Then the Shahbandar said: "I know that you are a charlatan. I am totally unprepared to believe you and I would not have come to this filthy place, to talk to a scoundrel like you, had I not, literally, been forced to do so. I have lost two, pure-bred steeds. Someone has stolen the two horses, or perhaps he has acquired them or borrowed them from me without my permission or knowledge. What is important is that they are missing and that is it. So open your Mandal and inform me where I can find them."

Juha then produced from his bag an ancient, black bottle in the shape of the head of a snake. He opened it, and whilst continuing his mumblings he poured into the brass goblet, seven drops, one after the other.

As he did so he raised his voice, little by little, in his language, impossible to understand, until he completed his mutterings in a high scream, which practically shook the Bridge of the Massacres, whilst the whip of the Hikimdar almost dropped from his hand and fifty heads, with frightened and bewildered eyes, popped out of the huts of the fortune-tellers. And the one who the most frightened of them all was their leader, owner of the skull, who grabbed the skull with heavily veined, shaking hands as if he thought that it was going to fly away. Juha called out in a solemn voice: "Hayiii ... ayee ayee ayee. Yaa Qayuuum — you alone know the secrets." Then the voice of Juha began to drop again, lower and lower as he burst forth, as if it were the beat of a drum: "Araakaad, rasama, abraabeeshin, abruun katin, ayl, kalaa."

* * * * * *

All eyes were now on Juha, shining, fascinated. Even the men of the guard gathered together, watching the solemn sight. The Hikimdar was more smitten than anyone else as Juha realised by a quick glance from the corner of his eye whilst being completely absorbed in his ritual without, apparently, paying any attention to what was going on around him, just as if there was nobody else on the bridge except himself. He opened his big yellow book and began to turn over the pages until he found the page which he wanted. Half of it was covered with the drawing of a spider preying on a fly. He then began to move his gaze between his brass goblet and his book and went on until he was quite certain that their curiosity had reached the stage at which their patience would be exhausted. He said, sedately, without lifting his gaze from the goblet: "You say, two steeds? Yes, yes, there they are, I see them. One is white, as light as day, whilst the other is as black as the night."

The Hikimdar called out, spontaneously: "Those are the two missing horses."

But the Shahbandar of the merchants raged: "There is nothing new in that! Indeed, all Sindashah saw the two horses, the day that they arrived from the Arab lands."

Juha paid no attention to the sarcasm of the Shahbandar, but carried on with what he was saying, just as if he was reading from a book: "And on the tail of the white steed is a white, silk tape. Ah, indeed, this tape is a magic talisman, which the eye cannot see. Let us have a look at the tail of the black horse. Ah, it also has a black tape — the same magic talisman as the other, which cannot be seen by the eye." Then he raised his head to the dumbfounded Shahbandar, who appeared to be very agitated by a dangerous warning look from the Hikimdar. But Juha did not wait for the answer of the Shahbandar and carried on his reading from the brass goblet: "And, in the hoof of the right foreleg of the white steed is a golden nail, covered with black in order that it should not appear to be different from the rest. So it is also carrying another magic talisman; and the same applies to the black steed."

The voice of the very disturbed Shahbandar cut him off: "Yes, yes, they are the two steeds, but I don't know anything about the two tapes, the white and the black ... and ...."

Here, the Hikimdar spoke: "Or about the two golden nails. Do you know what the punishment is, Shahbandar, for practising magic?"

The Shahbandar replied, anxiously: "Perhaps the groom has done this, without my knowledge — or perhaps they came from the Arab lands like that."

The Hikimdar snorted, hissing like a snake: "Anyway, we can look into this matter after we have recovered the horses."

Juha was very much aware that his words had hit the Shahbandar at a very vulnerable point. The look of entreaty which appeared in his eyes did not go unnoticed by Juha. Nor did the fact that the Hikimdar wished to use this same opportunity to finish off his opponent, or at least, to humiliate him, right to the last breath. Juha also realised that the Hikimdar's desire to humiliate the merchant was not just because of the competition over the race, but also by reason of the lady, the chaste wife of the Shahbandar of the merchants of the land of Al Amar.

* * * * * *

The Shahbandar then said, making signs with his eyes towards Juha, indicating submission and dependence upon him: "I know nothing about the silk tapes or the golden nails. Perhaps this fortune-teller here is just saying that in order to raise his fee. Well then, how much do you want, my man, to lead us to the location of the two horses?"

Juha said, understanding the signs of the Shahbandar: "This should be a conversation which no one should hear, except four ears, and which no one should see, except four eyes. So come with me, some distance away, in order that we may settle this matter."

The Hikimdar, burning with officiousness, said: "Surely, I can be a witness?"

Juha replied in a conclusive tone: "This is impossible. Otherwise, the Mandal will immediately become blind. Come, oh your eminence the Shahbandar, may God lengthen your life and let you enjoy the youth of she whom you love."

The two had hardly got away before the Shahbandar spoke, in a tone which was almost an entreaty: "Woe unto you, do you want to be the cause for the loss of my head? How on earth did you know about the matter of the silk tapes and the golden nails. Even my groom himself doesn't know anything about this matter!"

Juha said, pointing to his Chinese book: "I knew from this book. All the symbols which the magic liquid makes on the surface of the water in the brass goblet, their secret is to be found in this book."

Then the merchant, being especially nice to Juha, said: "And now, tell me how much you want?"

Juha said, straightforwardly: "Twenty thousand pieces of silver. Not more — not less and the two steeds shall be with you in the period immediately before noon, tomorrow, as God wills."

There was something in his voice which made the Shahbandar realise that there was no point in trying to bargain. So, like any clever merchant, he moved to the other point: "I agree, but on condition that the two steeds are returned in exactly the same state as that in which God created them, that is, without anything added. Is that understood?"

And Juha replied, simply and calmly: "That will cost you ten thousand pieces more."

The merchant cried out, anxiously: "That is a great deal. Why it's more than half the price of the horses themselves."

Juha said: "Indeed, then this makes their price exactly half the figure which you quoted, yourself, two days ago, to His Honour, the Hikimdar himself."

* * * * * *

The mouth of the merchant gaped open in astonishment and he had no alternative but to surrender, whilst saying to himself: "It is true; that wise man was telling the truth when he said that it is sufficient for a man to surrender, just once, and the whole of his life becomes just one, long series of surrenders."

Juha said, whilst the two of them were returning to where the Hikimdar and his followers were, with their eyes practically popping out of their sockets with curiosity. "Tomorrow morning, in the period immediately before noon, the two steeds will be returned to you, complete, just as God created them, with nothing added or taken away. So have your money ready, in gold, and in one bag. I beg of you not to make any mistakes in counting out the money, like you did with one of your customers, two days ago, in an illegal transaction concerning some jewellery." That was the last slap in the face, for it killed all remaining ability for resistance which the Shahbandar had.

When the leader of the fortune-tellers the owner of the skull, heard the figure which the new delegate was receiving for the return of the two horses, he cried out with a piercing scream and fell unconscious on the ground with nobody there able to rouse him. For everybody was dumbfounded and bewildered, as if a volcano had erupted over their heads.

But the Hikimdar, as he turned the reins of his mare, had already cried out: "Remember, you fortune-teller, that the two steeds must be returned, according to the description given when you saw them in the Mandal, with two silk tapes and two golden nails. That is how you, yourself, described them. Otherwise I swear by God, and by His Majesty the Khan, I'll beat the skin off your back."

* * * * * *

Juha collected his belongings together — the bottle, the goblet and the book, and threw them into his bag, rolled up his prayer mat and left the Bridge of the Massacres, returning to the road-house, which he had selected as a place where he could spend the night, without paying any attention to the four spies which the Hikimdar had sent to follow him.

They set off behind him, right at his tail, like hunting dogs, until their noses were practically touching the nape of Juha's neck. He was even able to hear their breathing, panting behind his ears. When Juha took his place in the tea-shop of the roadhouse, they all took their places, right up against him, two on his right and two on his left.

The waiter brought dinner, tea and a glass of water to Juha. Four other heads bent over his plate, counting how many pieces of meat were on the plate and, also, what was the colour of the tea in the cup. At the moment when Juha had finished his meal, and had thanked God for it, Skinner, with his broad smile and his athletic figure, appeared at the door and his eyes met those of Juha. He realised, immediately, that the spies were present around his friend, so he entered and passed by them in a respectful manner, without turning to look at them or at Juha. He took his place behind a wooded screen, where it was not possible for them to see him.

Then Juha got up and laid down his matting and got out his book, the bottle and the goblet. He poured some of the water into the goblet and then seven drops from the bottle on to the water, then started his incantations, exactly as it had been during the day at the Bridge of the Massacres. The spies rushed to write down just what he was doing and not a thing escaped their notice. Even when the voice of Juha began to rise, they wrote that it had risen and they also wrote down how many times he moved his gaze between the goblet and the Chinese book. Yet, with all this diligence and detail they were unaware of the sound of Skinners nail, as he scratched on the back of the wooden partition which was between him and Juha, nor did they notice that the voice of Juha had risen even more and had become·clearer as he said, whilst observing the brass goblet: "Yaa hayii — ee — ee — Yaa Qayuuum — let me see — ah, now I see, let me hear — ah, now I hear." And the spies rushed to write down on their papers.

"Ah, now I hear the hoof beats of the two steeds. Ah, now I see them clearly, with my own eyes." Then came the sound of the scratching of the Thief of Baghdad, with his finger-nail on the wooden screen, as if he was saying that he too, could hear and understand. Then Juha resumed, saying in a resounding voice: "Ah, now I see the two steeds, the white one and the black. There they are, running to their place which is known. Yes, I see now the two long tails, flying out behind the quarters of the two steeds. The white one, it's all the hair of the tail, there are no silk or woollen tapes, and the black one, all the hair of the tail and there are no tapes of silk or wool. Ah! and there are the hooves of two steeds, even the nails of the shoes, I can see them. They are made of iron. The two steeds are in the same state as when God created them. Aabraakaad, aabraabeeshin, kaatin, rasama', aabruun, abil kala, aabraakaad, aabraabeeeshin, kaatin, aabraakaad." As the chanting of Juha died away, the sound of the finger-nail, scratching on the wooden screen came through to say that the message had been received and that everything was going to be as it should be. For a second time Juha gathered his things together, not forgetting to pray the evening prayer before lying down to sleep.

* * * * * *

At the forenoon of the next day the whole of the city had gathered at the Bridge of the Massacres. All eyes were centred on the fortune-teller, the opener of the Mandal. Those who gave him the lie and did not believe, and those who had faith in him and believed that he was a person from whom the veil of inability to understand life's mysteries had been lifted. Then the Shahbandar of the merchants, in the company of the Hikimdar, arrived and no sooner was he face to face with Juha, sitting confidently in his place, than he promptly started speaking to him, saying: "Where are my two steeds, oh fortune-teller? We are now at the forenoon, just as you said."

Said Juha, without rising from his place: "Did you bring the money?" The merchant, in a shaky voice, replied as he was taking a heavy bag out of his saddlebag: "Here is the money, thirty thousand dirhams, exactly, in full, in gold." Juha turned to his talismans — the big Chinese book, the brass goblet and the bottle like a snakes head. And, just as he had done on the previous day, he mumbled, he cried out, he repeated the Islamic creed and burnt a quantity of incense. Then he poured out the drops of the magic liquid into the goblet and the oil spread out on the surface of the water in a circle as if it were a mirror on which would be reflected hundreds of pictures and forms. Then the voice of the Shahbandar came back, saying, insistingly: "Do you see the two steeds? Speak, where are they? Say!"

But Juha never raised his gaze from the goblet. For his attention was turned to it as if there was nothing else on earth except it. But there was an ant, which had climbed up the wall of the goblet. It appeared to have been attracted by the smell of the oil and when it had discovered that the matter was not worth all this trouble, or perhaps impossible to achieve, it returned, trying to climb to the lip of the goblet, to return to its place of safety on the floor.

And Juha said to himself, whilst observing the struggling ant, as the rattling in the throat of the Shahbandar and the raving of the Hikimdar blended into a continuous sequence in his imagination: "I swear, by God, that I will not open my mouth until the ant gets out of the goblet into the light." And Juha stuck to his oath. The insistence in the voice of the Shahbandar increased and the raging of the Hikimdar became more inflammatory. But the poor ant was still fighting to try and find a way out. For a time it lost its way, going horizontally back and forth, instead of going up, towards the top, until just as the patience of everybody was lost and the whip of the Hikimdar began shaking in his hand warningly, the ant finally clambered to the lip and rushed down to the ground and Juha cried out, sincerely: "Praise be to God, praise be to God, here are the two steeds, they have appeared. What's this? Ah — it's the old quarry next to the village of Shawlaq, there are three caves there. They are in the cave number..."

* * * * * *

The troop of the Shahbandar's grooms had gone off from the right side of the bridge, whilst a regiment of the Hikimdar's guards were rushing off from the left, all before Juha had finished his sentence, stirring up, behind themselves, a great cloud of dust. Everyone's eyes followed the two groups, a they raced each other, until they finally disappeared from sight at a bend in the road leading to Shawlaq.

Juha turned away to say his prayers, just as if nothing at all had happened, whilst a dreadful silence came over the people who remained, staring at the point from where the grooms of the Shahbandar and the guards of the Hikimdar had disappeared.

Half an hour went by. Then, suddenly, the silence was broken by the voice of a small boy who was standing erect at the top of the tallest date-palm at the head of the bridge: "There they are, coming..."

Everyone rushed off, in total confusion, trying to be the first to see, with the Shahbandar shouting in the middle. As for the Hikimdar, he set off, not caring who he knocked over or hit, to the other side of the bridge, preceding the main group, who were dashing about madly. Even the fifty fortune-tellers forgot their affected dignity and they were running along with everyone else, headed by their leader, the owner of the skull, who had forgotten all about it for the first time in his life, and went off running instead.

All this, whilst Juha was the only one who never moved from his place. Indeed, he turned his back on the whole scene. He began to collect his things together, and laid out his prayer mat preparatory to saying the noon prayer, the time for which was approaching. Except, there was something about the clamour of the crowd which was different from what he had been expecting. In spite of himself, he turned, to find that the gathering which had been blocking the bridge had dispersed. Some of them were just standing whilst others were running forward, but with uncertain steps, being somewhat in doubt. But the third group, led by His Honour the Hikimdar, were returning towards him very quickly. Juha could then see, through a gap in the crowd, the troop of the Shahbandar's grooms and the guards of the Hikimdar, returning from the quarry. And the boy on the top of the tall palm-tree, shouted out: "The two horses are not with them. They haven't found the horses."

Juha had not need to hear that. For he had seen for himself, with his own eyes, that the two steeds were not there. He almost went beserk. How did this happen? Had Skinner deceived him? Had he run off with the two horses? Have you got so old Juha, to such a degree that you are no longer able to judge men properly? Was all the talk of the Thief of Baghdad about repentance and about Abulayal Tahruddin, and — and — lies? Purely deception? Then there was something else which was even more important than all that. For Skinner knew who he was. The seven rewards waiting for whoever led to Juha Nasruddin were still valid, and their total value greatly exceeded the value of the two horses.

However, Juha did not get any time to think about this. For here was the Hikimdar in front of him, like a great mountain on his horse. And there was his whip, cracking a warning of evil to come, with two eyes emitting sparks whilst the two ends of his moustache really did look like the horns of an ox, trembling as if there was a fire burning beneath them. The voice of the Hikimdar was thick and coarse, as if he, in his turn, had just come out of a boiling cooking-pot. "Dog — imposter — trickster — thief — grab him — tie him up — beat him." A thousand hands reached out to do harm to the body of Juha: the guards, the grooms, the fortune-tellers, even their leader, and the volunteers from the sons of Sindashah, who were offended that the owner of the Mandal should have made such fools of them all. And in the flash of an eye, Juha had been stripped of his clothing apart from what covered his private parts, and tied to a tree. The Hikimdar got down from his horse in order to administer, himself, the first blow. But before the first lash could fall on the naked body of Juha, the voice of the

Shahbandar could be heard, as he appeared, running forward, preceded by the big, potbelly. "Wait — stop — release his bonds. The man did not lie."

The Hikimdar turned towards him, in protest, like a dog which had just had a piece of meat taken out of its mouth: "Whatever is this, oh Shahbandar? Who gives the orders around here, me or you?"

The Shahbandar, panting, replied: "I beg your pardon, Your Honour, the Hikimdar, but look what the grooms brought. They found both saddles of the two horses, in fact, in the cave by the village of Shawlaq. The two steeds were there. The man did not lie."

The Hikimdar hissed like a snake, lifting his whip and cracking it at the foot of the Shahbandar: "What we want is the two horses, not the two saddles, my dear Shahbandar. Now get out of the way or I'll tie you up beside him."

The Shahbandar drew back in fear, whilst the Hikimdar hesitated for a brief period, which gave the Shahbandar the chance to speak after he had found safety, away from the whip of the Hikimdar: "Take care not to cause him any injury. The man knew where the horses were, and they were there just a few minutes before you got there. Without any doubt, he is able to know what has happened to them and where they have gone. But it would appear that you, Your Honour the Hikimdar, do not wish to find the two horses, for some personal reason. Great — very good. This conversation will, no doubt, please the Khan when he hears it."

The Shahbandar left, followed by his grooms, not turning his head for anything, whilst an audible murmuring went on amongst the crowd, which caused the Hikimdar to give up the idea of the beating. He turned to the guard, saying: "Take him to the vault prison."

Whilst the guards were dragging Juha off to the prison, the Hikimdar leaped on the back of his horse, filled his lungs and said in a very loud voice, which everybody could hear: "Do you think that I did not know who you were, right from the first moment when you set foot in Sindashah? We have caught you in the end, you enemy of God, creator of sedition — go on — take him away."

* * * * * *

87

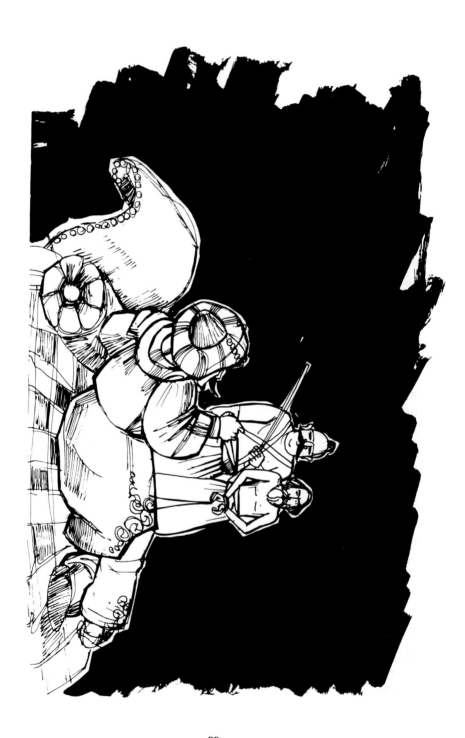

Chapter 7

Prison was nothing new as far as Juha was concerned. For he had known, before this, many prisons where Juha had been a guest for days or even weeks. But he had known, each time, how to relieve himself of the rather heavy hospitality, sometimes by just running away and other times by the use of artifice.

But the prison of Sindashah was different from any other prison. For it was set beneath the citadel of the city, in a deep vault which one entered by a ladder with fourteen rungs, most of them slippery and eaten away, so that almost each step would cause whoever was standing on it to fall down. Whenever the unfortunate prisoner reached the damp, musty bottom he would be met by clouds of insects, gnats and weak feeble voices — the muttering of imprisoned beasts in enclosed cages. The destructive darkness was only penetrated by a snooper, through a spy-hole in the faraway roof. Gradually, the eyes of Juha adjusted to being able to see in the darkness. He was able, with difficulty, to distinguish the spectres clinging to the walls. They looked as if they were bony skeletons from one of the cemeteries of the ancients.

Juha rested his back against the wall, weary and exhausted, whilst the gnats raced to his feet and lower legs, welcoming the new prey. But his attention was distracted from them by what was going round and round in his head — the question which was practically making his eyes pop out. How had this happened? Why had the grooms and the guards not found the two Arabian steeds in the cave of the quarry? Had the Thief of Baghdad renounced repentance and betrayed him? Was it possible that he was planning to betray him right from the beginning?

But the moment of doubt did not remain for long with Juha. It wasn't long before he heard something shouting from deep within himself: "Not so, and one thousand times, not so." Juha will not permit doubt to prey upon his mind. Indeed, he will remain trustful of the better side of the nature of mankind, all mankind. And in his ability to stir this good side of their nature within them.

If Skinner was unable to produce the two steeds in the place agreed upon, then, undoubtedly, something unknown had happened, unexpectedly. But what had happened? That was the question. What was important, was how to get out of this place.

Let us leave Juha to arrange his own affairs in his prison; after clarity had returned to his mind, when he had rejected the devil of doubt, with which his thoughts had been obsessed; and let us return to the premises of the Shahbandar of the merchants, to find him in an unexpected situation. The embroidered turban was on the ground, his bald head was covered in dust, his beard was ruffled like an old broom, his eyes were spinning, inflamed and angry, whilst his voice was like the howl of a hungry dog. "The two horses were there. The grooms found the two saddles of the two steeds in the cave of the quarry. Here are the two saddles. But, at the last minute, His Honour, the Hikimdar, was able to seize the fortune-teller, the reader of the Mandal, before he was able to say where they had gone. Indeed, it is clearly a plot. A plan, executed so that the field is now clear for him to win the race. But this will never be. I swear, by the glory and majesty of God, it shall not be. Does the General Mahmar believe that he is the only one who is capable of gaining entrance to the Khan in order to speak to him? I am not a stranger to the palace. I shall put my complaint up to the Khan and let what will be, be."

The spies rushed to the Hikimdar, General Mahmar, taking to him what the Shahbandar had said. Then another came to say that he had ordered his grooms to prepare his magnificent carriage. Then a third said that he had sent a message to the lady, his wife, to prepare for him the wool gown, embroidered with gold, the silk kaftan and the turban which was studded with precious stones. Then a fourth came to confirm that the Shahbandar had opened his strong-box and that he had taken from it the medals and decorations which he had been awarded on various occasions and that he was now working, cleaning and polishing them, in preparation for being received by the Khan.

The Hikimdar listened to all these reports with an appearance of complete indifference. But, in truth, he was becoming increasingly concerned, for the complaint of the Shahbandar to the Khan was likely to find a ready ear, especially as the story of the two prisoners who had escaped was still lingering on in the mind of the Khan.

He must, therefore, move fast. The Hikimdar took a long draw from the hookah whilst carefully studying the chessmen on the table before him, deep in thought as if he were playing an unseen opponent. But, when he lifted his head, his plan for meeting any likely danger had been completed and was only waiting to be executed.

* * * * * *

The first thing that must happen now is that the fortune-teller, the revealer of the contents of the Mandal, should confess to being a liar and an imposter, so that, under those circumstances, any complaint put forward by the Shahbandar would fail. Indeed, the Shahbandar himself might even be punished for giving false information. The way to the lady would then be clear. Ah, how sweet and delicious is the dear lady. And how His Honour the Hikimdar longs for you.

As for the two steeds, by the grace of God they will not return. And, therefore, you oh General Mahmar, will win the race and the favour of the Khan. However, the confession by the fortune-teller, that he is a liar and an imposter, will not lead to him being given a severe sentence.

The Khan is likely to find it sufficient simply to expel him from the city or to imprison him for a year or two, at the most. After which it would be possible for the man to talk and what he says may reach the ears of the Khan. Therefore, what is required now, oh General Mahmar, is that you should find a charge against the fortune-teller which would warrant execution by hanging or by khazuq, or at the very least, imprisonment in the prison of the vault of the citadel for life. And he must also confess to this new charge.

The confession itself is not a problem. The head of the undercover intelligence unit is capable of making him confess to anything that you wish, oh General, that he should confess about. But what is to be the charge which he is going to confess about? The General took another long pull on the hookah, and like the cloud of smoke which came out of his mouth, twisting and turning like a pit full of snakes, the charge had similarly come to fruition in the mind of the Hikimdar.

This fortune-teller was an agent of Ar Ramali. He had been sent by

him to spread sedition in Sindashah. Indeed, he is also one of his closest assistants and it was he who had arranged the escape of the two
prisoners, only two days ago. The smile of the Hikimdar spread,
whilst taking yet a third pull on the hookah; for just the mention of the
name, Ar Ramali, would be sufficient to shake the very essence of the
Khan, for he was his mortal enemy, sitting on his own borders, spreading sedition and dissension among the people and making destructive
plots for the downfall of the Khan.

* * * * * *

The Hikimdar clapped his hands and his orderly came to him: "Bring
the file of that heretic, Ar Ramali, and also call the head of the undercover unit." The file and the head of the undercover unit quickly arrived. The latter entered, with silent footsteps, like a cat. With his
clean-shaven face, his woven and embroidered clothing on his slender
frame, and his high-pitched, taut, squeaky voice with which he greeted
the Hikimdar, he resembled one of the slave girls. The Hikimdar signalled to him with his hand, to wait, and he began to look through the
file for a time until he raised his head towards the chief of the undercover unit, who was standing there with humility, and said: "Have the
executioner standing by, for at this moment we have a catch of considerable importance. We have uncovered a new plot of the heretic Ar
Ramali. And do you know who is its leader? It is that imposter of a
fortune-teller whom we caught just a short time ago. He was sent by
Ar Ramali; he is also his cousin and one of the main leaders of his
gang. Do you understand?"

"Certainly, certainly, my master the Hikimdar. I shall make him
confess everything."

"The uncovering of this plot, before the heretics have been able to
execute it, is a splendid job and the whole department will be rewarded. Do you understand?"

"Naturally, naturally, oh my master the Hikimdar, I understand.
Rest assured, my master, the confession will be just as you wish or
even better."

"Right, then bring that stupid fool of a fortune-teller here." And the lips of the Hikimdar spread out into a wide smile, in which the head of the undercover unit joined.

* * * * * *

The guard pushed Juha in through the door, roughly, so that he almost fell flat on his face. His eyes went quickly round the hall into which he had been hauled. The hall was flooded with light from four chandeliers, one in each of the four corners, and at the top was the Hikimdar, settled comfortably on his couch, looking at his papers. The mouthpiece of the hookah was stuck in his mouth and in front of him was the Chinese book and equipment of Juha. In another corner was a flaming brazier, attending to which was a hunchbacked dwarf with distorted features, pumping away at the fire with a set of foot-operated bellows. On the fire were two iron bars and rods of various shapes and sizes whilst behind the brazier, on the wall, were leg-irons and heavy chains. On the ground was a small carpet, shining on the top of which was a set of scalpels, tweezers and pincers, which you would not normally see except with surgeons.

In the other corner of the hall was the head of the undercover unit, in his woven clothing, with his facial expressions of femininity, whilst two paces away from him was the executioner, playing with the ends of a cat-o'-nine tails, as if it were an octopus.

Before Juha knew where he was, the executioner, with a quick hand, stripped off his shirt from his back, and Juha felt the touch of his fingers, like claws on his back, as if he was choosing the best places to receive the lashes from the whip. The foot of the hunchbacked dwarf, working on the bellows, became more enthusiastic. Juha felt a cold shudder go through his body whilst his heart called out to Julshan and his children, to all the people whom he loved and who loved him. For a moment his mind dwelt on the deaf, dumb and blind hermit, and his conversation which he never completed, about the spring in the mountain and the shedder of blood, Haji Agha. Like a flash of lightning, tens of difficult situations, which he had faced and overcome, passed through his mind. And now, was this the end for Juha? And he using an assumed name, in a situation where he was a fortune-teller, naked, or practically so. But Juha's face remained normal, calm, giving nothing away about the tempest which was raging inside of him, whilst he stood in his place, watching the head of the Hikimdar bent over the papers before him.

Finally, the Hikimdar raised his head, gave Juha a piercing look over the horns of his moustache before he said: "Of course, you are aware why my men arrested you and threw you into prison. Indeed, I know all about you and you have not been out of my sight for a single moment since you set foot in my city. It will be better for you that you do not prevaricate, and that you admit your true name."

This was not the first time that Juha had been interrogated, and it was also certain that it was not the first time that the Hikimdar had interrogated a man whom he wished to send to the gallows or to the khazuq. But it was also certain that it was the first time that he had faced someone of the calibre of Juha.

Juha was silent and said not a word as he tried to discover, from the mien of the man, whether the papers in front of him had anything in them which referred to his own name. Then the voice of the Hikimdar came again, provocatively, as he said in a threatening tone: "What is it now? Have you become dumb? Or perhaps you have lost your memory? We can reactivate it at any moment." The chin of the executioner went up whilst his hand holding the cat-o'-nine tails began to swing, in anticipation of the banquet to come. And as the eyes of the head of the undercover unit began to dance with joy, the enthusiasm of the foot of the malformed hunchback on the bellows of the brazier increased. But not an eye of Juha blinked, despite the question which was worrying him. Did they know who he was? Had the Thief of Baghdad given him away? Not at all. Impossible.

* * * * * *

When Juha spoke, the intonation of his voice was firm and confident, as if he was giving a lecture at a university.

"I am neither a liar nor an imposter. What the Mandal said was true, Your Honour the Hikimdar. My Mandal never lies."

The Hikimdar was unaware of the fact that behind these simple words was a little trap which Juha had set up in order to confirm that his true name was not the subject of the interrogation. He fell into the trap easily as he answered, furiously and mockingly: "Mandal, Mandal, your Mandal is a pretence and a liar, you imposter. All the fortune-tellers, I know them to be cheats and imposters. You are no different from the fifty imposters by whom the Bridge of the Massacres is congested."

The mind of Juha calmed down. When he spoke again, after that, his tone was much more confident and relaxed: "My Lord, the Hikimdar, you yourself have already witnessed the two saddles which the grooms brought. And the horses were there too, in the cave of the quarry, just a few minutes before the arrival of the guards and the grooms. I saw them myself in the Mandal and in front of each horse was a bundle of green lucerne." And General Mahmar slipped into the little trap up to his ears when he said: "Why, therefore, did they not find them there? Where did they hide themselves? Speak up!"

"I thought that you had realised what had happened, my Lord, especially as you know the extent of my loyalty towards you. For I carried out exactly what I had read in the eyes of a great man who had spoken to me concerning the two steeds on the previous day."

The Hikimdar asked, with some concern: "And what was it that you read in the eyes of this great man of whom you speak?"

"I read, my master, and my book confirmed what I had read, that the great man, for whose wishes I have great respect, was not eager for the two horses to be returned immediately." The shot in the dark was a direct hit which shook the Hikimdar. A look of dismay·shot out from his eyes in the direction of the head of the undercover unit and the executioner. Then it settled for a moment on Juha's face, questioning, before the Hikimdar's head bent down again over his papers, as if he was looking for something amongst them. But Juha beat him to it with yet another arrow: "My book, my Lord, also related to me details of a great danger, to which a noble beautiful lady is exposed, one who is entitled to all esteem and protection, especially from His Honour, the great Lord, who was the first to open the subject of the two steeds to me on the bridge. For black jealousy has gone to the heart of her husband who has become suspicious of the existence of a relationship between her and the great Lord for whom I have total respect. He has begun to send after her spies and agents in order to provide proof of a charge against her, the punishment for which is to be stoned to death. I have also understood from my book..."

But the Hikimdar was no longer able to bear it. If this conversation were to go on in the hearing of the head of the undercover unit and the executioner it would result in the greatest danger possible. As for the hunchback on the bellows, there was no danger from him for he was deaf and dumb. He had been specially selected for this job because he would be unable to speak about what he might see or feel of the agitation of those being tortured.

The Hikimdar was quick to cut off Juha, saying, as he went through his papers: "Hold on, a moment. What is this mix-up?" Then he directed what he had to say to the head of the undercover unit: "Where is the letter that came to us from the Bukhara Khan about the assistants of Ar Ramali? Go and look for it everywhere. It ought to have been in this file."

Off went the man, quickly, and Juha resumed what he was saying: "Then, my master the Hikimdar..."

But the Hikimdar cut him off, saying: "Wait!"

Then he directed what he had to say this time to the executioner: "Go down to the head of the undercover unit and tell him also to bring the memo which was put up to us by the Commander of the Frontier Guards. Assist him in the search, and neither of you come back without them." Juha did not need all that in order to realise that both the letter and the report which had been asked for were there, in the file in front of the Hikimdar, and that he had fabricated the loss of them for their conversation to be secure from other ears.

The Hikimdar then said, in an attempt to recover from his embarrassment: "It would appear that you smoked too much hasheesh last night. What is this mix-up that you are going on about concerning the lady who is being exposed to danger as the result of the jealousy of her husband?"

Juha replied, keeping down the hypocrisy, for which there was no need: "I am speaking, my Lord, about the lady and the Shahbandar, whom jealousy has caused to lose his senses, and about a third person, highly placed, you probably know who it is, my Lord, better than I do."

The slap in the face pulverised him, from which all the remaining resistance of General Mahmar collapsed. He then said, completely unguardedly: "But — does the Shahbandar really know?"

Juha replied, in confirmation: "No, but he almost does. For he has already sent off spies and look-outs to the two of them. And he is preparing, even now, to be received by the Khan to complain about two matters, not one matter."

At this point the Hikimdar had decided on a view. It would be necessary to come to an understanding with this fortune-teller at any cost. His tone of voice changed completely, and he said, forcing a laugh, which seemed strange and without purpose: "Come closer to me, you fortune-teller. In fact, I believed, on the whole, that you were really telling the truth. But I just wanted to test your loyalty. Take a pull on the hookah."

Juha moved closer to the Hikimdar until he was sitting beside him but excused himself from the hookah. The hunchbacked dwarf was watching what was going on with his mouth wide open as if he was seeing a miracle. His foot began to go slower and slower on the bellows until it stopped altogether. Juha said, transferring the matter to the Hikimdar: "My book has told me that if you can get over a specific danger to which you will be exposed during this week, it will not be very long before you will be the number one man in this country. And you are entitled to this and more and, therefore, I wish to place all my experience at your disposal. For this book which you see, reads what is behind the heart and what the eye and the breast conceal, but none can read its symbols other than I."

Then the Hikimdar said, his greed having carried him away, incautiously: "Yes, yes, I will be able to get great benefit from you. Let us work together, my good fortune-teller. Indeed, I am aware, from what you say, of a loyalty which man finds missing in so many persons today."

"My loyalty to you, my Lord, knows no bounds."

"I shall appoint you, as of now, as the head of the fortune-tellers guild of those who are on the Bridge of the Massacres. I shall instruct

97

that the skull and the mace of the guild should be placed in your tent." Juha was the last person to want such a promotion but he thought it imprudent to show any opposition and the Hikimdar continued with his conversation: "The present head of the guild receives from the other fortune-tellers, a fee amounting to a tenth of all that they receive in fees. I shall make it one-fifth instead of one-tenth."

Juha said: "May God lengthen the life of my Lord and give him the pleasure of all that he desires."

The voice of the Hikimdar came back again, saying, anxiously: "But can your book tell just when and how the Shahbandar of the merchants began to have fears of a liaison between his wife and ... that great person of whom you were speaking."

"Allow me to see, sir." Juha put out his hand for the great Chinese book and he began to turn over the pages whilst repeating in his hollow voice: "Abrakad, Ibrabishin, Katin." He then began to mutter strange mumblings, not capable of being understood. Then his condition changed and suddenly his eyes began to protrude and his hands shake whilst his voice was clothed in a fearful ringing which made the hunchbacked dwarf draw back in fear until his back was up against the wall. Suddenly, Juha cried out, as if he had seen a spectre: "The dog, the despicable and vile beast, now I see him. The time is approaching sunset. He is sitting at the door of his premises. The drums roll. The great Master dismounts from his horse to greet him. He smiles at the great Master and asks him to sit down; but behind the smile is bitter hatred and a stabbing in the back. The Shahbandar rogue — the rogue, he entertains the great Master with pleasant conversation, hiding his deep resentment."

"And what are they talking about?"

"Yes, about horses and the race. The great Master is talking honestly and with good intention. The Shahbandar gives the appearance of friendliness but in his heart are ten venomous snakes. God is greatest — God is greatest — what is this bright light which shines from the shop? It is like the full moon come down to the earth. What is this diffused scent, the fragrance of which would intoxicate anyone who approached it? The great Master greets the grand lady, whilst behind his back, all forms of intense dislike and jealousy creep out of the yellow eyes of the Shahbandar. Oh, what black hatred there is in the eyes of the man.

"Ah — oh, you scoundrel — oh, you despicable merchant and usurer — I can see that you are arranging something, you are asking your wife to uncover her face in the presence of the great Master. The two hearts are set alight with the highest and most holy of emotions, whilst you, oh repulsive one, are striving to create a scandal. Indeed, I see the Shahbandar, son of a viper, noting the loving looks exchanged between the two angels. Indeed, he is up to something — the accursed scoundrel is up to something — he's up to something."

The excitement in the voice of Juha became more and more inaudible until, when he had said the last word like a whisper, he folded the book and the sweat was pouring from him in profusion and his inhalations of breath were following each other so quickly that it was as if he had been running. The Hikimdar was so fascinated and confused that he cried out, hardly aware that he was doing so: "I swear, by God, that it is as if you were the fourth of us. So, therefore, the scoundrel of a merchant wants to set me up. I swear to God that I will pulverise him, I'll make minced meat of him. Listen, oh fortune-teller, let your first mission be, as from now, that you follow up the movements of this stupid Shahbandar and observe his places of abode."

"Nothing shall escape me, my Lord, from the very moment when I shall leave this prison."

"Worry not, worry not, you shall leave it immediately. I shall put up my report to the Khan."

"Perhaps the Khan will not approve my release?"

"Do not worry about a thing. Just leave the matter of the Khan to me."

"One other thing, my Lord, I'll probably need some money, especially as you have torn all my clothes."

"You will leave here with new clothes and two thousand dirhams."

* * * * * *

On the same day, when Juha was leaving the fort, after he had been released, he met, at the door, the Shahbandar of the merchants who was going in to ask for an appointment to see the Khan. No sooner had he spotted Juha than his eyes were dancing with delight and he cried out, at the top of his voice: "So, they have let you out, oh fortune-teller? Praise be to God for your safe-keeping. How happy I am, truly, how happy I am. You will recover my two steeds for me, is that not so? You will get them back for me? Eh? Look, this is the petition which I had intended to present to the Khan in order that he should pardon you from hanging until you had found my two steeds for me. Take it, read for yourself if you wish."

Juha said: "I can only read the Chinese language, but thank you for your kindness, anyhow."

"So, let us get on with it and complete the reading of the Mandal. Hopefully, we should be able to get the two horses back before the end of the afternoon."

Said Juha: "Why all this hurry? I do not like being rushed in this fashion. Let us put off the opening of the Mandal until tomorrow, or even the day after tomorrow."

The Shahbandar stepped back, flabbergasted, and the happiness disappeared from his eyes. "What do you mean by saying, tomorrow, or the day after tomorrow? Have you forgotten that only three days remain, before the day of the race?"

"Then, petition the Khan to postpone the day of the race. I'm very tired and I couldn't possibly open the Mandal now."

Juha turned round to be on his way but the Shahbandar grabbed him by the collar as he shouted out, angrily: "Indeed, say that you have been bribed not to return the two steeds to me. I have understood, but be on your guard, for the Shahbandar of the merchants of Sindashah will not take this lying down. Woe be on you, you cheat. And woe be on whoever bribed you."

Juha was in a hurry in respect of his own affairs and he pushed the man away from him and set off on his way, not turning to look at a thing but going straight to the roadhouse. And there he spotted Skinner, who had taken his place next to the wooden partition. Their eyes met, for a fleeting moment, without any of the visitors to the place noticing anything. Then Juha laid out his matting in his place on the other side of the partition.

He put his head back on the partition and whispered, in a voice which could not be heard by anyone else: "I am pleased that my confidence in you was justified, but tell me, why were the two steeds not in their place at the appointed time?"

"I had no alternative but to move them from the cave at the quarry after I spotted some spies approaching the place. I moved them to an abandoned hut behind the mountain. Then I came back immediately to inform you, but found that you had gone off to the Bridge of the Massacres. There, I was watching for an opportunity to talk to you but they arrested you and took you off to the prison, whilst I was pulling my hair out like a lunatic."

"In general, what has happened has been good; and the early bird catches the worm." Then Juha rolled over on his side and it wasn't long before he was fast asleep.

* * * * * *

Chapter 8

Juha returned to the Bridge of the Massacres to find that the news of his appointment as the head of the fortune-tellers had preceded him. For, on the site of his old, threadbare matting was now a new tent of brilliant colours. And, around and inside it were at least ten fortune-tellers who were sweeping, sprinkling water to keep the dust down, and hanging up presents on the walls of the tent. No sooner had Juha made his appearance than all the fifty fortune-tellers rushed forward towards him, with each of them trying to beat the others in showing loyalty towards him. One of them grabbed his sandals from his feet and started to polish them with his turban, whilst another began to dust the ancient Chinese book, removing therefrom the dust of centuries and a third shook out his small prayer mat in the wind as if he were a fisherman, casting his net in the water. He then laid it out with great care at the feet of Juha. All this was going on and our friend was silent as he watched the enthusiasm of the hypocrites.

Then his eye fell on the leader of the fortune-tellers, the owner of the skull, who had set himself down in a remote corner, squatting on his own, after the people had removed themselves away from him and only an old, mangy dog remained to share his pain with him. With the skull between his hands, he was looking at it intently, in tears sometimes, and with indignation at other times, as if it had abandoned him and had handed him over to be ruined.

The sound of drums was then heard from the direction of the head of the bridge, and a troop of horsemen, dressed in black uniforms and led by His Honour the Hikimdar mounted on his grey horse, appeared. The two ends of his moustache, the ox horns, appeared to be even longer, whilst the usual whip and the feather of his turban were swaying with the wind and the steps of the horse.

The fortune-tellers were suddenly surprised to see the fearful Hikimdar dismount from his horse in front of Juha's tent. Juha came out to welcome him without any ceremony or affectation, and they exchanged greetings as if they were two old friends, then they went into the tent, together, and dropped the curtain behind them.

One of the fortune-tellers whispered in the ear of his neighbour: "I read the sand last night and the seashells said that this fortune-teller is well connected and that he enjoys the support of the Khan himself."

Another answered: "Did you notice how he shook hands with the Hikimdar, without even bending down and kissing his hand." But the conversation inside the tent was of a different nature.

The Hikimdar said, and he was showing signs of concern: "What is the latest news of the Shahbandar that you have? Have you read his innermost thoughts like you promised me? Have you found out what he is concealing? Have ...?"

Juha answered, cutting him off: "I opened the very depths of his heart yesterday, just as I open the pages of this book, and I read it all. There is nothing in it except evil, resentment and the worst of intentions. The rancour which is in his heart towards you would suffice to burn a thousand cities like Sindashah. He is now arranging to be received by the Khan in order to spread his poison. At the same time he is arranging an ambush for a beautiful lady whose affairs are of great concern to you. But, rest assured, everything is going to be all right. He will be unable to cause you any harm for your star is the one which is in ascendency, oh General Mahmar. But on one condition: that you dispel the thought that has just come back into your mind."

The face of the Hikimdar went red, as if he had just been caught, red-handed, at one of his crimes. For what he had been thinking of at that very moment, was that this man who was talking to him was dangerous, in the extreme, and that just as soon as he had got himself out of this difficult situation with the Shahbandar, he would have to rid himself of him. "Know this, oh powerful Hikimdar, I am extremely keen for your safety and victory over all who show enmity against you. Allow me to tell you, in total sincerity, that my keenness here, is not for your black eyes nor for any benefit or reward or even high position. The fact of the matter is, quite simply, that my book here, which tells no lies, informs me that your star and my star are combined together and that the fate of each of us is linked to the fate of the other. Any evil which touches you will reflect, immediately, on me, and of course, the reverse is also true. You yourself probably noted that I almost met my death in the vault prison at the moment when the plot of the Shahbandar to bring about your downfall almost succeeded. Indeed, our fate is as one, oh General Mahmar, so you can depend upon me."

The Hikimdar, with his mouth wide open like someone totally perplexed, but believing every word that Juha was saying, said: "Do you mean that we shall be delivered from the treachery of the Shahbandar?"

Juha replied, in a voice of certainty: "And the love and the glory shall be for you alone."

The Hikimdar was silent for a moment in consideration, being very cautious not to give free rein to his thoughts so that this amazing fortune-teller could pick them up, then he finally said: "I forgot to ask you, what happened to the two horses and why did the men not find them in the cave like you said?"

Juha replied, quite simply: "Because I removed them from there." Baffled, the Hikimdar asked: "What do you mean by saying that you removed them?"

Juha continued what he had been saying in the same simple tone; whilst readjusting his new turban on the top of his head: "It means that I coverted them to air and no man can see or touch them except myself."

The Hikimdar asked, in amazement: "But why did you do that?"

"I had no alternative but to do so after I discovered that the thieves who had stolen the two steeds had removed the golden nails from the hooves and the silk tapes from the tails. When it was my duty to defer the whole matter until I could find out what you wanted and what we ought to do."

The Hikimdar said: "You did very well — but — can you not remove the Shahbandar as well?"

"Regretfully, that I cannot do, yet. My experiments with animals have been a success but that has not been the case with humans. For certain there is something lacking in the magic talisman to enable me to make the son of Adam disappear into thin air. I am certain that I shall soon find the missing part."

"I hope that you do that — I hope that you do!" The Hikimdar said that in a fervent hope whilst his imagination ran through the long line of those whom he wished that this fortune-teller would be able to 're-move'. Naturally, there was the Shahbandar, first, the Commander of the Army, then the Chamberlain of the Treasury and the Chief Justice. Then, after him, was the Bearer of the Seals and, finally, the Chief Chamberlain. And the heart of the General Mahmar nearly fell through his ribs when he saw who the last one was in the line of those for 'removal', for it was the Khan himself. Let him get that thought out of his mind quickly, before this amazing fortune-teller got the chance to read it. At that very moment he was mumbling his magic words which could not be understood, which he concluded with a cau-tion, saying: "Do not hurry. Everything in due course."

A very grave and solemn Hikimdar left the tent of Juha, with his hopes and ambitions revived. But Juha did not get any rest for the for-tune-tellers presented themselves at his tent, giving commitments of loyalty and allegiance, with each one of them attempting to make his words more rhetorical and of finer meaning as regards the extent of his loyalty to the new leader, whilst competing with each other in bal-lads of panegyric, extolling his praises. Juha was able to discover that they had all prophesised his advent long before he had arrived and that he alone was the link between God and man, that if Muhammad had not been declared to be the final prophet, then he would certainly have been a prophet. When each of them departed he left behind his gifts, in both cash and kind, until Juha's tent was full of them, whilst he him-self was silent, not saying a word, bewildered as to what he should do.

It wasn't long before the look of disdain disappeared from his face to be replaced by a look of pity, and his eyes were wet with tears. A question was raging inside him, saying: "How can a man fall, any man, to this level of humiliation and degradation?" Then, at the tail-end of them all, came the chief fortune-teller — with a broken spirit, subjugated, he could hardly put one foot in front of the other, and with a terrible look of hatred springing from his yellow eye.

In his hands were the skull, his valuable treasure, and a bag, the contents of which he counted out — one hundred and fifty pieces of silver — three times as much as any one before him. He placed the skull and the bag on Juha's prayer rug, without saying a word, then he turned away, with a bent back as if all the worries of the world were on his shoulders. This moved the compassionate feelings of the heart of Juha and he called to him, just as he reached the door of the tent: "Wait, take these things which you have brought, I do not want anything from you."

The man whipped round, like someone bitten by a snake, and the hatred appeared, almost, like a cloud in front of his eyes: "Why? Is it not enough for you? Do you see this as just a little? Is it not enough what you have done to me? You — you —"

Juha said simply, ignoring the insults of the chief fortune-teller: "I have no need for either your skull or your money. Give me your hand and allow me to tell you your fortune."

The man practically exploded: "Who, you, you imposter? You who have brought upon us disgrace by your failure to find the two horses, yesterday. You, want to read *my* fortune?"

* * * * * *

Said Juha, kindly, catching hold of the hand of the man. "Your fortune says that this hard period will disappear, very quickly. You will return to your tent and your leadership. The man who has caused your misfortune will disappear as if he never was and nothing will remain of him on this bridge except a memory. One day you might come to know his name and will rename the bridge after him."

But the man did not stop to hear the remainder of Juha's prophecies. However, he had hardly left before he was made to realise that there were still some drops of bitterness left in his cup of misery to drink. For he was received by all the fortune-tellers with a stream of insults and invective just as if they had never, ever flattered him, never mind just yesterday. Even those who had been closest to him, those whom he had long believed would remain by his side until the last breath of life, even though the whole world might abandon him, they were the ones leading the campaign of invective against him and were exchanging comments in a loud voice in order that he would hear them:

"Why do you think that the chief refused his magic skull? No doubt he had discovered that it couldn't do anything. He no doubt knew that it was the skull of a mangy ape, like its owner."

"And he loathed its putrid smell."

"Get far enough away, you beast. For we are not going to let you stay amongst us. There is an empty place at the other end of the bridge. Take your place there and don't let your smell get down to us."

This was more than he could stand and he burst out, in an angry voice, mixed with tears: "Even you, Luqman, how can you manage to keep your food down, you scoundrel. Have you forgotten the day when you arrived at this place, hungry and deprived, when I sheltered you and treated you as my own son, and taught you the art of magic and astrology and fortune-telling? Is this, then, my reward?"

"Go to the devil, you scabby old chatterbox."

"And you, Sa'fan, did I not cover up for you, concealed your name and paid your debts, saving you from the anger of the Khan?

"Is this my reward from you, Majdhub? You, whom I had considered to be my successor? Listen, oh you, the new chief. Listen carefully to these hypocrites. For they will pay the last honours to the dead in respect of you tomorrow, just as they are paying the last honours to me today. For that is the way of the world and you will drink from the same glass."

Juha said, compassionately, knowing full well the pain of the old man: "Indeed, they will come back to you tomorrow, begging your pardon, petitioning for your favours."

* * * * * *

The day of the race arrived and the whole city gathered around the course whilst the Khan, his guests, his chamberlain and his senior assistants sat in an elevated pavilion, shaded by flags and banners. The race was won by the two horses of the Hikimdar and the people all cheered, congratulating the great victory. The General Mahmar came forward, full of elation, to receive the prize and the race trophy. The Chamberlain stretched out his hand with the heavy bag in order to hand it over to the Khan amidst a storm of jubilation, clapping and shouting. The Hikimdar took another step forward towards the Khan as the drums echoed with a rapid roll, leading up to the crucial moment. Suddenly, there was a piercing scream, cutting through the air, from the direction of the general public. The hand of the Chamberlain, with the heavy bag of gold, froze and the outstretched hand of the Khan went rigid as his eyes went in the direction of the voice which went above the sound of the drums and the general hubbub. And there was a man, slipping between the guards and rushing towards the enclosure. Behind him dozens of men carrying whips and cudgels were chasing after him and he was running barefooted and bareheaded, as if there was a touch of the devil inside him, as he screamed: "I demand safe-custody and justice, my Lord, security and justice, my Lord." And when the man arrived at the foot of the enclosure there were dozens of hands, grabbing at his collar, but his voice was still calling out: "I am seeking security and justice, my Lord."

His voice reached the Khan, who said, indicating with his hand: "Let him come. Bring him here."

In a flash the man was lying on the ground, at the feet of the Khan, who was shaking with anger, whilst the man was screaming, as he tried to get to his feet: "Safe-keeping and justice, my Lord."

"Who are you, my man, and how could you allow yourself to disturb our serenity on the day of the race?" But the man continued his screaming as if he had not heard, whilst the Chamberlain of the Ministry of Commerce leaned over to the ear of the Khan, whispering and pointing to the man asking for safe-keeping and justice.

The eyes of the Khan widened, as he said, in astonishment: "You say he's the Shahbandar of the merchants. Yes, yes, I can distinguish his features. But what has brought him to this state, barefooted, bareheaded and with threadbare clothing? Stand up, Shahbandar, you have safe-keeping, without doubt, despite the inconvenience which you have caused us. What injustice has been inflicted upon you? And who do you consider was able to inflict this wrong upon you?"

At this very moment, Juha was sitting at the door of his tent, asking himself why the Shahbandar was late and why he had not come to him till now. For he had waited for him from before the race. But he did not come. And now the race was over and the two horses of the Hikimdar had won but of the Shahbandar there was no trace. He had already lost the prize and it was certain that he would seek him out now in order to recover the two steeds so that his losses would not be doubled.

* * * * * *

But Juha was not correct on this occasion. For the hatred of the Shahbandar for the Hikimdar, and also for the fortune-teller, was even greater than his greed. The appetite for revenge had totally overcome him and he could see nothing but avenging himself against the Hikimdar and the disclosure of his plots together with the fortune-teller. However, Juha came round from his daydreams to see dozens of guards, falling upon him, seizing him and pulling him along to the enclosure of the Khan at the racecourse, leaving the fifty fortune-tellers and their chief with their mouths agape at the change of circumstances in this strange manner.

It was the three main hypocrites who were the first to realise the significance of what was happening and they rushed to the owner of the skull, once again flattering him, dusting his sandals and the skull, and then they carried him, on their shoulders, along to the empty tent of Juha as they cheered him. He smiled, suffering, knowing that all that they did was merely lipservice. But he did not speak, for the bitter mocking in his smile was more eloquent than all the talking. Despite this, the hypocrites continued with their dissembling as if nothing had ever happened.

* * * * * *

The guards threw Juha at the feet of the Khan. With difficulty he pulled himself together to try to stand, whilst his flashing eyes were looking round quickly amongst the faces of the people in the enclosure.

He knew, immediately, that a fierce quarrel had taken place between the Hikimdar and the Shahbandar for both their faces were aflame with anger. Even the two ends of the Hikimdar's moustache, the horns of the ox, were bristling with anger, and the potbelly of the Shahbandar shook with irritation. Sweat was pouring profusely from both of them whilst the Khan himself was no less angry as he raged

110

like a volcano: "It has never happened, in the history of our court, that such obscene pronouncements and vulgar, low insults have been witnessed. It has never happened before that a single creature has dared to disturb our serenity in this disgusting manner."

Here, his eyes fell on Juha Nasruddin, who was still pulling himself together in an effort to stand up, and he said, with a clear ring indicating that his anger had increased: "And who might this beast be?"

The Head of the Ministry of Commerce hurriedly said: "He is the fortune-teller, the reader of the Mandal, my Lord, the reason for ..."

But the angry voice of the Khan, as sharp as a sword, cut him off: "What do you say? A fortune-teller? Here, in my court? Whatever brought him here, to this place?"

The face of the Head of the Ministry of Commerce went grey, as he replied, stuttering: "It was I who sent to call for him, my Lord. I thought — I mean I envisaged — I mean — it entered my mind, that Your Highness might — perhaps — I mean you might like to listen to his testimony — I mean, to make certain of — I believed, my Lord— "

The Head of the Ministry of Commerce began to stammer, moving his frightened eyes between the Khan, the Shahbandar and the Hikimdar, whilst he pleaded through his eyes with his colleagues who were packed together behind the Khan. But it appeared that not one of them was prepared to rescue him.

Once again the Khan snorted as he threw out his hand, addressing his assistants: "His Excellency was thinking! — It struck his mind! — His Excellency was imagining! Do you hear, Your Excellencies? His Honour, the Head of the Ministry of Commerce thought that I should gather together in my court, the fortune-tellers, the magicians and every Tom, Dick and Harry of the rabble." He then turned to the Head of the Ministry of Commerce, as the sparks flew from his eyes: "As long as your ideas are at this level of genius, oh Head of the Ministry of Commerce, you should interrogate him yourself and call upon him to open and read the Mandal, at this moment, and tell where the two missing steeds are. Or, he should confess that he is an imposter and a trickster — now — at once, or I shall have both of your heads off, together." The Khan fell silent after he had got his outburst off his chest, and returned to his seat to take his ease amongst dozens of cushions as he signalled to the fan bearers to be more active with the ventilation. The eyes of Juha Nasruddin met with the eyes of the Shahbandar and although Juha tried to give his look something of significance for encouragement or understanding the Shahbandar found it sufficient to pull a couple more hairs out of his chin without it appearing, from his attitude, that he had understood anything.

Then came the voice of the Head of the Ministry of Commerce, shaking and trembling, saying: "Oh fortune-teller, you yourself have heard the wishes of our Lord, which cannot be refuted, so speak clearly and tell everything, leaving out nothing at all." And, in fact, Juha did speak out, clearly and confidently. In a very few words he said that he was capable of returning the horses and revealing their position with just a glance at his goblet and his book which the guards had taken. Nor did he forget to mention that the Shahbandar had promised him the payment of thirty thousand pieces of silver for the return of the two steeds.

The Head of the Ministry of Commerce then said, directing his words to the Shahbandar: "Did you both agree on this?"

The Shahbandar took a heavy bag out of his pocket and handed it to the Head of the Ministry of Commerce, without saying a word, who then shouted to his guards to bring the goblet and the book.

Again, Juha asked for water and poured it into the goblet and then he poured a number of drops from his black bottle, which he had kept hidden in his breast. He began to watch the drops of liquid which drew a thousand shining forms on the surface of the water whilst he was muttering: "Abrakad abrakishin katin —" Everybody was fascinated, perplexed, silent with awe. Then, suddenly, Juha screamed out loudly: "There they are, there are the two steeds, I see them both now, in the garden of an old abandoned palace below the mountain, on the door of which are two carved crocodiles. In the front of it is a little stream of water, dropping down from the mountain above, on the right bank of which are seven willow trees."

The Shahbandar cried out in disbelief: "But that is the description of my winter palace which I abandoned a long time ago."

Said Juha, calmly, as he folded away his book: "The two steeds are there."

* * * * * *

A murmuring of disbelief arose between the members of the inner circle of the Khan, whilst a squad of horsemen was setting off, as a result of a signal from the Hikimdar, in the direction of the palace to which Juha had referred.

The Khan said, sedately: "The fortune-teller is an imposter. I can smell the stench of skulduggery in his words. But, we must eradicate doubt with certainty."

The Hikimdar said, certain that his chance had now come: "And if it appears that the two steeds were hidden in the palace of the Shahbandar himself, for the whole of this period, then the matter would have a different aspect, my Lord."

The Head of the Ministry of Commerce, getting his breath back, said: "And until the guards return with the certain information, it is up to you, oh fortune-teller, to inform us how it was that you were unable to return the two horses until now. And who it was who bribed you so that the finding of the two of them would be delayed until after the race.

"Speak up and do not be afraid, tell the whole truth and no evil will become of you — and if we find the two steeds —"

Said Juha, calmly: "My Mandal does not lie, ever. They are both there, and the guards will bring them back. And you, oh Head of the Ministry of Commerce, will give me my reward, by your own hand."

The Head of the Ministry of Commerce replied: "Indeed, I will add ten thousand other pieces of silver to it if you will admit everything. Just say, who was it who bribed you so that the finding of the two steeds would be delayed?"

The Hikimdar rushed to cut him off: "Did you hear my Lord? He wishes to force false confessions from the fortune-teller and he is enticing him with ten thousand pieces of silver, in front of us, and in the hearing of my Lord? This, I swear by God, is the height of crime."

The Head of the Ministry of Commerce replied in a voice with no less anger and indignation: "Do you dare, you criminal, you heathen, to accuse me of crimes? Have you forgotten the taxes which you impose on the merchants? Have you forgotten the widow, whose house you took away from her by force, in order that you could present it to one of your lovers? Have ..."

The irritation of the Hikimdar increased and he screamed: "Do you think that we don't know what you are doing? Indeed, I know all about the deal with the camels which you contracted in Hadishtan, and the carts pulled by mules, and the other carts without mules and your conspiracy with the Chief Chamberlain ..."

The Chief Chamberlain cried out: "How dare you mention my name, you criminal, you rapist, do you think that I don't know that it was you who put the poison for..."

But the voice of the Khan came roaring high above all the other voices: "Enough, enough, do you wish to publicise all your scandals in front of the rabble? Do you realise what this exchange of accusations means? Does it not mean that I am surrounded by a gang of thieves? By God, in whose hands lies my soul, I shall make an example of you all. Wait until I return to my office. Have you gone mad, oh Head of the Ministry of Commerce? And you, oh Hikimdar, have you lost your reason? I shall undertake an investigation into everything that you do. I shall..."

But the Khan did not finish what he was saying for he was cut off by a cry from behind, saying: "There they are, they've come back."

And Juha cried out, in his turn: "And the two steeds are with them."

And a third shouted: "One of them is as white as day whilst the other is as black as night."

Said Juha: "I believe that I am entitled to my reward now, oh chief of the Ministry of Commerce."

But the Minister drew back a pace to the rear as he said: "Not before you explain to us and confess as to who bribed you."

But the Khan said, crossly: "Give him his money. For he has already found the two steeds. The money has become his by right. Go on."

The Head of the Ministry of Commerce threw the heavy bag at the feet of Juha, who bent down to pick it up at the very same moment as the Shahbandar grabbed at the bag and attempted to snatch it away. The two of them rolled over on the ground several times before the guards managed to separate the two of them. But the bag finished up in Juha's hand. The Khan cried out in a strangled voice: "What is this comedy? How could you permit the court to be turned into a bunch of vagabonds? Who is responsible for this infringement of law and order?"

The Shahbandar called out: "It is the Hikimdar, my Lord. It was he who bribed the fortune-teller so that he would not find the two steeds before the race, so that he could prevent my Lord from the pleasure of seeing them, whilst they were running and winning."

The Hikimdar then shouted out: "Indeed, you are the sinful criminal. How can you dare to speak about the theft of the two horses when it was yourself who hid them in your own palace? Do you think that our Lord would be deceived by you with such a trick."

The Head of the Ministry of Commerce cried out: "The Shahbandar tells the truth. The Hikimdar is the one to be accused."

The Chief Aide-de-Camp shouted: "Indeed, he was the one who hid the horses."

Once again the clamour and the tumult was raised and the corners of the court were rocked by the exchange of accusations whilst the voice of the Khan was lost in the babble of sounds. Indeed, the insults had given over to slaps and everything became very confused until nobody was able to see anyone but himself. Then suddenly a voice was raised, saying: "The Khan, the Khan, get to the Khan, he's having one of his fits again."

Everyone became involved with the Khan. Nobody paid any attention to Juha as he slipped far away. When the Khan finally opened his eyes, after about an hour or more, stretched out on his bed in his palace, Juha was two leagues away, or more, exchanging smiles with Skinner, the Thief of Baghdad.

* * * * * *

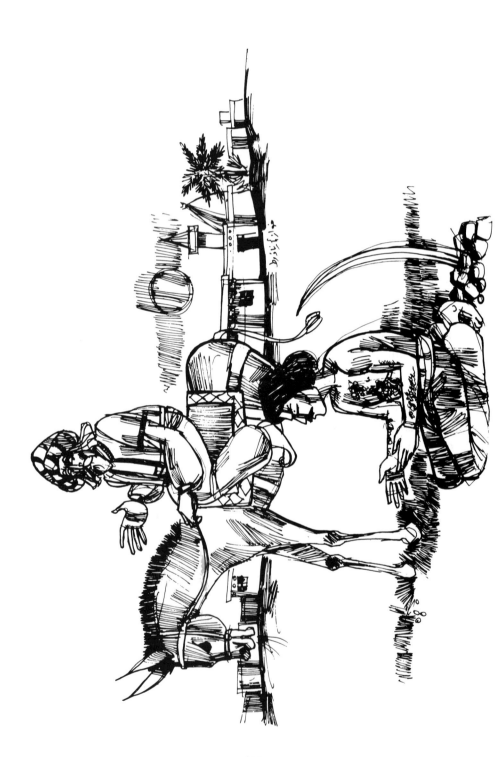

Chapter 9

The city of Sindashah arose to the most astounding news, which shook it like an earthquake and caused its people to forget, in an instant, the events of the previous two days. They forget the extraordinary events which surrounded the big race. They forgot the loss of the two horses of the Shabandar and the miracles of the fortune-teller, who read the Mandal, the sting of the whips of the Hikimdar and the quarrels of the chamberlains and also the fit by which the Khan had been afflicted. They only had one subject to discuss.

For the holy man Abulayal Tahruddin, had returned the previous night after an absence which had lasted for more than one hundred years. He had returned and had distributed his presents, as had been his custom, in the children's bags, suspended behind the doors. And there were the children, filling the streets and alleys of Sindashah, with joy, merriment and rejoicing, with bunches of flowers and tunes of songs, in their new, brilliantly coloured clothes; whilst in their hands were toys, toffees and sweetmeats of all kinds and colours. In their eyes was a look of confidence with which they challenged the guards and undercover men, perplexed and alarmed by what they could see and hear.

Some people swore that they had seen Abulayal Tahruddin with their own eyes, before dawn, whilst he was flying from house to house, above the tops of them and between the trees, with dozens of bags and baskets behind him, also in the air, carrying the presents. Others said that the bags and baskets were not flying on their own in the air, but were attached to a winged steed, whilst a third group claimed that it wasn't a steed but a donkey. They even added to this that they had heard our Master Abulayal Tahruddin calling to his flying donkey, using the name 'Masoud'.

At this very moment, exactly, Masoud was tethered at a mulberry tree which spread plenty of shade, outside the gates of the city. And Juha was beside him, leaning his back on the trunk of the tree, resting after the labour of a long night, whilst quite close to him was

Skinner, the Thief of Baghdad, plunged into a deep sleep, with a smile on his face that was almost wide enough for the whole of creation.

A beam of sunshine slipped through the branches of the mulberry tree and fell on the face of Skinner, creating a halo around his face, as if he was one of the angels. The lips of Juha parted in a happy smile too, but it was not long before it disappeared, leaving behind it the look of a big question. How would he be able to find his way to Haji Agha and the water well?

When Skinner opened his eyes the question was still going round and round in Juha'a head, as the breeze carried to him the sounds of the rejoicing and the songs of the children from the city, hidden behind the walls.

Skinner, whilst in a discussion with his friend, said: "I dreamt that Abulayal Tahruddin was patting me on the shoulder and giving me a necklace of jasmine flowers and saying: 'These are from your bush which you planted at my tomb'."

Juha said, simply, as he was turning up the corners of his long garment and undoing the tether of Masoud: "That is a dream of clear meaning. Be of good cheer, my friend, about the favours of Abulayal, and now, let us get on our way towards the north. Hopefully, we will be able to find our way to Haji Agha and the water well."

Skinner said: "Not before we visit the tomb of Abulayal. Not before I satisfy myself that the jasmine bush really has already blossomed and that he has forgiven me."

"Is that dream not enough for you?"

"Yes, but I need to satisfy my heart." Then Juha said, in an attempt to convince his friend that there was no necessity to visit the tomb: "After all that you did yesterday there is no question but that our holy man Abulayal is pleased with you." In reality, Juha was afraid that the jasmine plant at the tomb would have dried up like the previous ones. He was afraid of the effect of such a blow on the Thief of Baghdad.

However, the other insisted as he led Masoud on the road to the tomb: "Indeed, we must visit it. Only God knows if I shall come this way again. If you are tired, wait for me here and I will go and visit it and come back."

Juha said, surrendering: "Indeed, we'll go together." And he lifted his eyes to the heavens, praying for a miracle to happen.

And it was as if the heavens had listened to the prayers of Juha for the three had no sooner got close to the tomb than Skinner screamed, shrilly, rattling the walls of the tomb, whilst he was leaping about like a madman until he fell flat on his face, to get up and jump about again whilst continuing to cry: "Allahu Akbar — Allahu Akbar — Allahu Akbar."

* * * * * *

Juha looked, and in the place where Skinner had set the plant, he found a flowering jasmine bush, its fine branches entwined, as if they were necklaces of turquoise. He left his friend, praying with humility, in response to the invitation of the old Sheikh, caretaker of the tomb, who said: "The joy cannot be too much for your friend after he has seen that his plant has grown and flowered."

Juha said, and his words, too, were almost dancing with joy, regarding the old man with love: "I do not know how I can thank you. For it is you who have done this, without doubt. The plant which he set would not have grown and flowered had it not been for you."

The Sheikh said, with pleasure, as he asked Juha to sit next to him on the step of the tomb: "The matter gave me no more trouble than bringing a few handfuls of fertile soil from the back of the tomb to the same place. It would have been too hard for me to have seen the young man distressed again by the failure of his plant to grow. I wish you could have seen, last year, when he came back after a few days to find that his plant had dried like a stick, but, praise be to God, he will not know, after this, tears other than tears of joy."

"You have done a miracle, oh venerated Sheikh." The smile of the Sheikh widened and disclosed his toothless mouth.

"Indeed, the miracle was what happened yesterday, in Sindashah.

Have you heard the news of the return of Abulayal Tahruddin?"

"Do you think that this news is correct?"

"It is true, one hundred per cent, oh venerable sir."

"So what the lady says is true then?"

"Which lady?"

"A widow from Sindashah, who came here today to make a vow in the name of our Master, Abulayal Tahruddin, to spend the whole of today in prayer at his tomb after he had visited her home yesterday and left presents for her three children, beautiful toys such as he had left for all the other children. But he gave her more, she says, twenty thousand pieces of silver, together with a card which said: 'This is half of what is due to you, which was lost in the market, some days ago'."

Juha nodded his head, without speaking a word, whilst the Sheikh continued, saying: "It is apparent that miracles do not happen singly these days, for the widow has already told me, today, that she has decided to bring up an orphan child who has lost both its parents, as an acknowledgment from her of the kindness of our Master, Abulayal."

Juha said, and there was a ring of delight in his voice which did not escape the ear of the old man: "Only goodness gives rise to more goodness, like the jasmine plant only produces the jasmine flowers."

The Sheikh said, interrupting: "On condition that the goodness is sown only in fertile ground. Whoever said, 'Do no favours except for people who deserve them,' was telling the truth."

"Indeed, he who said, 'Do favours and then throw them in the sea,' was even more truthful. Because, venerable, old man, I believe that each one of God's creatures on this earth has some good in him, which may be hidden for years, under the thick cover of ignorance, necessity or circumstances. But as soon as it is struck in a sensitive spot it bursts out, like a torch, burning with love, truth and the effort to make other people happy. "

The Sheikh shook his head in opposition: "That was my belief, until some years ago, when a person entered my life who was the devil himself. All the light of the universe could not remove the veils of evil amassed over his heart whilst the fires of harm and in-jury have milled around in his head until every atom of humanity there has been burnt up. This man, if it is possible to call him a man, is he who has made me a nonbeliever in the theory that there is good in all men."

Juha, who was captivated by what the old man had to say, said: "And how was that?"

The Sheikh continued with his conversation, and it was as if his recollections had been stirred: "It will be sufficient for you to ima-gine that the greed, rancour and pleasure in hearing the sufferings of others, which exists collectively amongst the whole of mankind should all be held by just one single person. This is the octopus, the wild beast, of whom I was talking. He was the man in whose hands my bad luck caused me to fall, and for whom I worked, as a clerk and a watchman, on a mountain spring which he owned, and on which he had erected an iron door in order to sell its water, drop by drop, to the peasants."

Juha jerked himself, as a spark of hope suddenly came to his mind: "You say, a mountain spring? With an iron gate on it? Tell me, what's the name of this man?"

The Sheikh replied, wondering about the reaction of Juha: "His name is Haji Agha, but what is important about knowing his name?"

"You will know, soon enough, but tell me, how did the well come into the possession of this person?"

"They say he won it over a bet in a game of backgammon."

Juha cried out, as he grabbed the forearm of the man with such force that it almost hurt him: "God is greatest, for I swear by God that this is yet another miracle at your hands, my father. Tell me, my father, tell me everything about this Haji Agha. What is he like? How tall is he? Is he clean shaven or bearded? I beg of you to for-give me for my reaction, it is not simply a matter of curiosity. Where did he come from? Where exactly is this spring?"

The Sheikh said, in protestation: "Hold on, my son, hold on. For your questions are coming at me as if they were a swarm of bees fleeing from the hive. Ask whatever you like and I will answer every question but give me the chance to answer one question at a time so that my answers will be unequivocal on the subject and balanced as befits a man of my age."

* * * * * *

They say when a man is the subject of a discussion going on in his absence, he is struck by a fit of coughing. And if this be true, then it is more than likely that Haji Agha remained the victim of a sudden fit of coughing for that whole day, from sunrise until the sun set. And when the Sheikh said goodbye to Juha and his friend, and patted the head of Masoud as they were preparing to go off in a northerly direction, as he had indicated, Juha said: "This has been, I swear by God, a blessed day, my father, for we have all received blessings — our Master Abulayal Tahruddin, the children, the widow, my friend Skinner, and me, but you alone, have not received any present, so take this garment." And Juha took off the long shirt which had been presented to him by the Hikimdar, when he was coming out of the vault prison.

The old man refused to accept the present and protested that the long shirt which he was wearing had been with him for more than ten years and that he would not be showing good faith if he abandoned it now. But Juha insisted and Skinner went forward and removed from the Sheikh the old, tattered shirt and threw it on to the fire and dressed him in the new garment, in spite of his protests. A cloud of smoke went up which was soon dispersed by the spring breezes. Then Juha cried out, exhuberantly, whilst he goaded on his donkey with his heel in the belly: "Get on Masoud, for after today we'll not lose our way."

* * * * * *

After travelling some days along the narrow mountain tracks, Juha's party stopped, one morning, on the summit of a high hill, extending from the foot of which was the village of Sikriya with about one hundred and fifty huts of the same size, looking as if they were pretending to be frightened phantoms, supporting each other. Beyond the huts extended the green fields and gardens of the village with blossoming flowers and sprouts of produce. In front of them shimmered the water of the spring. The base was enclosed between two mountains and its head was at the entrance to the village where it was surrounded by a wood of evergreen oak trees. Appearing from behind the trees was a yellow-coloured building of two parts which resembled sails or wings, and which surrounded the head of the spring, as if they were embracing it.

Juha poked his friend with his elbow, as he pointed to the yellow house, the features of which appeared between the branches of the trees: "That is the lair of the viper and this is the spring."

"It's bad luck that it's not something small that one could carry away."

Juha scolded him, playfully: "Can't you think of any method except stealing?"

"No doubt, you would prefer to go to him begging and submitting to him a petition, bending down on your knees in front of him, imploring him to withdraw from the spring and hand it over to us out of the goodness of his heart."

Juha then said, calmly: "That is exactly what will happen, he will hand over the spring out of the goodness of his heart. But, we shall not bend down on our knees nor shall we beg of him. It is more than likely that it will be he who implores us to take over the spring from him and relieve him from the burden of it."

Skinner shook his head in disbelief, whilst Juha continued with what he had to say: "The matter is, quite simply, if it is impossible to take away the spring from this viper, then the only solution is that we move him away from it. And this, with the help of God, is what we are going to do."

"You mean, we get rid of him? Like drowning him in the spring, for example? Or we throw him off the top of the mountain?"

"It never occurred to me nor will I even permit you to let such a thing cross your mind."

"I beg your pardon, my master, I just want to understand."

Said Juha: "Give me your ear and listen. For I fear that the wind may carry our whispering to the viper himself." Some moments later, Juha came down from the top of the hill, on his donkey, going towards As Sikriya, but he was alone.

* * * * * *

Let us leave Juha, on the back of his donkey, going forward, slowly and quietly, to the field of battle, which was the reason why he had left Nahawand some weeks before, and precede him to the village of As Sikriya, where the people were going through a period of great difficulty, through which they had forgotten those happy days, before the spring fell into the hands of Haji Agha.

The previous owner of the spring was a rich, spendthrift youth, who lived for most of the year travelling between Samarkand, Isphahan and Basra, leaving the spring in the charge of a venerable Sheikh, whom it was said had been his teacher and who had brought him up and who was no less generous than he himself was. His job was to arrange the distribution of the water of the spring amongst the peasants, and not its sale. For this they, the peasants, paid him his salary which never exceeded twenty pieces of silver per annum. The benefit was great and the value of the produce of the land all went to the peasants.

But the memory of those days has faded today as a dream of long ago which has no reality under the heel of Haji Agha who began to raise the price of the water, year by year, until even the total produce of the ground would hardly be sufficient to meet the demands of the octopus of an owner.

And on that morning, whilst Juha and his friend were on top of the hill, getting their first glimpse of the village of As Sikriya, the elders of the people had agreed to meet in the village teashop after Haji Agha had informed them that, this year, he had decided to relieve them from paying their dues for the water but that he was asking, instead, that Laila, the only daughter of Muhammad Ali, the headman of the village, should be taken to his house, in order that he could use her as his concubine. But Muhammad Ali had refused and had informed Wardani, the messenger informer and 'parrot' of

124

Haji Agha, that Laila was not for sale and that she was engaged to be married to her cousin, Hassan.

Wardani went to his master and returned to say that in that case, the people of the village would pay, collectively and totally, to the master, the sum of twenty thousand pieces of silver.

On this basis, the elders of the village gathered together in the teashop, to look into the matter. Either Laila or twenty thousand pieces of silver, which could hardly be paid using everything that they owned. They would have to sell all the goats and cattle which they owned, they would have to forego the storing of rice, wheat and barley and they would have to sell all the produce of the land whilst it was still on the trees, in order to be able to meet the large sum which the master required.

How great is the effect of poverty and degradation upon the dignity of man!

Those who had backed up Muhammad Ali yesterday, and had supported him in his refusal to sell his daughter to Haji Agha had changed their minds from one day to the next.

And when Muhammad Ali arrived at the teashop, the disgraceful thoughts and inability to do anything about their situation had driven out what remained of the dignity of the clan.

How many of them had had the thought come to his mind that Laila wasn't his daughter, what did she matter to him? Praise be to God that Haji Agha did not want his wife or one of his daughters. And how many a revered old man received a whisper in the mind that the correct action should be that Muhammad Ali should sacrifice his daughter for the saving of the ground which was dying of thirst?

Today all heads were lowered, looking at the ground, and backs were bent as if time itself was riding on them. The eyes were down, not wishing to meet the gaze of Muhammad Ali who had shuffled to the teashop, dragging his feet as if each one was tied to a mountain. When Muhammad took his place, alongside the owner of the teashop, he too, dropped his head and lowered his eyes until it seemed that his chin was almost touching the ground.

Some moments of heavy silence passed and everyone was hoping that someone else would begin the talking. For there was no solution other than that Muhammad Ali should present his daughter for slaughter. But nobody wanted to talk, even though amongst them there were those who gave out looks of regret and from whose hearts were sighs of sad resignation, released with regret or sorrow, or by way of mourning. He would then be able to go home with his mind at peace. For the misfortune would not fall on him, or on any member of his family. Suddenly, the silence was broken by the voice of Hassan, bursting out like the blows of a hammer.

"What is the matter with you all, sitting there silently? Which of you is going to be able to be the first to lick the shoes of Haji Agha? Surely, some one of you wants to be the first to have this honour?"

He then turned to Muhammad Ali, excitedly: "And you, uncle — just a few days ago, you approved my betrothal to Laila, gave your promise, clearly, and we read the opening chapter of the Quran, together. What will you do now, uncle, about your commitment to the opening chapter of the Quran?"

Amongst the gathering arose a murmuring, the words of which were not clear, whilst Muhammad Ali screamed out: "What do you want us to do son? As you know we are but poor people, without power or strength."

"You are not poor, you are cowards. Frightened rabbits in the face of the wealth and standing of the master."

Muhammad Ali did not answer with anything more than a couple of tears which wet his white beard.

But all the others present erupted at Hassan, upbraiding and insulting, for they found that erupting in the face of Hassan was less of a burden than challenging Haji Agha, in any case. And this storm was more repulsive than the young man could bear and he slipped away from the teashop without a glance at anything or anybody.

* * * * * *

Not long after this Juha was going slowly along from the corner of

126

the village on his donkey, considering the situation. Suddenly, he saw a young man, naked to the waist, kneeling down as if he were praying, whilst behind him was a long blade, buried by its handle, with the sharp end upright, gleaming in the rays of the sun. And the pleading of the youth reached the ears of Juha: "Oh Lord, forgive me for what I am about to do. Be kind to me, oh Lord, in your punishment of me. I know that to kill oneself is sinful. But here I am before you. You, oh Lord, you see, you hear and you know. What else is left for me in this world after I have been denied Laila?"

The young man was totally absorbed in his plea, with his eyes closed. He did not notice Juha, who slipped in behind him, pulled the sharp blade from the ground, and threw it far away. The young man completed his petitioning and shrieked out loudly, leaping up into the air. He fell flat out on his face, in the very place where he had buried his blade, without noticing that the blade was no longer there.

A few moments passed, with the young man stretched out on the ground making no movement until Juha put his question, in a quiet voice, like the cooing of a pigeon: "Do you intend to lie there, stretched out like that, for ever?" The young man shuddered, startled, when he heard this voice of a human being. For he had imagined that the voices of the two angels of death, Munkar and Nakir, would sound different from the voices of human beings. And then he opened his eyes to be even more startled. For instead of seeing the faces of the two angels of death, the first thing that he saw was a scraggy, white, dusty beard, and a face, scorched by the sun and covered in sand, with two deep eyes, shining with kindness and compassion.

"Where am I? Who are you?"

"You are at the gates of Hell, of course. Where did you think that you were going, after doing what you did to yourself? As for me, I am the head of the Myrmidons, who has come to carry you away to where all the insipid young men, who flee from life at the first upset, must go."

The young man said, as he realised what had happened: "Woe be to you; you stranger. Why did you save my life when there is no place on earth for me? Why did you not abandon me, to leave this transitory abode, where there is nothing but torture, pain and deprivation?"

Said Juha: "And how do you know, my son, what the future has in store for you? Who knows, my son, but that God is saving you for another matter about which you know nothing yet? Tell me, what has made the world become so dark in your eyes? Tell me, talk; perhaps I will be able to help you."

"Nobody can help me."

"For sure, there is someone who can help you. Every problem in creation has a solution. The only problem which has no solution is death and that is what you were trying to do to yourself. Come on, I shall help you. I promise you that."

"I beg of you, sir, leave me alone with my affair. For even the Sultan himself could not help me."

"I have told you. If the Sultan cannot help you, I can."

Then the young man said, mockingly: "So, can you give me twenty thousand pieces of silver."

"Have you lost it gambling?"

"There is no call for you to poke fun at me, sir!"

"Poke fun at you? God forbid that I should poke fun at the pains of man. I may poke fun at my own problems, sometimes, but I never poke fun at the problems of others. But let me ask you quite simply, what do you need the twenty thousand pieces of silver for?"

"The story is all about the fact that I love a young woman."

"Ahh, now I understand, no doubt that she is from a well-to-do family and that her severe father is asking this large dowry for her."

"No, indeed, she is my cousin and her father is not asking for a dowry. At least, he is not asking for anything that is beyond my ability to pay, for he wishes, for her and for me, happiness together."

"You confuse me, my son, what is the problem then?"

The youth sighed, in torment: "May the curse of God be upon him, the black-faced one, Haji Agha, the owner of this well, he is the secret of my trouble."

Juha cried out at the top of his voice, so much so that the youth

128

jumped in dismay. "What do you say? Haji Agha, he is the cause of your trouble? Then praise God, my son, that he set you in my way, or perhaps he set me in your way. Whatever! What is important is that our meeting now, holds the secret to your release."

A glance of the young man strayed into the deep eyes of Juha and he sensed a calm coming over his soul, as if he had known this stranger for years. Then Juha said: "Now, tell me your story."

* * * * * *

Now, Juha was leaping with joy with the approach of the battle. He had not, up to this moment, ever set eyes on Haji Agha. But just the mention of his name from the young man who had been on the point of committing suicide, had been enough to set alight, in the heart of Juha, all the instincts for the fight to come. And Juha listened to every word and asked all the questions that he wanted to ask, receiving an unequivocable answer to every question.

And after Hassan had finished his story, Juha asked him: "How many days remain before the time for the irrigation of the land?"

"Ten days."

"Then we have plenty of time ahead of us. Be of good cheer, my son, for Laila will never be a concubine of Haji Agha, never. This is a promise which I set upon myself and may God, who is the third of our secret meeting, make me accountable for it. And if Haji Agha should intervene then I shall also interfere, and woe be upon him."

On yet another occasion did Hassan's gaze wander to the face of this amazing stranger, without understanding why he was becoming more confident in him, until he said, almost apologetically: "Forgive me for saying, sir, but this is not going to be the only time for the irrigation of the land. It will be followed by a second, and a third, and a fourth occasion. And each time Haji Agha will ask for my Laila, or perhaps his black lust will ask for some other girl of the village, and perhaps he will raise the ransom from twenty thousand pieces to forty."

"Do you think that I came here just to add to the fortune of that

129

octopus, black of face and heart, the sum of twenty thousand pieces of silver on each occasion of the irrigation of the land? No, my son, I came to take back from him what he has stolen, not in order to increase it. Put your mind at peace, and leave the future to God. But now, I have a request to make of you, which I hope you will fulfil."

"I am under your command."

"Our meeting must remain a secret. No creature must know of it. I realise, of course, that you cannot keep it from your Laila. Let that be so. But, warn her; she must not open her mouth to any third person, not even to her father. For everything depends on our meeting remaining a secret. It must not be known to anyone in the village at all. Do you promise me?"

"I promise you, and I guarantee Laila."

At this point the eye of Juha fell on Skinner, the Thief of Baghdad, who was beckoning to him from behind the delapidated wall, and he said: "And the second condition is that you should stay in this place of yours, and not leave it until after half an hour, and the third condition is that you should never, at any time, try to find out who I am."

"Every one of your instructions will be obeyed."

When Juha was alone with his friend, the Thief of Baghdad, their conversation revolved around the sum of twenty thousand pieces of silver, which Juha required to have before ten days had passed, and on condition that he should obtain them lawfully.

Skinner began to bang one hand against the other. How, in the name of God, could he get possession of twenty thousand pieces of silver lawfully? Should he sit at the door of the mosque and shout out: "In the name of God, calling all benefactors."

Juha said: "Indeed not. Go at once to Sindashah. No doubt you will remember that we still have money owed to us there. You need, for going and coming, six days; and for doing the job, two days. So off you go, in the keeping of God."

The Thief of Baghdad cried out, as he was departing, knowing full well what it was that Juha wanted him to say: "Farewell, my friend, I shall be back, and what you require will be with me."

Juha followed his friend with his eyes, until he disappeared.

Then he turned in the other direction, where the house of the Octopus stood, hidden behind the oak trees, and took his way towards the village, repeating, as he did so, as if it was an anthem:
"Haji Agha,
You robber, bloodsucker,
I am coming for you."

* * * * * *

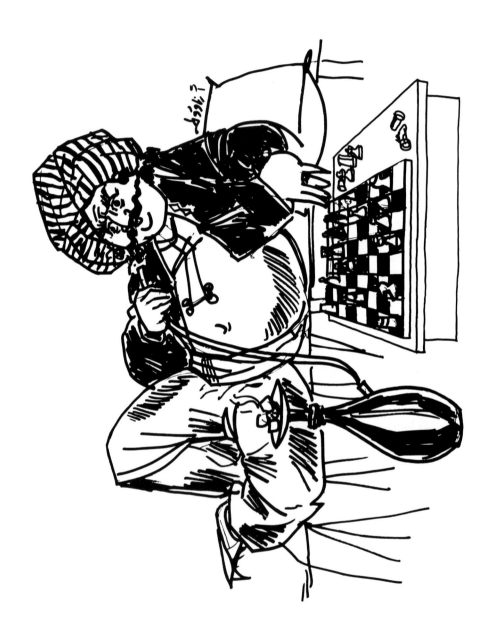

أحسن تدبير

Chapter 10

Juha took the glass of tea from the hand of Wahdan, the owner of the teashop, thanking him with a smile and ignoring the questioning look in his eye. But the man had hardly turned around, going away from him, when it appeared as if he had suddenly been struck with a touch of madness. For he rushed to the door of the teashop, shading his eyes with his hand as if he wished to make certain about something, far away, on the road. Then he came running back in, moving around in confusion, collecting all the cushions he could find in the teashop to put them on the single couch to be found there. Then he asked the few customers he had to get back from the couch or to leave the place altogether. He wiped off a table with the bottom of his long shirt, and placed it carefully in front of the comfortable couch. Then he rushed to put a hookah beside it, on the top of which was a cone of tobacco and then went to the door a second time, bowing repeatedly as he did so.

A look went out from the eye of Juha, along the road extending from the door, and his heart began to pound in his rib cage, so much so that he could almost hear it beating like a drum. For he was now certain that the person approaching, to whom Wahdan was doing all this bowing, was none other than his opponent, Haji Agha.

He entered the teashop, surrounded by a halo of pride, looking with a disdainful haughtiness around the place, passing over Juha as if he were a fly, to settle, with disgust, on the small number of customers who had withdrawn into a far corner. Then he sat himself down on the couch, preceded by heavy breathing, which reached the ears of Juha sounding as if it was coming from a working mule. His follower came forward and sat down in a place not very far from the place which Juha had chosen for himself.

The Master clapped his hands a couple of times, with an artificial movement of a person of some standing, and Wahdan went to him quickly, in answer, putting hot embers on the tobacco cone of the hookah. Then he ran again to put a chess board in front of Haji Agha and was preparing it for a game whilst the Master was taking long pulls on the hookah, sending clouds of smoke to form a network of twisting snakes around his black, pockmarked face.

* * * * * *

Juha, from his place, began to observe his opponent as he played, noting his movements. Yes, everything that he had heard, from the caretaker of the tomb of Abulayal Tahruddin and then from Hassan, the betrothed of Laila, was true and correct. The man had covetous eyes which plainly revealed unlimited greed, only equalled by an enormous arrogance, shown by his mocking, disdainful glances towards everything and everybody around him. His hands were veined and claw-like, as if they were ready, at any moment, to strangle someone. Then, he was playing chess with Wahdan as if he had made a great concession and that it was sufficient honour for Wahdan just to be playing with him. Every time he moved a piece it was either a threat or a new insult, whilst the other just smiled at the insults, humbly accepting the degradation.

Haji Agha was playing with the black pieces. Nevertheless, he still began to attack, savagely, from the movement of the first piece.

Juha noted that he played impetuously, rashly, so that he would miss checking the white king a couple of times in order that he could, each time, capture a mere pawn. The white pieces began to shrink in number, piece by piece whilst the black pieces were entire, apart from one pawn. Flushed with success, Haji Agha said: "It would be better for you, you stupid fool, to concede, so that we can play another game. Look at you, you have only got the bishop, one knight and a pawn of no value whilst I have my forces totally, or almost, with my bishop holding your king by the throat. Checkmate, you donkey."

Wahdan appeared confused, his shaking hand stretching out to touch the king, then pulled back to touch the bishop, then it left it to come down on the knight whilst Haji Agha continued with his exultation: "Why don't you play, you coward, you ass? I've told you, concede and let us play a second game. It's bad luck that we do not have a

134

bet on the game. I swear by God, if there had been a bet I would have taken the teashop, and everything in it, from you."

"Praise be to God that we did not agree on a bet."

"Naturally, no betting on this game. What do you think about a bet on the next game? I'll give you five to one?"

Wahdan's feeble voice came back: "I beg you pardon, my Master, but I never gamble."

* * * * * *

At this point a new voice entered into the conversation: "I'll accept the bet, sir, and on this self-same game too. I'm prepared to complete the game and I offer one hundred pieces of silver. What do you say?"

The owner of the voice was Juha who stood up in his place and then went over and stood at the side of the chess-board, between the two men.

Haji Agha looked at Juha, dismissively in the beginning and then mockingly: "It would appear that you have a lot of money, stranger."

Said Juha, taking a bag of silver out of his pocket: "It's not a great deal, but it's sufficient for a gamble, from time to time."

The Master took a long, quick pull on the hookah, with his eye on the bag of money, then he blew out his words with the smoke: "Are you serious? I advise you to hold on to your money."

Juha said, as he threw the bag on to the table: "I am very serious, except, perhaps you want to withdraw." Juha did not miss the greedy look, mixed with anger, in the eye of Haji Agha, as he ordered Wahdan to vacate his place to this stranger who had no need for his money. Then he took from his pocket five bags of money and threw them on to the table next to Juha's bag. And as Wahdan moved out of his place he said to himself: "My guess was right. This stranger is mad, without doubt, or perhaps he smoked too much hashish before he came here."

Juha said, as he settled into his place, studying the chess board: "If I had more than one hundred pieces I would have wagered it with you. Regretfully, I do not have another fil more."

Wahdan then cried out: "Then how are you going to pay for your tea and your bed tonight?"

135

Juha said, smiling, as he moved his king to a more secure position: "Do not be afraid, I shall not lose, and in any case, if I should lose, the Master here, may God be generous to him, will probably pay you, on my behalf, one piece of silver."

Haji Agha, after he had made his move, then stormed: "Oh no, you can give him your sandals and go away from here barefoot, as a lesson to you, for I am not paying anything."

Juha said, as he moved his bishop: "In that case, I cannot lose. For, my dear sir, I cannot travel barefoot, even in the face of all the lessons in the world, and now, if you will permit, check."

Haji Agha cried out: "Well, I swear by God, I do not think that I have seen anybody in my life more stupid than you. Do you not realise that this move means the loss of your bishop?"

Juha said: "Are we playing a game for a wager, or just talking?"

Haji Agha snorted as he grabbed the bishop with his claw, just like it was an insect, and threw it into the box: "That's your bishop gone too, what are you going to do now?"

Juha answered, quite simply, as he moved his knight: "No, you tell me; what are you going to do now? Check, sir, checkmate." The look of Haji Agha froze over the chess-board, and his pockmarked face became dark blue, compared with the tongues of fire burning in his eyes, whilst his lecherous lips began to shake as he looked very deeply at the chess pieces as if they were poisonous scorpions.

Juha began to gather together the six bags off the table as he said: "The game has finished, brother Wahdan, and these are now mine." All this was going on whilst Haji Agha was still in his place, just as if a thunderbolt had dropped on him and had paralysed him.

Finally, he muttered in a cracked voice: "It was very strange that I did not notice that trick. For you tricked me, stranger. It was as if you had blinded my eyes and I did not see how my king had come to that end."

"Then let us play another game, even money this time."

"You can cut off my hand if I ever play you again. And now, on your way. The five hundred pieces of silver which you have robbed me of will be all. And it might be better that you set off now, for I couldn't stand the sight of your face again."

Juha, almost crying, called out: "Set off? It goes on. Does my journeying have no end? Will I never be able to settle in some place? Oh Lord, am I destined to be pursued for ever and ever? Is there not one place in the world where I can take refuge?"

His words hit their target. For Haji Agha spoke almost kindly, for the words of the stranger had pricked his ears up: "You say that you are being chased? Who is chasing you? Why?"

Juha said: "It is just bad luck, sir. My bad fortune is pursuing me. Do you know what eternal misfortune is? For that is what I have."

* * * * * *

These phrases were sufficient to extend the course of the conversation between the two men. It had already occurred to Haji Agha that the stranger might well be an absconded criminal or someone else of that nature. In this case it would be quite easy to go along with him until he could come to know his secret and the name of the town where he was wanted. He could then hand him over and get back the five hundred pieces which he had robbed him of.

Juha was reading all these thoughts as they passed through the mind of Haji Agha, just as if he was reading from the pages of an open book. Juha continued with his complaint of the ages: "Know this, oh great Master, that I held, until quite recently, a very important post in Misrabad. I was the concessionaire of the great market. It was I who collected the taxes and gathered the rents of the shops and the profits from all the deals made. In my work I had no rival. I was able to rent the small premises at the rent of the medium sized premises, and for the medium sized I took the rent of the large sized premises.

"The taxes which I collected, on every deal of buying and selling, were greater than the profits of both the buyer and the seller. I swear that the Khan of Misrabad, had as much confidence in me as he had in any of his chamberlains. Many times I was entitled to be made a chamberlain, but the Khan had no confidence in anyone else to take over the market from me. My income was enormous, but more important still, was the goodwill of the Khan, for this was my greatest wish and desire. After eight years had passed, the Khan died suddenly, and the world, for me, became dark. I felt that I could not remain in Misrabad any longer.

"For I had a thirst for knowledge, especially in one particular branch of the sciences, which I don't want to explain about, so I travelled to the country of Khusrawan, where the greatest sources of this tremendous science were to be found, together with the most distinguished of its scholars. Would that I had not travelled! Indeed, would that I had died, before I went there! For in Khusrawan my knowledge was the cause of my misfortune and the weak position which I am now in. This was the reason why I went roaming around the countryside, aimlessly. I hardly settle in one place when I am off, finding myself to be always travelling. When I came here, and I tell you the truth, I came here intentionally. It was my intention to spend a period of study and rest until, with the permission of God, my journey of castigation would end. But not all that man hopes for is realised."

Haji Agha took a deep pull on the hookah, thinking and studying the stranger with a look of scrutiny before he asked him: "And what are you going to do now?"

"Praise be to God. I now have six hundred pieces of silver with me, through which I shall attempt to make my living."

"Do you intend to take up gambling as a profession?"

"God forbid that I should do so. That was just a stroke of luck, and I don't think that this will happen again."

"Perhaps you wish to enter commerce — buy from here and sell there, making a profit."

"I do not think that I am capable of trading. On top of which trading requires the merchant to travel about a lot. What I want is to settle in one place and get on with my studies. The sort of job most suitable for me would be that of a storekeeper or an accounts clerk with a modest merchant. These six hundred pieces of silver are my capital. That is, a deposit that I would be required to pay to the employer."

Haji Agha blew the smoke out of his nose and his mouth at the same time, whilst turning round in his mind some sort of a problem, whilst the eyes of Juha were watching what was going round in his mind: "Now sir, I will say goodbye, may God protect you. I thank you for your present, if I may be permitted to call it a present. My companion has now had a rest and the time has come for us to go."

"Companion? Do you have a companion with you? Where is he?"

Juha said, pointing to his donkey: "This creature, he of the long ears."

* * * * * *

Chapter 11

Juha pointed to his donkey Masoud, saying: "This is my friend and travelling companion. Oh, well — may peace be upon you — we have placed our trust in God." Juha said this as he was getting up and he went slowly to leave by the door of the teashop. The two red eyes of Haji Agha were almost holding him back by the collar, for he was going away carrying with him the five hundred pieces of silver, no, six hundred.

The look on Juha's face, as he was putting the saddle on his donkey, Masoud, preparatory to departure, was sufficient for Haji Agha to make up his mind about the matter which he had been considering and he called out, apprehensively: "Wait a moment, stranger!"

Juha turned his head towards him, without stopping what he was doing: "Any service that I can perform, sir?"

"You say that you are looking for work, as a storekeeper or something like that! Perhaps I can help you."

Juha dropped the saddle of the donkey and turned towards him, this time giving him all his attention: "May God bless you, sir, and prolong your life. Do you know someone with whom you can intercede on my behalf? I swear to God, if you do that I shall remain grateful to you for as long as I live."

"Yes, I know someone. Come, sit beside me and I'll lead you to him."

"Where sir, where?"

"In this place, itself."

Signs of bewilderment appeared clearly on the face of Juha, so that even Haji Agha understood their significance without difficulty. He began to look around the teashop, at the bare walls, the roof made of palm fronds, the pigeon cotes hanging by the door and his eyes, showing great concern, finally came to rest on the face of Haji Agha: "I beg, sir, to explain a little more. For I can see that the teashop can barely support its owner, never mind the hiring of a clerk." "Of course, it's not in the teashop, stranger. No, I mean here, in this place." Then Juha said, shaking his head sorrowfully: "My Master speaks in a language which is beyond my level of comprehension.

Please explain, so that I can understand."

Haji Agha giggled, pleased with his own wit: "I shall make my words simple, and I shall explain everything to you. It is just that I first want you to answer a few questions."

"Ask whatever you like, sir."

"Have you ever visited this village, before?"

"I have not had that honour."

"Have you any relatives here, or people that you know?"

"All my relatives and acquaintances are in Misrabad."

"Will you swear to that?" "I swear, by the mercy of God in respect of my father and all my ancestors, that I know no one in this place and that I have no relatives or friends here and that this is the first time that I have come to this blessed village. But why all these questions?"

"I shall explain that to you later. And now, the final question. Are you one of those foolish people who succumb to their emotions? Those who collapse in the face of tears?"

"I'll tell you the truth, sir. Nothing is of importance to me in this world apart from myself and my studies, although I am compelled at the present time to show concern, also, for my friend here, the one with the long ears."

"That is a personal matter, even if I cannot understand the reason for your great concern in respect of this donkey, but that is your own concern. But now, oh stranger, let your heart dance with joy. By the way, what is your name?" "Abdussabur." (As Sabur means 'the Most Patient', one of the glorious names of God. Abdussabur means 'the slave/servant of God'.)

"Indeed. Abdussabur is a very suitable name indeed. I'm saying, dance with joy, Abdussabur, for you have found the job which you want."

"Truly, sir?"

"Yes, do you see this spring? Do you know who owns it?"

"The spring I can see, yes, it is beautiful, an inexhaustible wonderful source of wealth. Who is its owner then, sir?"

"Me — yes, I am the owner. So what do you think, oh Abdussabur, about being, from this very moment, the watchman of this spring and its water tank?" There was no need for Juha to hide his pleasure. From the very moment when he arrived at the slopes overlooking the village of Sikriya, he had been arranging matters so that they would conclude with this end, or, it would be better to say, that they would begin at this beginning. And there was the man himself, offering to employ him as a watchman for the well and its water tank.

Juha scratched his beard, as if he was weighing up his words before he spoke: "Of course, you will need a cash deposit on this job?"

Haji Agha then said, with excessive generosity: "I would not normally be satisfied with less than five thousand pieces of silver but I am pleased with you and I need you, therefore I will accept from you the five hundred pieces of silver." As he said this he put out his hand to the baggage of Juha, taking from it the five bags and congratulating himself on his cleverness, for his money had returned to him. This stupid man had returned it himself. But in spite of that he would keep his word. He would appoint him as a keeper of the spring and its water tank. If he proved to have ability, then he would have the benefit of his services. If not, he would get rid of him in no uncertain terms.

Not ten minutes had passed before the whole village was talking about the new misfortune which had befallen it: "Haji Agha had appointed a new keeper for the spring."

One of them said: "It is as if it was not enough for us to have one executioner, so now we have two."

Another said: "What other evil awaits us on the morrow?"

But Hassan said: "No one knows what the fates are hiding from us. But, for some reason, I just do not seem to be able to be pessimistic."

Then Wahdan cried out: "How great is God. Now Hassan, the imbecile, speaks in the tone of the wise men. Be gentle, Lord."

Haji Agha led his new follower to the place where the water came out from the spring. It was in the form of a narrow pass, enclosed between two high mountains. On it the man had erected an iron gate, which was encircled by a heavy chain and which was locked by an even heavier padlock.

And the Master said to Juha, as he handed him the enormous key: "You are, from this moment, the watchman of the spring. Do not open its gate to allow the water to pass through this channel, except on permission from me."

Juha said to himself: "This, is the gate through which all the injustice

143

which has torn apart the people of As Sikriya, has passed." Then he raised his voice and said: "I belong to it, oh great Master, I belong to it."

The Master then continued with his instructions, for he had been pleased by the tone of Juha's voice: "Do not give anyone a single drop of water on credit. Pay first, then take the water for which you have paid. This is the principle to which you must pay full attention."

Then the Master and his employee, went to the nearby hut, over the door of which were lots of spiders webs: "You will live in this hut. The key of the gate of the spring is with you and should not be allowed out of your sight."

Two complete days passed before the watchman of the spring appeared in front of the teashop. The sun had set and Haji Agha had played the usual two games of chess with Wahdan, the owner of the teashop, and beaten him, as usual. Then he had departed with his servant, Wardani, just two paces behind him.

Juha did not go into the teashop but passed by quietly, ignoring the greetings of the few customers which reminded him of the hypocrisy of the fortune-tellers on the Bridge of the Masacres on the day the Hikimdar Mahmar appointed him as their leader.

Looks of hatred and disgust from those to whose greetings to him he had not replied, followed him down the road until, when he reached the nearby bakery he bought the whole of a large basket of top quality white bread, and then turned to a man selling vegetables and bought from him the whole of a basket of onions, green beans, cucumber and lettuce and then added to all that two bundles of mint.

Then, carrying the two heavy baskets on a stick across his shoulders, he made his way back, being followed by a lot of eyes which were almost popping out of their sockets. "What was the abominable watchman of the spring going to do with that quantity of bread and vegetables which would be sufficient for ten persons when he, as far as they knew, lived on his own in the hut near the gate of the spring?" The next day the same thing happened and he was watched by perplexed eyes as he carefully selected each loaf of bread and then the best kind of cucumber and onions and also as he placed his purchases, with great care, in the two baskets and hung them on the two ends of the stick, to carry them on his shoulders as he went on his way to the hut.

On the third day there were hundreds of eyes watching Juha as he went and came back. But Wardani did more, for he followed him, keeping well away, to make sure that he did not see him. He slipped through to the fence from which he could observe the watchman of the spring and see what he got up to. By good luck the door of the hut was left open, or perhaps it was from the excessive inattention of the new watchman, believing that he was secluded, far from any eye.

In the light of the oil lamp which Juha had lit, Wardani was able to see him as he took from his large bag, a brilliantly coloured carpet, probably silk, which he laid out on the ground. Then, taking each loaf of top quality white bread, one after the other, he carefully wiped it with the end of the turban and placed it, with great care, on the beautiful carpet. He also brought two buckets full of water and placing one of them on each side, he moistened the stalks of the spring onions, the cucumbers and the leaves of the lettuce with the water, wiped them and then placed them also, beside the loaves of bread, as if he were laying out a guest table.

Wardani observed all this and he was extremely astonished but when he realised that this feast was being prepared for the donkey which was standing in the other corner of the sizeable room, his eyes nearly popped out of their sockets. And he saw, from where he was standing, the watchman of the spring exchanging whispers with his donkey, bending down suddenly, to kiss the right fetlock of the donkey, and then the left, and finally, he saw him giving it loaves of bread, bundles of onions and cucumbers, wiping them on each occasion with great care, and bending down so low in front of the donkey's feet that he touched the ground from time to time.

The strange sight was more than the mind of Al Wardani could stand and, before he knew where he was he had leaped in the air, away from the fence as if he was crazy. Then he was off, running like the very devil, and he did not stop running until he was in front of Haji Agha. He was panting, unable to speak, until Haji Agha cried out to him, excitedly: "What is the matter with you, speak up?"

Finally, the confused words came from the mouth of Wardani: "Master, you won't believe what I am going to tell you, until you have seen it for yourself."

145

Chapter 12

Juha was not unaware of the dozens of perplexed eyes which were furtively watching him from behind the fence and from the top of the mulberry tree, facing the open door. Indeed, he was probably expecting some of the ears to reach so far as to be able to actually hear him breathing.

For this was how he was playing the part which he had planned and which he had carried out yesterday and the day before yesterday. He swept the place, under the feet of his donkey, Masoud, and sprinkled rose water on the ground. Then he began feeding his donkey by hand, whilst kneeling beside his forelegs, and every time he extended his two hands under the nose of Masoud, he said, with humility: "Be so kind as to partake of this food, my Lord, with, I hope, pleasure and satisfaction, Sire."

The words of Juha reached the ears which were pricked up behind the fence and on top of the mulberry tree, situated in front of the hut, and they doubled the consternation of the people. Those spying on Juha held their breath as they watched over his every movement and action, unable to believe their own eyes. Then they saw him raise his head suddenly, at the sound of 'Abdun falling from the top of the mulberry tree. He ran to the open door to close it and everyone heard the sound of the bolts as he locked it tight.

At this moment, Haji Agha lost his patience, for he was no longer able to keep quiet and he rushed at the locked door, banging it with both hands. His follower, Al Wardani, was with him as he cried out: "Open up, oh Abdussabur, open up or I'll break down the door!" A few moments passed before everybody heard the sounds of the bolts as they were being drawn, then they saw the door opening and everyone noted that the brilliantly coloured carpet had disappeared, together with the silver plates that he had been using. But the donkey was still in its place and Haji Agha, not wishing to give Juha any scope to do anything, pushed him out of the way roughly, bursting into the hut. Behind him entered Al Wardani, whilst everyone else gathered at the door, watching and listening. Haji Agha then said, as he flung his arms about in the air: "What on earth are you doing, oh Abdussabur? Have you gone completely mad that you should feed the donkey with the finest bread and turnips?"

Juha hesitated for a moment and he appeared clearly distressed, as if he had been caught red-handed, committing a crime. His words came, hoarsely, strangled: "My Master, I — did not — do — anything — but — who are all these people that you have brought with you?"

Haji Agha turned crazily towards the door to scold his follower, Al Wardani, in a voice like that of a roaring ox!

"What in the devil are you doing here. Get rid of that mob and get away, yourself also, out of my sight." Then he turned to the watchman of the spring, Juha; carrying on with his tirade, whilst Al Wardani was chasing away all the parasites, as if he were driving a flock of sheep. "Now, you; explain to me, immediately, this madness which I have seen, or I'll throw you down in the bottom of the spring."

Juha answered, as he was still, apparently, trying to overcome his confusion: "Please, Master; make yourself at home, please sit down."

"I don't want to sit down, but I want to point out to you that my eye has never left you. I watched you yesterday, and the day before yesterday, as you bought those quantities of the finest white bread, and bundles of lettuce, onions, cucumbers, peaches, apricots and apples."

"That is true, Master, I do buy my provisions every day in the market."

"Your provisions? Those provisions were enough for ten men."

"You know, sir, I'm a very big eater."

"Don't try to lie. For I have seen you, with my own eyes, feeding the donkey."

Juha interrupted him, in trepidation: "I beg of you, Master, do not use this word. Do not put us in jeopardy."

"What? What do you want me to call this creature then? Perhaps you want me to call it a horse, or a gazelle?"

Juha raised his arms in the air, imploringly: "I earnestly entreat you, in the name of everyone dear to you, do not use this word. You can refer to him by saying, 'our friend with the long ears', for example, or any other form of description that you like, but not the sort of name

148

which is totally unsuitable for one who is one of the most outstanding and greatest of persons."

Haji Agha burst out, angrily: "The most outstanding and greatest of persons, you stupid idiot. Where are the great people here? You, you imbecile? What other great person is there here, apart from myself? I am the Master of this village and its owner."

Juha begged him, and he was almost in tears, looking around himself in consternation, for his confusion had increased: "Sir, sir, please do not raise your voice like that, I beg of you."

"Perhaps you do not want to upset your friend here, the donkey."

Juha slapped his own face as he moaned: "There you go, saying it again, sir. I swear, by God, you are trying to destroy me."

The man screamed, as he almost went out of his mind: "Are you trying to play with my mind, you so and so? What destruction is there here if I call things by their proper names? I say about the donkey that he is a donkey — a donkey, a donkey!"

At this very moment, Masoud brayed loudly. Juha rushed to him, knelt down at his feet, and said, entreatingly: "I beg your pardon, my Lord; forgiveness; for he does not know."

Then he turned to the bewildered Haji Agha and said to him, in a sharp voice as he pulled him outside: "Listen, sir, let us go outside and talk there."

"Not before you give me an explanation for this madness. For I have rights over you by the fact that I am your Master."

Juha tore his garments as he cried out: "Alas, alas, what can I do? I cannot, oh my Master, I cannot. For it is a fearful secret which nobody must know of."

"Secret? What secret? And why should I not know it? Indeed, it is inevitable that I should know it. There will be no secrets hidden from me on my land and under the roof of my own house."

Then Juha said, as he shook his head in pain, as if he was being torn apart by a fatal helplessness: "What a severe affliction it is for a man to find himself torn between two problems, each one of them bitter. Will you not take pity on me, my Master?"

"I don't know anything except one thing. That is that I was kind to you, I granted you work and lodging and I prepared the way for you to have rest and stability. And here you are, you return all this with evasion and ingratitude. It is correct, he who said, 'Beware of evil from those to whom you have been kind,' was telling the truth. But I shall not permit you to do this, never, ever. So, speak up! It will be better for you to speak now, before I lose my patience with you."

Juha replied, in a moaning voice: "Yes, my Master, you have been kind to me. This I can never deny or forget. This is what is worrying me now. For my father, may God rest his soul, would say to me that to hide a secret from your benefactor is to show ingratitude."

"The very highest wisdom. Your father, it appears, was a wise man. Do not neglect his advice."

"But the revealing of this secret, sir, involves a very real danger. Your life, and my life, would not be worth a pinch of snuff. Indeed, we could be transformed, in a single moment, to mere chaff, to be scattered by the wind."

"What you tell me will remain a secret between us. A third person will never know it."

Juha hesitated for a moment before he said, as he took his old, Chinese book out of his bag: "What I am about to ask may be offensive and I beg of you your pardon, in advance. But you must swear, on oath, on this book, that nothing of any conversation between us, will be divulged to any creature, whatsoever. Say, 'I swear by all the secrets of the universe, on this book'. "

"I swear, by all the secrets of the universe, on this book." "That I will maintain special and holy secrecy, in respect of he of the long ears, as if it were a bottomless well, as God is my witness."

* * * * * *

Haji Agha repeated the oath and he remained with open mouth, whilst his eyes exhibited a strange mixture of curiosity, consternation and greed. Juha's eyes looked deeply into the eyes of Haji Agha and, in his view, greed was the predominant factor and Juha was sure the man had become like putty in his hands. So he opened his book and quickly turned over the pages until he came to a page which was decorated by extraordinary pictures of men, dogs, frogs and donkeys. Juha stopped at this for a moment, without paying any attention to Haji Agha who had turned his head, attempting to understand the riddles and the Chinese characters, whilst his heavy breathing was following on like the death rattle of a slaughtered beast.

Finally, Juha said: "What day is this?"

Haji Agha replied, quickly: "Sunday, no, it's Monday. Why do you ask?"

Juha said, as he closed his book: "That is good, sir. I shall reveal to you my secret, and my destiny shall be in the hands of God. However, you will have to wait until next Saturday."

Haji Agha tried, without success, to convince Juha that he should tell him now. Until, as he continued his insistence, begging at one time and threatening at another, Juha said resolutely: "I have no ability to do other than this, sir. Either you wait until Saturday, or I shall move on from this place."

This was more than Haji Agha could bear the thought of and he said, submissively: "Move away, never. You will not move from here. So you can take your time until Saturday, even though I do not understand why we have to wait."

Said Juha, and he was bent over in pain: "You will excuse me when you actually know. But now, the time has come for this torture to end. I beg of you, Master, leave me now. And our appointment is for Saturday."

Haji Agha hesitated for a moment, then he turned away towards the door, completely baffled, not knowing how he would have the patience to wait until Saturday. But before he went out he turned to Juha and said, threateningly: "I shall wait until Saturday, but beware of trying to leave this place. For I swear, by God, if you do I shall kill you." Then he slipped outside, leaving Juha flat on his face whilst Masoud was in his corner, lifting his head towards him as if he was studying him with two wide, intelligent eyes.

* * * * * *

At that very moment, Skinner, the Thief of Baghdad, was in Sindashah seeking to carry out Juha's instructions to obtain the sum of

151

twenty thousand pieces of silver, on the condition that it should be money obtained legally. Skinner had arrived one day before this, and all the way along the road to Sindashah he had been asking himself: "What does Juha mean when he says, 'This money should be money which has been legally obtained.'?" Juha had told him this as he was handing over to him a bag containing six hundred and fifty pieces of silver, saying that these dirhams would help him in his task. How could that be? What was the relationship between the six hundred and fifty pieces of silver and the money to be obtained legally? How, in the name of God, could he invest it commercially for two days only, and make it twenty thousand silver pieces, without the means of doing so being totally illegal? Then why six hundred and fifty? Why not seven hundred, or a thousand, or even five hundred?"

And suddenly, the thought alighted in the mind of Skinner, just like the sun setting on the sea. This six hundred and fifty pieces of silver was the price that the Shahbandar had paid for the jewellery which he had estimated, at the time, to be worth more than forty thousand pieces of silver. Skinner banged his forehead with his hand as he cried out to himself: "Well of course, that is the wealth to be obtained by legal means."

And so it was, when he took his place at a nearly teashop, to observe from his position the premises of the Shahbandar of the merchants of Sindashah, that he knew exactly where he was going and what it was that he had to do.

By good luck, the Shahbandar closed his premises before closing time and went away, carrying with him his black suitcase. Skinner followed him, creeping along in his tracks, so that hardly an ear could hear him or an eye see him, until the Shahbandar arrived at his residence at the other side of the city, knocked on the door three times, and an old man opened the door for him. Skinner then said to himself as he took a place for himself amongst the branches of a willow tree facing the door: "I wonder how many servants there are in this palace." Skinner stayed up the tree for more than an hour, waiting patiently, like a leopard waiting for its prey. But he was rewarded for his patience when the door opened suddenly, and the Shahbandar appeared, with his potbelly and his bald head and his inflated pride, in a different garment from the one which he had been wearing when he entered the house. Behind him, between the two sides of the door, could be seen the beautiful face of the lady.

Her words reached Skinner's ears, as she said, coquettishly: "When will you come back, dearest? I shall remain waiting for you, with longing, until you come back, and I hope that you will not be so late as to come back after midnight."

"I really do not know when I shall be back. I may possibly be a little late. You know very well that my friend Taimur won thirty pieces of silver from me yesterday, playing backgammon, and I shall not come back tonight before I have recovered my losses."

"That is how you are. You leave me on my own every night. All day you are at business and all night with Taimur, whilst you have no time at all for me. I am your loving wife, who longs for you, night and day, and you are always busy with backgammon, horses, racing and the market."

The Shahbandar went away, sighing as he did so: "I shall not be very late tonight, so go to sleep and when I get back I'll wake you up." The lady closed the door whilst the Shahbandar quickened his pace, panting slightly, to recover what he had lost to his friend Taimur. All this was going on as Skinner was perched in his place up the tree, hidden amongst the branches, as the darkness crept in swiftly.

Then the door opened again and a beam of light came out as Skinner saw three men. One of them was the old man whom he had seen at the time of the arrival of the Shahbandar, and there were two younger men with him. Then the old man said to his two companions: "May the curse of God be on this woman and her unending demands. She wants me to go, at this time, and bring her a sackful of that Egyptian henna from the shop of the perfume vendor, Khadar. Why from Khadar, the perfume vendor, only? I don't know. His shop is at the far end of the city. It takes two hours to get there, and at this time of the night too."

"May the devil take her, and her husband as well, the mule. She wants me to bring her six bottles of tamarind, as if anyone would want tamarind at this hour of the day. And from where? From the Peacock Market and from nowhere else."

And the third one said: "I just do not know what has come over this woman. She wants me, now at this hour, to bring her two quarters of Damascus dates. And this isn't the season for dates, yet she says, 'Don't come back without them'. "

The old man said: "Look, I've got an idea. What do you think if we all go to Madkur's teashop, drink tea and pass the time away, and then, about midnight, we'll go back, one at a time, and say we haven't found what she wanted?"

And so Skinner saw them, turning off at the first corner that they came to in the road, to go the teashop of Madkur. Their laughter had hardly faded away before the door opened again, and Skinner saw three young girls, flitting out like birds getting out of a cage. One of them said, as she went swinging along: "Our lady has gone mad, there's no doubt about it! She has instructed me to go now, this moment, to the seamstress, and I'm not to come back until I have got her four new dresses."

A second one said: "And me, she wants me to go to the embroidery place and bring the counterpanes which I myself took there only a week ago. I'm certain that he will not have finished them yet."

"But me, she didn't want anything from me. She just told me to go and visit my auntie, whom I haven't seen for a month, and come back in the morning. What do you both think? How about you both coming with me and we'll spend the evening together there, with my auntie. Indeed, why don't we spend the whole night there and not come back until the morning?"

The first one said: "No, we can't stay all night. She is now on her own in the palace; the men have gone out and here we are, going out. It will be enough that we spend a pleasant couple of hours, or three, and we come back before she dies of fright."

Then the voice of the second one came, as they were going away: "That one, frightened, she's the devil himself!"

The sound of the girls faded away as the heart of Skinner was dancing with joy. The lady was now alone and his task had become quite simple. All he had to do was to find a way to get her out of the palace. Or would it be better to enter now and take his chances? But he did not have to think for long for the door opened, yet again, and the lady herself came out. She looked to the right once, and then to the left, before she dropped her veil over her face, locked the door with the key, and went away at a quick pace, followed by the eyes of Skinner, until she disappeared at the nearby corner, leaving behind her the fragrant scent of her perfume.

* * * * * *

The palace was now empty of both its owners and their servants. As for the closed doors, these did not present, for a single moment, an impediment in the path of Skinner. And so it was that not many minutes passed before the Thief of Baghdad was going around all parts of the palace as if he owned it, looking for the lawful wealth which Juha wanted the jewellery of the widow.

For he understood perfectly what he had to do. He had to take the jewellery, and leave in its place the six hundred and fifty pieces of silver which the Shahbandar had paid as the price for it. But where would he find the jewellery?

Skinner searched the first room he came across, and the second, then the third, without finding anything. But when he entered the fourth room he became certain that this was the bedchamber of the lady. For there was the fragrance of the perfume, the women's clothing, the comfortable bed, together with the hidden candles, the mirrors covering the walls and the big clothing box in the far corner. Then — what was this small box, inlaid with ivory?

The box was locked. But this, naturally, was not a problem, and it was not long before it was open and the eyes of Skinner struck by the sparkling jewellery inside it. Our friend heaved a deep sigh: "Here, Skinner, is the lawful wealth."

But he had hardly lifted up the box in his hands, after he had closed it preparatory to departure, when he heard the sound of a door opening and closing, and footsteps approaching. He looked around him, seeking a way out. What sort of an ambush have you dropped into, Skinner?

There are no windows in the room from which you can jump out. There is only the door and the footsteps are approaching it, with sounds of a conversation and whispering. Where would he go?

His eyes fell on the large box in the corner of the room. Ah — this is the only hiding place. He must jump into it. And so, he leapt in, pulling the lid down over himself, to find himself sinking into a pile of silk. Then he quietly stretched himself out, holding his breath. Not a moment passed before he heard the door of the bedchamber open and the voice of the lady of the house saying: "Do come in, darling. Don't be afraid of anything. You won't find anyone here." Then a metallic rattling reached the ears of Skinner, with the rustling of clothing and coquettish laughter and a coarse mumbling. It wasn't long before he was able to identify in it a voice which he knew well. The voice of General Mahmar, His Honour the Hikimdar. As for the metallic rattling, that was, no doubt, his sword, his belt and his innumerable medals and decorations.

Now, his talking and laughing came to the ear of Skinner: "How cross you are, love of my life. I swear on every oath, there is nothing in my heart except you nor do my dreams contain anything except the vision of you."

"Liar — liar, be truthful for once in your life."

"Don't raise your voice like that."

"There's nobody to be found here. Be reassured, your friend, the mule, has gone to play backgammon with Taimur and he will not return, as usual, until nearly dawn, whilst all the servants are out. We are on our own Mahmar; alone darling."

"Are you sure?"

"What, His Honour the Hikimdar, afraid? The most powerful man in Sindashah, afraid?"

"Dearest, you know what awaits us if ever our affair is discovered?"

"When a man is truly in love he should not be afraid, but this is not the subject for which I sent for you. I want to know why you abandoned me?"

"I haven't abandoned you at all. Love of my life, I am pledged to you, even though it was necessary to keep out of your way for a time, for your own safety, breath of my life, for the safety of both of us."

"Why? Why? Tell me."

"Your husband, the Shahbandar, my dearest, he is the reason."

The lady cried out, bitterly: "What's happened to him? What is new with you? He was always there and we were always meeting."

"Yes, yes, that's true. But the situation is different now, dearest. Do you remember our quarrel about the horses?"

"Are you trying to say that your heart has hardened towards me because of your quarrel with my husband?"

"No, no, never. My heart will not harden in respect of you, ever. Love of my life, it does not beat except at the sound of your name and it only lives for your love."

"Well then, what has happened? What has kept you away from me?"

"Your husband suspects that something is going on between us. In fact, he is making arrangements to try and catch us 'flagrante delicto'."

The box shook as musical laughter rang out from the lady: "What? He suspects? That imbecile of a mule suspects? It appears to me, my friend, that you do not know him at all. Or perhaps you do not know me. So you had better learn that in my hand, he is just like this ring. For he is unable to think about anything, unless I suggest it to him."

"But, my dearest, the fortune-teller, the one who can read the Mandal, he said to me that ..."

"Let all the fortune-tellers go to hell — forget all these misgivings, my Mahmar and come here — come over here, beside me — fear nothing, my beloved."

Skinner closed his eyes, smiling, imagining what might happen, when the Hikimdar Mahmar moved over next to her. What Skinner was imagining had hardly begun when it was mixed up with the sound of heavy banging on the outside door, accompanied by utter confusion in the bedchamber. A thick, loud voice was screaming: "Why doesn't someone open the door? Is everybody sound asleep?"

Then there was the voice of the Hikimdar, mumbling in dismay, as he went around the bedchamber like someone demented: "Your husband — the Shahbandar — we are lost — I am lost — finished — I'm finished — finished." Then he started wailing like a child. But the lady was made of sterner stuff. For after just one second she had become totally prepared to deal with the situation.

She cried out, at the top of her voice: "Wait — what has happened to you — are you drunk? I'm coming down to open up for you." Then she dropped her voice whilst she whispered: "Why are you running around in circles like that? You're like a dizzy fly. Come here, get in this box, quickly." Then she raised her voice again: "I'm ready — I'm coming down now — God, do you want me to come down naked, in my nightdress? Why didn't you take the key with you?"

The Hikimdar whispered, as he was getting into the box: "Then there is something in here."

"Fiddlesticks — whoever said that you were a coward was telling the truth — clumsy oaf." And out went the lady to open the door.

* * * * * *

The Hikimdar, General Mahmar, piled into the box, burying his chin between his knees. Then he attempted to stretch out his lower leg a little but it struck something which prevented it from further movement. He almost lost the ability to speak when a voice came out the darkness to him, saying, in a whisper: "Take care, respected sir, your foot nearly put my eye out."

The Hikimdar suppressed a scream of terror, with difficulty, and a whisper came out of his mouth like a faint rattle: "What? Who is here? How ...?"

But he didn't finish his sentence, for a hard slap came down on his jaw which deafened him and rattled his ear, through which came a whisper with a frightening warning: "Silence your voice, you idiot. Can you not hear the fall of their footsteps? Shut up, or I'll bury my knife in your neck." And the Hikimdar felt the point of the knife on his neck. He became more aware of the fall of the footsteps of the Shahbandar and his wife as they were entering the bedchamber. The voice of the lady could be heard, saying: "It is nice of you to come home early. I will reward you for that."

"I didn't find Taimur at home. The old fox slipped away from me this evening." The Shahbandar said this as he sat down on top of the box to take off his sandals.

The lady then said: "I have got a fearful headache. I was dreaming a very strange dream when I was awakened by the banging on the door."

"Where are all the servants?"

"They have all gone out. They were disturbing me with their hollow chattering so I got rid of all of them, to leave me to go to sleep in peace. The headache was almost killing me. There is some medicine, I think, in your safebox downstairs. Would you mind?"

"With pleasure, my dearest. I am sorry that I woke you up from your sleep. At once — I'll come back with the medicine." The man jumped up off the box. The two men inside held their breath when they heard him say. "There's something moving in this box."

The lady quickly said: "Ahh, it must be a mouse. I did see a mouse before I went to sleep. It got away from me before I could kill it. We need a cat, my dearest."

"I must kill this pest of a mouse first."

"Ohh, my head, the medicine, my darling, I beg of you. My head is almost bursting."

"Of course — of course — just as you say my darling. Watch that it doesn't come out of the box before I come back."

The Thief of Baghdad heard the steps of the Shahbandar as he was going away, then he heard him stop, and a strange rattle came out of the chest of the Shahbandar, or perhaps it was from some other place, accompanied by a low scream of terror from the lady. Something or other had happened! What on earth could it be? Then came the voice of the Shahbandar, roaring, raging like a mad bull: "Whose is this inlaid breastplate? Where did this gold sword come from? Speak, woman, before I throttle you with my own hands."

* * * * * *

Chapter 13

A curse almost fell from the lips of the Thief of Baghdad as he felt the body of the Hikimdar fall upon him, like a lifeless corpse, inside the box. And on the outside the storm heightened rapidly — the voice of the Shahbandar roaring, the frightened movements of the feet and the breathing in quick succession.

"Speak woman, whose is this golden sword, whose is this breast-plate, embellished with precious stones and decorations?"

Finally, the lady of the house found her tongue. But her words came out, trembling and stuttering: "This? This? You say the sword? What sword? And — the breastplate? You ask whose they are? They are yours, naturally, my dearest. I bought them from the market as a present for you — unexpectedly!"

"A present? For me? A sword? And a breastplate, embellished with precious stones, and decorations also? Do you think that I am simple-minded, you unfaithful woman?"

This Shahbandar knows all the insulting terms and each expression of them comes out, sharp and offensive, like spittle.

As the uproar grew louder than before it became apparent from the movement of the feet outside, and the heavy breathing, that the Shah-bandar was chasing his wife, who was screaming in a high-pitched voice: "Yes, a present for you. I swear that they are both a present for you. And don't raise your voice so much. Do you want all the neigh-bours to gather round us? I swear ..."

"Neighbours? What neighbours? Let all the people in the city come and witness your disgrace. Speak up. Who was here? Who was here?"

The Thief of Baghdad, inside the box, pushed the heavy body of the Hikimdar away from himself, with disgust, whilst he wrestled with every atom of his brain: How was he going to get out of this situation? The screams of the lady grew sharper, mixed with the roaring of the Shahbandar which was now becoming more like the bellowing of a bull: "I'll kill you, you bitch. I'll pulverise you, you faithless hussy." It was clear now that he had got hold of her. "I'll kill you. Speak up, who was here? How did he get out of here? No — your lover didn't go out of here, he's hidden here!"

And if fear was causing the lady to let out screams with a maddened hysteria, it was causing the thinking mechanism of the Thief of Baghdad to move at a speed which was even more frantic.

The bellowing of the Shahbandar became louder, blending with the screaming and the sound of angry hands slapping soft flesh. "Where have you hidden him. Talk. Did —? He might be here, in this box."

Now there was no value in hanging about. Skinner did not know how the idea sprang into his mind, like a passing beam from behind a cloud. It is possible, for he was a well-practised thief, who had been through dozens of scrapes and experiences, that he simply acted on an instinctive inspiration. It could also have been a flash of genius from inspirations of Juha himself, which found its way to him over the great distances, across mountains and valleys. Whatever; the Shahbandar, bellowing like a bull, and the frightened lady, like a mouse in the presence of a hungry cat, were surprised by the lid of the box opening suddenly, and by a handsome, broadshouldered, virile youth leaping out of it, and then closing the lid behind himself noisily. The outstretched arms of the Shahbandar sagged whilst the lady let out a short scream. All the blood left her face with just two, wide, black, bewildered eyes staring out: How had the form of the General Mahmar, whom she had placed, with her own hands, in the box just a few minutes ago, been converted into what she now saw before her?

The Shahbandar was the first to come to his senses and he leapt into the air with a roar in the direction of Skinner. However, a flashing, intimidating knife in the hand of the Thief of Baghdad was sufficient for him to reconsider his position. And when the lady of the house found her voice she said: "Who are you? Who are you?" Naturally, she did not need an answer.

The Shahbandar raged: "You are asking, who? Do you not know, you whore?"

"I swear; and may God turn me into a statue of stone, here and now, if I break my oath; I do not know this man and I have never seen his face before."

Skinner waved his gleaming knife in their faces as he said: "There is no point in denial, lady, for everything has been revealed and it will be better for us not to continue to deny it. Indeed, we should repent and ask for pardon and forgiveness from your honourable husband."

The lady screamed, and drew back, unbelievingly: "What is this that you are saying, you lunatic?"

Skinner continued, directing what he was saying to the Shahbandar: "I have woken up to myself, Sire. I swear, by God, that I am full of remorse and do repent, most sincerely, to you. For I have heard with my own ears the words of love and endearment with which you compliment your wife, and this has truly filled me with remorse."

The lady screamed: "You are a liar, a liar. Do not believe him. I swear that I have never seen his face before this moment."

The Shahbandar puffed out from between his teeth: "Be silent, you abominable woman. Is this to be my reward because I removed you from the slums and made a lady out of you? You cheat on me? And with whom? With this scoundrel?"

Then Skinner said, consolingly: "Women sometimes have strange tastes. The main thing is that I have repented, Sire. Dear lady, there is nothing to be gained by denial. There is no salvation for us but in confession — in repentance. For was it not you who invited me here, tonight? Did you not tell me that the palace was empty that you had sent all the servants far away and that your honourable husband had gone to play backgammon with his friend Taimur, in order to recover the money which he had lost to him yesterday?"

The merchant snorted: "Did you tell him all this, you despicable woman?"

Skinner continued, with firmness and truth: "I swear that I shall never set foot in this place again, after today. I swear that I will never permit my eyes to set on the face of this woman after today. With your permission, Sire, allow me to swallow this remorse, for the rest of my life."

Skinner stepped towards the door calmly, with a bent back and tearful eyes, as if he were carrying his whole lifetime on his back. But the Shahbandar yelled, as he came forward to block his way, as if he did not care about the knife being flourished: "I will not permit you to leave this place."

Skinner leaped sideways, as he waved the knife about threateningly, then he said: "Leave me to my conscience, Sire. For it is harsher than any punishment which might occur to you. Do not allow me to be responsible for what may affect your position in the market and your reputation because of the scandal. You are the greatest merchant in the city and it is incumbent that you should maintain your established place within it. No, no, no Sire. My conscience could not bear, ever, that evil should befall your commercial activities or cause you to lose the title of Shahbandar, just because of some rash act. And now, I commend you to the protection of God. As for you, my lady, may you be eternally damned. It is you who have tempted me and caused me to rebel against God and to betray this great man here."

The lady's throat rattled as she burst into tears: "Liar, liar, I swear that I do not know this creature."

The Shahbandar roared, in disgust: "Hold your tongue, you whore. As for you, get out of my sight, before I change my mind. Get out, and take this with you, and this too."

Skinner was not in need of anyone to urge him on to leap outside, whilst behind and above him, from the door, came the sword and the breastplate of the Hikimdar.

* * * * * *

In the flash of an eye, the Thief of Baghdad was in the street, running so fast that his feet hardly touched the ground. He didn't stop running until his foot stumbled on something, only to find that he had fallen on the edge of one of the graves in the cemetery of the city. Only here did he feel certain that he had escaped and he breathed a deep sigh of relief. However, in the palace of the Shahbandar, the storm was still raging, but with little thunder and lightening and lots of wailing and raining.

Now the Shahbandar was sitting on the box in a state of confusion, sometimes slapping his cheeks and at others pounding on his knees, whilst his words were an incomprehensible combination of the bellow of a bull and the babble of a brook, with his head going from side to side like the pendulum of a wall clock. His turban, lying by his side, was half undone and his bald head was shining under the light of the candles whilst his belly was twitching nervously, as if it was the stomach of a freshly slaughtered rabbit: "And I, who took you from the slums and made you into more of a lady than any of the others. I, who believed in your fidelity, more than I believed in myself. Is this, then, my punishment? You are planting, in my head, two horns for me?" He raised his fingers to his bald head, and it was as if he was feeling for the horns. "You, are unfaithful, to me? And with whom? With a scoundrel who is not even worth a mustard seed? What did you see in him? Uhh? What did you find in him that was better than me? Uhh? Uhh?"

Through the tears and the sobbing of the lady her moaning increased: "I swear to God, I do not know him, I swear to God I do not know him. I swear to God that I have never, ever seen him in my life."

But the Shahbandar did not listen to her. For by now, he was not thinking of anything but one thing. What was he going to do with this woman? Should he drag her to the Court of Justice to be sentenced to the statutory punishment, to be stoned to death? Should he whip her himself, now? But what could he do about the scandal and the disgrace? How could he face the merchants and the agents in the market? The scandal might well cause him to lose the title of Shahbandar, to become no more than his old opponent, Hasbullah Al Hasawi? No, he would not let the secret leak out from the door of the palace. Nevertheless, she must be punished. She must not be allowed to get away with her crime without punishment.

Here the anger returned, like a tempest, raging in the head of the Shahbandar, for he suddenly leaped off the top of the box with a cry that practically burst the eardrums of the Hikimdar, inside it, and almost stopped his heart. Then he rushed forward, like a rocket, to the large mirror. He pulled it down to the ground for it to smash, totally destroyed, and be scattered around, whilst bottles of scent and containers of perfume which were in front of it were thrown to the ground with a terrible noise which to the ears of the Hikimdar, trembling inside the box, were as if they were successive waves of thunder. Then the Shahbandar turned round to the curtains, tearing them to shreds, and then to the wardrobe, taking the silk dresses out of it and tearing

165

them with his teeth and nails, just as if he was a hungry hyena which had just come out from the depths of the forest, ranting and raving. The lady was cowering, on her own, in a corner of the spacious room, still sobbing in perplexity: "I am being wronged — I swear by God that I do not know him. I swear to God that I do not know him."

* * * * * *

The Shahbandar was still going round the room in a frenzy, destroying and tearing up everything that he could lay his hands on. In just a few moments, all the comfortable bedding was reduced to a pile of rubbish. The floor was covered with splinters of broken mirror and glass bottles, torn clothes and curtains, and the eyes of the hyena were looking round the place, searching for a fresh victim.

Then the eyes of the Shahbandar fell on the clothing box and stopped there. He began to go forwards towards it, panting, and only God knows what it was that he was intending to do with it. As for the lady of the house, at that very moment, she dropped to the floor, unconscious.

The Shahbandar reached out with his gnarled hand to the lid of the box and opened it. But he had hardly begun to put his hand into the box when he had snatched it away quickly, letting out a high pitched scream of pain. It was just as if a crocodile in there had closed its jaws on his hand, or perhaps it was a wolf or a snake. However, the Shahbandar did not have long to think about the matter, for suddenly, from inside the box, arose a spectre, covered in a sheet, surrounded by a halo of dust. The eyes of the Shahbandar opened in consternation and terror, and before he had realised what was happening, the spectre had thrown something heavy into his face which caught him a sharp blow and he almost fell to the floor. Before he could recover his balance, the spectre was leaping out through the door whilst the Shahbandar was letting out wild screams which shook the very sides of the palace, and the spectre set off down the road at a frantic pace, without a glance sideways.

Notwithstanding, fate had many more, uncompleted surprises for the Hikimdar, General Mahmar. For his rapidly moving feet led him,

166

also, to the cemetery, to fall, in his turn, at the same spot where, only a few minutes before, our friend Skinner, the Thief of Baghdad, had fallen. The fleeing Hikimdar, like the Thief of Baghdad before him, rested his back against the stone of the grave, in order to recover his wind and to allow the drum beats of his heart to calm down. But he had hardly stretched out his legs to rest, unable to believe that he had survived, when suddenly, there were two bright eyes looking at him out of the darkness, with beneath them two rows of gleaming white teeth shining out from two smiling lips. The Hikimdar attempted to get to his feet to renew his flight, but two strong hands on his shoulders pushed him back to the ground, which killed a scream of terror on his lips. A whisper then came out of the darkness which he immediately recognised as that of his companion in the box: "How did you leave things there, my friend, in the palace of the Shahbandar? Oh, by the way, your sword, your breastplate set in precious stones and your decorations are with me. You can take them with you if you wish, but do please, permit me to hold on to the trousers, as a keepsake."

But the terrified Hikimdar was not prepared to give any thought to the trousers, or the sword or the decorations, nor to listen any more to this strange creature, under whom the ground had opened whilst he was in the lady's clothing box. From the mouth of General Mahmar came a strangled yell, as he leapt into the air in a graceful movement which a high diving champion would have envied, and went flying between the graves, with his feet going faster than the wind, followed by the laughter of the Thief of Baghdad, and leaving behind him the sword, the breastplate and the trousers.

* * * * * *

In the palace the Shahbandar had come out of his stupor, and he was clutching the jewellery box which the fleeing spectre had thrown at him and from which the lid had fallen. Naturally, the box was empty because the jewellery, at that moment, was held in a bag tied to the belt of the Thief of Baghdad. The Shahbandar's words came stumbling out: "Where — where are the jewels? My jewels — my gold, my sapphires, my emeralds."

And at this time the shackles of fear which had restrained the tongue of the lady were released, and she hastened to the attack: "Oh, you stupid numbskull, you clumsy mule. It would have been better if instead of accusing me of being unfaithful, the most horrible accusation which can be levelled at an honest woman; instead of chasing after your filthy suspicions, you had run after the thieves. Had you not realised that they were a couple of thieves who had slipped into the palace whilst I was asleep, and they have run off, one after the other, in front of your very eyes, carrying with them your jewels, our jewels?"

The Shahbandar went off again to the clothing box, for the disappearance of the jewels had done something to him which not even the discovery of the sword and the breastplate in his wife's bedchamber had done, and he began searching feverishly in the corners of the box, and he emptied everything that was in it: sheets, blankets, old dusty clothes and a bag, on to the floor. This last made a sound and he picked it up, with trembling fingers, for a handful of golden dinars to fall out. The moans of the lady of the house increased: "Have you realised now, how you have wronged me? Stupid simpleton! You allow the thieves to get away, so easily, and then you accuse me. Me, the most respectable woman in the whole of Sindashah. May God forgive you. As for me, I'll never forgive you, ever. As if it wasn't enough for you to lose my jewellery through your inattentiveness, you then have to go and destroy my bedchamber and tear all my clothes to shreds." The Shahbandar did not need a great deal of intelligence to realise that the thieves had stolen his jewellery. Otherwise, how could it have disappeared. He had certainly wronged the lady, but he could be excused, in the circumstances. As for what happened in the palace of the Shahbandar after that, it was an unending flood of tears from the wife who had been wrongly accused whilst the raging of the husband gradually changed to remorse and the asking for forgiveness.

The torn clothing and carpets were given a temporary home in the box and the intact bottles of perfume were restored to their place on top of the dressing table with the smashed mirror. Then the Shahbandar himself began sweeping up the remainder of the broken glass and the results of the storm, with promises of a new mirror, decorated this time; containers of perfume, more and of better quality than those before which had been destroyed; and new sets of clothing, bracelets, ear-rings, necklaces and handkerchiefs for the lady of the house to mop up all those tears.

As for the jewellery, to hell with it, if you can forgive me, dearest! By the very best of luck, and this is a secret that the lady of the house knows nothing about, nor will she ever know anything about it, he had only paid six hundred and fifty dirhams for it, the same amount as had been dropped by the two thieves in the clothing box.

God be praised, it was as if his inner self had been speaking to him, when he did not pay any more than that sum to the widow who had sold it to him, just a few weeks before. It was by this sort of instinctive action that he had achieved his rank, Shahbandar of the merchants of Sindashah!

* * * * * *

The village of Sikriya. The strange secret behind the relationship between the new watchman of the spring and his donkey was dominating the mind of Haji Agha and occupying it day and night, so that he had no other concern than it. So much so that he had become a daily visitor to Juha, or Al Haj Abdussabur, anxious to be able to persuade him to reveal his secret, believing, day after day, that it was inevitable that behind this was some astounding information. He used all means and wit available to him in order to speed up obtaining that which had been hidden from him. But Juha was making him wait, from one angle to increase his impatience and from another to keep him waiting until Skinner got back from his trip to Sindashah.

Juha said: "Ease up, Master — do not be in a hurry. Everything in due course. I have already promised you that I will reveal the secret when it is due. If I were to open my mouth for one single word, before its appointed time, then a great misfortune would befall both you and me. And the damage will not be restricted to us but will be the cause of a tremendous disaster in respect of a very highly placed personage. There is no point in mentioning his name but it is sufficient for you to know that it could change the fate of a whole country, indeed, perhaps the fate of the world in its entirety."

169

The impatience of Haji Agha was doubled but there was nothing that he could do except to change the course of the discussion. Perhaps he might be able to entice Juha into revealing another word or making another slip of the tongue which would shed yet another ray of light on all this uncertainty. He said to his friend whilst discussing with him: "You told me that you were compelled to abandon your senior post in Khasruwan and that, from that day, you have been roaming from place to place in the company of this donk — I mean this anim — I mean this creature with the long ears. So what did you do that you should be banished from there?"

Juha wiped a fresh apple with the corner of his turban and then gave it to his donkey, Masoud, with all due respect, but attempting to conceal from the eyes of Haji Agha the great respect shown, before he replied: "No one banished me for I left on an important mission for a period of three years. And when the mission is finished we shall return — I mean, I shall return."

Haji Agha made it appear as if he had not noticed this slip of Juha's tongue, as he said: "No doubt that it is a very important mission if you have to spend three years over it."

"It is, in fact, a very important mission, and difficult also, at least in the part that affects me personally."

Haji Agha very cleverly picked up the end of the thread: "You mean that the mission has two sides. One part affects you whilst the other affects another party. Perhaps it has some connection with that donkey of yours?"

Juha cried out in protest, reprimandingly, his voice sharp at the beginning, then ending his remarks beseechingly: "Sir, I have asked you, politely, more than once, not to let that word out of your mouth. You don't know what harm it does to me. I beg of you —"

"Take it easy — take it easy. I forgot, my brother. Does not someone, who has been what I have been, have the right to forget occasionally. I will not mention that word, even though I do not know why it makes you so angry that things should be called by their proper names. Is the other half of your talk connected with — the long-eared one here?"

"You are trying to lead me on again, sir. I can see that you are very sharp in these matters. In fact, your intelligence is of the unusually dangerous type, especially for one like me."

These words aroused the arrogance of Haji Agha and he attempted to appear even more intelligent as he moved his interrogation to yet another angle: "Let us leave this part of your mission, which does not affect you, for what does affect you. Do you not think that this is another secret which you wish to hide from me, after we have partaken of bread and salt together, and have become friends? Tell me — what have you been doing for all these three years."

"I have been seeking knowledge; about an ancient book, to be precise, which was written on papyrus by the old, wise man of the Pharaohs, Hur Mahib."

"And did you find it?"

"I found a copy of a translation of it in Chinese, in which I have found something of what I am looking for, but the complete knowledge requires that I should devote all my time to studying this book, and that is what I am not yet able to do. It would appear, regretfully, that I am likely to remain incapable of doing so. Without returning to Khusrawan, that is —. But no —. There you go, sir, you have succeeded, yet again, in leading me on. I will not say another word.'

"I do not wish to entice you into saying anything. It is simple that you have aroused my curiosity concerning the book. Now then, I swear to God, I love discussing books, even though I am, by nature, of the type which creates the events which are related in books, rather than one who wastes his time in reading them."

Juha sighed, painfully, as he said quietly, as if he was talking to himself: "May God be praised. Whoever said: 'Voices are given to those who have no ears,' was telling the truth."

"What do you mean?"

"No — no — I don't mean anything, just a thought passing through my mind, like a solitary cloud in the summer."

"You were talking to me about your book. What does this book deal with? Which branch of knowledge does it handle?"

"I told you. It deals with knowledge as a whole, but I have not yet seen in it but one half, which is, in fact, the least that concerns me personally."

The brain cells of Haji Agha became active: he was getting very near to the secret, or at least he was on the very edges of it: "So, the part that you have studied, what does it deal with?"

Juha then said, uncautiously: "It deals with the practices of sorcery — black magic and white magic."

"Ahh, then you are a magician?"

"No, I am studying sorcery in order to overcome it, to negate its effectiveness. It means, briefly, that I do not practise sorcery, but that I eliminate it and put an end to its effects."

Here Haji Agha was approaching another stage towards the revelation of the great secret: "And what is the sorcery, the effects of which you are now trying to eliminate? Speak up."

The palm of Juha was raised to his mouth in a quick movement, as if he was wishing that he could put back into it, words which had come out from it in spite of himself. And his eyes plunged into the very depths of Haji Agha for a moment, before he said, in something like a rebuke: "Sir, you do, truly, have an extraordinary ability to draw out a person to whom you are talking, to make him say that which he really does not want to say. Someone like you really ought to have been a judge, indeed, a chamberlain and a minister, for you have, with tremendous ease, extracted from me things which I ought not to have revealed. But once again I appeal to you to limit the use of your intelligence with me — no — I will not say another word." Haji Agha became inflated with pride, so much so that he was almost laughing out loud from the extent of his delight. He perceived himself as one playing with the person with whom he was talking in the same way as a hungry cat plays with a fat mouse.

A short period passed before he picked up the thread of the conversation again: "Do you know what I was doing before I became the owner of this well? I was the Head of Police in Khuwarazim."

Juha said, enthusiastically: "Only now have I come to understand. A man of your ability could not possibly be satisfied with this position. For it is far below your level. Believe me, I have been on intimate terms with many chamberlains and rulers and have known them well, from inside, yet I did not find a single one of them who had half the level of your intelligence. You, sir, are of that rare class of people who were born to rule."

Haji Agha swelled with pride again, as he reached out his hand and began to twist the end of his moustache with pleasure.

"Do you know the appointment which would be suitable for you, and you for it? It is that of Chamberlain of the Treasury, in fact, Chamberlain of the Treasury in a large state. Any Khan in the world would hope to have a chamberlain of your quality, for the treasury. With you there, not a single subject of his would escape the payment of his taxes and customs dues."

Haji Agha cried out, giving full rein to his imagination: "I swear by God, you tell the truth. This is the only post which would be suitable for me. Yes, I am capable of creating new taxes. What would you think, for instance, if I should institute a tax on tears? That is an idea which has come to me now, off the top of my head! Every time anybody sheds tears, money enters the treasury. And the more taxes they pay, the more tears they will shed!"

"What a marvellous idea! Did I not tell you, sir, that you are the most intelligent person I have ever known?"

"And, I have another idea, that we should set a tax on laughter. For people cannot live without laughing, in this way we can provide the Treasury with a new and inexhaustible source of income."

Juha cried out: "God is greatest, God is greatest. However did the Khan of Khuwarazim fail to notice this deep perception and understanding."

"Then there is a third idea, a tax on beards, every man who lets his beard grow pays a tax on it. And in order that men should not refrain from growing beards we should impose an even greater tax on those who are clean shaven. And, in passing, a tax on women's hair seems a good idea. The longer a woman's hair is, the more tax she pays."

Juha clapped his hands together in amazement: "Praise be to God. How stupid that man was."

"Which man?"

"Why the Khan of Khuwarazim, of course! Look at the money that he has lost by allowing you to retire from his service?"

* * * * * *

Chapter 14

It was not an uncommon occurrence that the rain clouds should have avoided the village of As Sikriya that summer and that its land should have been deprived of rainfall. The ground began to crack, appearing as if it was opening its mouth and screaming out for water. The conversation of the peasants was still the same — for the trouble caused by Haji Agha had descended upon them — a mixture of complaints, exchanging views on their anxieties and the hope that, some day, the mercy of God would include them. But when would that day be? And how?

After three days, it would be the appointed day for irrigation and the Headman would go to Haji Agha, taking to him his daughter Laila, to be his concubine. And only when the snake would be left alone with the pigeon, would the water start to flow from below the dam, to bring the greenery back to the fields.

Probably there were some of them feeling; with a tightening of his chest, like a stone in his gullet; some sorrow and distress at the fate which had been decreed should befall Laila, the most pretty and chaste of the maidens of As Sikriya. But, was there any other solution? Would it have been possible for them to have paid the twenty thousand pieces of silver to Haji Agha as the price for the water, even if they all sold everything that they possessed, from goats, cows, hens and even their hoes?

Yes, there were probably some of them who were prepared to turn their faces away from the Headman, Muhammad Ali and his nephew, Hassan, the betrothed of Laila, whose attitude had suddenly changed from the mad, bitter outburst which had become prolonged against his uncles, in-laws and the old and wise men of the village on the day that it was decided that his Laila should be offered as a sacrifice at the altar of Haji Agha. For today, he rarely appeared at the teashop or along the paths. If he appeared he was totally silent, he did not speak to anyone nor did he answer if he was spoken to.

Indeed, there were probably one or two who were prepared to swear

175

that they had seen something approaching a smile on his face which they were unable to explain and they finally came to the conclusion that the shock had affected the mind of the poor chap. One of them said that it was better for him, and for us, and that it was better for a man to lose his mind if the bitter actuality of things was more than he could bear.

As for the talk of the village about the eccentric new watchman of the spring and about the royal meals which he used to serve to the donkey, this had faded, once they had arrived at an explanation. For if some people could worship cows, then what was strange about one of them worshipping a donkey?

But Haji Agha, and he, naturally, was more intelligent, was in no way satisfied by this explanation. He continued to believe that, behind the respect shown by the watchman of the spring to the donkey, was a very important secret that he must eventually get to know. For it was not only because of curiosity and a keen appetite for knowing the unknown, but also because he believed that the secret, in the hands of an intelligent man, was a guaranteed way of getting rich quickly. And the more important the secret, the greater was the opportunity to make money.

Even though the watchman of the spring had already promised him that he would reveal his secret to him on Saturday, which was now only a few days away, he continued to make his visits and to spend a longer time with him, attempting to gain his friendship and confidence. He touched upon many subjects, hoping that he could pick up from him, by slips of the tongue, that which would take him closer to the secret, or reveal to him some of its aspects.

And, at every meeting, Haji Agha would pick up a reasonable number of slips of the tongue of Abdussabur, without it ever occurring to him, for one single moment, that these slips of the tongue were calculated and planned and that it was Abdussabur who was playing with him, and guiding his thoughts, in the direction which he required.

* * * * * *

And so it was, that by the time Friday had arrived, Haji Agha was really certain, without his watchman being aware of it, that the big secret which the latter was so careful about, was an activity connected with magic, but what was the connection of this magic with the donkey? And, the royal feasts which were held in his honour every day? This was what remained for him to find out, for certain, even though he might even be able to guess what it was now.

And on that afternoon, Haji Agha, whilst having a discussion with the watchman of the spring, said to him: "I really am of that class of person who are meant to rule others. For people are continually in need of those who can rule them and I do not doubt, for a single moment, that my ability is over and above the limits of this small village. Nevertheless, I have been able to achieve a model here, which even the greatest states on earth would do well to follow."

The watchman, whose thoughts appeared to be miles away, as if he was trying to recall some distant memory, said: "That is true, that is true. Would that those there understood that."

Here was yet another of those slips of the tongue and Haji Agha was quick to seize upon it: "And who are they, about whom you are speaking?"

The watchman of the spring was quick to recover his poise: "I? Them? No, no, I did not intend anybody specifically. What I really meant was all those who are concerned with the affairs of ruling."

Then Al Haj Abdussabur closed his mouth before another word should escape and Haji Agha was forced to submit to the wishes of his partner in the conversation, but the slip of the tongue left its mark.

Then the conversation moved to another aspect. "The business of ruling, my friend, is the total submission of people in general, to the degree that they actually become slaves whilst the ruler becomes some sort of god. Look at me, for instance. I am only one person, but I control the destinies of all the people of this village. I even control their emotions. If I so wish, I can make them cry. When I desire, I make them laugh. In my hand, alone, is their life and their death. Not one of them can even breathe unless I say so. I could take the total product of their labour on the land for the whole year but I am careful to leave them with enough to keep them alive, so that they will be able to pay to me the price of the water for the following year. And so on. As you can see, I am compassionate with them. Take this season, for instance. I could see that they were probably not going to be able pay the cost of the water in cash, so I suggested that they paid me, instead of cash, by one of their maidens, in order that I could take her to myself as a concubine. Do you see how I am compassionate with them? For I found them a solution which would never have occurred to any of them. This is one of the responsibilities of a ruler, to find solutions for the problems of the general public which they themselves, through their natural backwardness, are unable to find solutions for. Is this not so?"

Juha, telling the absolute truth, said: "I understand your point of view completely. It is a point of view which ought to receive its due reward."

Haji Agha then continued: "And this, in fact, is what is happening. For the money which I decreed that they should pay to me does not increase my wealth. But it is imperative, for maintaining the prestige of the rule and for ensuring that the general public remain submissive to my wishes, that I should impose payment for the water upon them. From another point of view, I really do have a need for a girl with whom to relieve my solitude, and I have chosen the girl who is suitable for this purpose."

Juha, in the tone of one very concerned about what he was listening to, then said: "No doubt, she is beautiful, well-built and of suitable station?"

"Well, naturally she is not of the standard which is really suitable for me but she is beautiful, indeed, she is the most beautiful girl in the whole village. I used to see her a lot when she was working in the field or the apricot garden; her father keeps a small garden of apricots, next to the other side of the spring. I can testify that she is, by purely artistic standards, of a very high level of gracefulness and shapeliness of form. I cannot conceal from you that I desire her and it is for this reason that I have given up the payment for the water, this season, in order that I can obtain her. The fact is, I have bought her for twenty thousand pieces of silver. And that is a very good price for a pretty concubine, don't you agree?"

Then Juha said, in philosophical terms: "What is important is that the interior should be as good as the exterior."

"What do you mean by that?"

"I used to have a friend in Khusrawan, from a good family, who acquired a concubine from the common people. He is now on the lepers' island."

The mouth of Haji Agha dropped open in consternation, for he realised what Juha was getting at and a thousand thoughts went around in his imagination before he found his tongue: "Do you mean ...?"

"This likelihood is always possible. There is no doubt that those commoners live in a state of poverty and backwardness, so that it is possible that all kinds of sickness, particularly contagious diseases, should exist amongst them."

Haji Agha, in an attempt to dispel the thought which Juha had provoked and which was now beginning to take root in the depths of his mind, then said: "But — but this girl, specifically, appears to be of sound health and mind. For she is like a green shoot that is just waiting for someone to pluck for its flower to blossom and give off its fragrance."

Juha said: "This is just where the danger lies. Most of these commoners have a natural immunity against these malignant diseases. But this does not prevent them from being carriers of contagious diseases wherever they go."

"This never even occurred to me. I continually saw this young girl as a pearl, for whom the time was right to be lifted from the soil, polished and then set in a ring of gold. But now you have activated all my worst fears."

"If you really desire her to this extent, then try it. You might be lucky!"

"Luck, what luck? It is only stupid people who surrender their affairs to chance and good fortune. Oh no, my friend, for what you said is the absolute truth. And who knows? Perhaps this girl was insane and possessed by the jinns. Did you know that this girl has a cousin, whose name is Hassan. It is said that he has recently been affected by a touch of madness, which came to him suddenly, whereas previously he appeared to be normal, just like everybody else."

Juha, or Al Haj Abdussabur, as Haji Agha knew him, said: "Diseases like this are normally hereditary. Nevertheless, the girl may ..."

"No — no — I will never permit this girl to enter my home."

"What will you do then?"

"I shall force them to pay the price of the water. And if they fail, then I shall take Laila and sell her, at once, in the slave market."

* * * * * *

Haji Agha went off, returning to his palace, leaving the watchman of the spring to go up to his donkey to give him what gave delight and pleasure to the donkey. He had hardly left him when the sky was lit up by lightning, followed by peels of thunder. But the rain fell far away from the ground which was thirsting for it. Whilst, in the dead of the stormy night, the thoughts of Juha went far away, to seek out Skinner, the Thief of Baghdad. "I wonder what he has done, where he is now."

At that very moment, Skinner was in the box, his knife at the throat of the Hikimdar, General Mahmar. His scared ears were listening to the roaring of the Shahbandar of the merchants and the moaning of the frightened lady whilst he was working his brain at top speed, attempting to find a means of escape.

* * * * * *

Juha heard a light tapping on the door and quickly went to open it, to find Hassan, appearing pale and disturbed. And he had hardly closed the door behind him when he whispered, gasping out his words: "I beg of you to forgive me, sir, for failing to keep my promise that I would not attempt to contact you, but — only three days remain before the appointed time for handing Laila over to that savage beast." "I know that well, oh Hassan."

"The eyes of Laila have dried up and she has no more tears. It appears that she has completely lost hope."

"This is the worst thing that can happen to anyone. No, oh Hassan, it is not permissible to let her lose her hope, ever."

"I have found a way out, sir. Laila and I will flee, before it is too late. We can cross the mountain, to the other side, before anyone notices that we are missing. In fact, we have already prepared the necessary provisions for the road."

"If the only solution is to flee, then you must prepare provisions for more than two persons, for I must accompany you both. For my donkey also, because I cannot possibly leave him here. There is a fifth person also; you do not know him but it will not be long before he is here. Thus it is not just a matter of two persons fleeing. It is the migration of a whole group, my friend. Not so, oh Hassan. There is no need to flee, for everything is going well."

Then Juha caught the hands of Hassan, between his hands, saying: "Tell this to your Laila. Tell her not to despair. Tell her that everything will come right in the end. In a manner which will please both her and you."

"She will not believe it."

"Tell her this from me."

"But she does not know you, even I myself don't know you."

Juha looked into the eyes of Hassan, whilst pressing firmly on his hands, saying: "But you, oh Hassan, you have confidence in me, isn't that so?"

Hassan cried out, excitedly: "I believed in you from the very moment when I opened my eyes to see your face on the day in which you rescued me from killing myself. My faith in you has never been shaken, even in the moments when I am possessed by despair about everything. I see your face looking at me and it causes hope, and certainty about things, to rise within me. Who are you? Who can you be that you are capable of setting such faith in the hearts of others? I swear to God, that if Juha had not already died, years ago, I would have said that you were Juha and nobody else."

A lively song sang in the breast of Juha but his voice was calm as he asked his companion: "Are you certain that Juha has already died."

Hassan said, painfully: "The criers went through the village, years ago, announcing that and many people wore mourning for him after that time."

"Did you know him? Have you ever seen him?"

"Not really, but many of my people had seen him whilst others had heard of him and everybody loved him. How many an oppressed person has there been, overcome by his unjust treatment, who has remained undaunted, certain that Juha was there and that he would come, one day, to right the wrong and punish the transgressors."

Juha bowed his head in silence, for one moment, to cover up how moved he was, and then he put out his hand to touch the shoulder of Hassan, saying: "The likes of Juha, my son, do not die. For as long as injustice and transgressors of justice exist, there will always be a Juha there, also, to bring justice to those who have been wronged. Who knows? Perhaps his spirit has settled in my body."

Hassan opened his mouth to speak but Juha interrupted him, saying: "Go now, to your Laila, and pass on to her your faith. But beware, do not pass on what you conjecture."

* * * * * *

Another day passed by, whilst Juha, with an eye on the road, was watching for the return of Skinner. Suddenly, there he was, appearing before him in his unique fashion, as if the ground had opened up to reveal him or as if he had dropped down from the sky. His face was covered in dust, as were his hair and clothes, but the happy smile on his face and in his eyes was saying that he had succeeded.

Juha received his friend with an embrace and then rushed to close the door behind him and pulled him over to a place where an infiltrating eye would be unable to see and a sneaking ear unable to hear.

And after he had listened to his whole tale, and had lived through every minute and detail of it, he said: "Now, we have to act quickly. Tomorrow is the last day before the irrigation of the land, but it is necessary that we should agree on a few matters first."

"Whatever you think, oh Juha, that is what has to be correct."

"First of all, I consider that the jewellery which you have brought with you is the property of the poor widow and must be returned to her. Do you agree about that?"

"That is exactly what I believe."

"However, we are going to need the jewellery for a day or two, or perhaps even for a week, for use in a good deed. Do you agree with me that such a use cannot be considered to be unlawful?"

182

"No, it is absolutely legal."

"So, let us go ahead, with the blessing of God."

"I can probably understand, now, what you are aiming at. There is a heathen city on the other side of the mountain, where there is gambling. If I were to take the jewellery there, I would be able to double its value in a few hours. As you know, I have considerable knowledge in all the various games of backgammon and cards. And I have enough tricks for someone to write several books about. And ..."

"No, oh Skinner. We will not resort to anything illegal in order that we may do good. I do not support, in any way, the belief that the end justifies the means. It is incumbent upon anyone who seeks to do good that he does so in an honest manner. Gambling is a sin into which we must not slip."

"Then, what are you going to do, sir?"

"I shall play another game with the jewellery which is not a game of gambling but a much more delightful game and which is more thrilling.

Come with me.

Juha and his friend slipped into the apricot garden, which was floating in the light of the moon. And there, in a corner of the garden, was Muhammad Ali, working with his hoe, in a slow, regular movement, as if the hoe itself was carrying all the worries of the world, or as if his hand no longer had any life in it, until his footsteps ended at a tree in the garden which was the most beautiful, and with the most blossoms, of them all. He collapsed below it like a heap of wood, burying his head between his knees, weeping.

Juha knew, from a story which Hassan had told him, describing it, that the tree at which Muhammad Ali sat, was the same tree which Muhammad Ali had planted on the day that Laila was born, and to which he had given the name of the new-born child.

And since Laila had reached the age of ten she had come to know her tree and had developed, in respect of it, a tradition which she would never give up, ever.

And on every day of the week Laila would tie a distinctive tape on its branches, and for each day she made a specific colour; red for Saturdays, white for Sundays, yellow for Mondays, blue for Tuesdays, crimson for Wednesdays and green for Thursdays, and then all of them together for Fridays.

Juha's eye flitted through the branches of the tree, looking for the bundle of coloured tapes, for today was Friday, but he could not find it. Then a lump came in his throat when he spotted a black tape at the very spot where he was expecting to find the six brightly coloured tapes. It was clear that Laila was intending to indicate by that, that she was mourning for herself. For tomorrow, Saturday, was the day when she was to be handed over, as a concubine, to the palace of Haji Agha, or as a fly in the web of the spider. Juha poked at his friend, whispering: "Skinner, do you see that black tape, well it will not remain in its place for very long. It will be changed for the most brilliant colours in a short time. For you will see for yourself, Skinner, how the exchange will take place, in a flash, in one of the most delightful moments of life."

Skinner looked at his friend in a dull-witted fashion and said: "I don't understand!"

"You will understand everything, very soon. Is the bag of jewellery with you?"

The Thief of Baghdad whispered: "Yes."

"Right, be prepared, and the very moment that you see that the man sitting despondently under the apricot tree, is preoccupied, you must get in there, without him being aware of you, and bury the bag of jewellery under the tree, but in such a fashion that it can be easily discovered."

At that moment, the voice of Hassan came from the other side of the garden, calling "Laila."

The voice reached the ears of Muhammad Ali, who lifted his head and then pulled himself together, to stand and then stumble on his heavy feet, in the direction of the voice. Juha nudged his friend and said: "Now." And in the flash of an eye, with the agility of a leopard, the Thief of Baghdad was under the apricot tree, burying the bag of jewellery, careful to leave a corner of it visible, next to the hoe, then he leaped back to his place beside Juha. Then the voice of Muhammad Ali, coming closer, could be heard saying to his nephew: "I've told you, son, leave Laila to her own devices, and don't break my heart any more than it is already broken. Laila can no longer be counted as belonging to you."

But Hassan sounded very confident as he answered: "Tomorrow has not arrived yet, uncle. And by the time that it does come, many things may have changed."

"What, then, is going to change? Are we in the time of miracles? Do you think that a miracle is possible, then?"

Hassan then said: "Who knows? Tell me, uncle, do you believe that Juha is still alive?"

"Juha, my son, died years ago, if you really want the answer. And Laila goes, tomorrow, to the palace of Haji Agha, if you need me to remind you. Just as Juha cannot return to life, except by a miracle, similarly, my daughter Laila can only be delivered by a like miracle."

Hassan said, without thinking, as he turned to go back from whence he came: "And perhaps it will be the same miracle."

"What do you mean? Have you really gone out of your mind? Are you...?"

* * * * * *

But Muhammad Ali never completed his sentence for his eye fell, that moment, on something strange, below the tree, next to the hoe. He bent down, feeling round what he had seen. Then he rushed to strike the ground with his hoe, as if the red jinni had taken possession of his hands. And it wasn't many moments before he was taking a bag out of the soil. He began to open it with two shaking hands as he held his breath. Then his legs gave way and he sank to his knees as he emptied the bag of its contents. Then he opened his mouth in sheer amazement, for he could hardly believe what he saw.

For suddenly, gushing out of the bag were thousands of beams, blue, white and red, like the haloes of the angels. The trembling fingers of the man allowed the bag to slip out of his hands, beside the pile of jewels. He opened and closed his mouth several times before his scream erupted, shaking the corners of the garden, and echoing amongst the trees: "Laila ... Laila ... Laila ..."

Then came Laila's voice, sad and depressed: "What is wrong, father?"

185

Laila appeared, dragging her feet as if there was a weight tied to each one of them. And before she reached the place where her father was standing under the tree, raising the wonderful things up to his face, wetting them with his tears and laughing, she stopped, suddenly, as if her feet had become nailed to the ground: "What? — What is this, father?"

"Look, Laila, at what I have found? I have found this treasure, here, under this tree — your tree, Laila. Oh, how great is your glory, Lord. But Laila, I had been digging here, in this very same place, just moments ago, and there was nothing here. It is God, Laila, God alone, oh Laila, who has answered my prayers and who has sent one of his angels to deliver us. This treasure, oh Laila, will deliver us."

But Laila was not there. The astonishment had bridled her tongue, even if it hadn't already shackled her legs. But finally, with her eyes popping out of her head, as she realised what the treasure, wet with tears in the hands of her father, really was, she let out a long scream and as it died away, set off running, like a filly off the bit, crying out: "Hassan — Hassan — Hassan —"

Then she ran, retracing her footsteps to where her father was kneeling down. She bent down, in her turn, playing with the treasure with her trembling fingers and stroking the necklaces and bracelets, as her mood changed. At one moment she was kissing the jewels and the next kissing the beard of her father. Then she would change and set off, running like a sparrow, all around the garden with her joyous shouts shaking the trees: "Hassan — Hassan — Hassan—"

And when she came back the following time there was a bunch of tapes in her hand, red, yellow, white, green, crimson and blue. She jumped up and cut down the black tape from the apricot tree, to hang, in its place, the coloured tapes. Then the voice of her father could be heard, as he prayed to God in humility: "God is greatest, praise be to you, oh God." The moist eyes of the Thief of Baghdad met those of Juha and he said: "It is on days like this that life becomes worth living."

Then they both went off, letting their presence disappear in the shade of a cloud passing below the moon, as the song of a curlew above As Sikriya could be heard, repeating itself: Al milk lika lika lika ya sahib al milk, (the fortune is yours, is yours, is yours, oh owner of the fortune).

Juha said to his friend: "You must find yourself a hiding place nearby, where nobody can see you or know of your presence here and from where you will be able to come to me, quickly, when you see a white cloth hanging on top of the willow tree which overlooks the hut where I am living."

"I hear and I obey, Sire."

And it was only a few moments before the Thief of Baghdad was hidden out of sight, just as if the ground had swallowed him up, for he had found a cave not far away which some Indian fig bushes concealed from view and which nobody could climb up to unless he had the agility of the Thief of Baghdad.

The following day witnessed an exciting morning which Haji Agha introduced in a happy voice, he was singing as if to his friend, the watchman of the spring: "Today, the irrigation of the land begins. After a short time the peasants will arrive to beg for the water gate to be opened. They will bring with them, naturally, that girl. Do not let her get anywhere near me but take her at once to the slave market in Ishiqbad and sell her there. But the price must not be less than twenty thousand."

Juha looked in the direction of the village and he said: "I can see them coming but I don't see any girl with them."

Haji Agha rushed up to him to look down the road for himself and he said: "How can that be? I do not believe that they could have arranged twenty thousand pieces of silver. It is most likely that they have come to petition me to delay payment. But that is impossible. They will not get a single drop of water unless they have paid in advance." Haji Agha then drew himself up where he was standing, put his feet further apart and crossed his arms across his chest, like a statue of one of the Pharaohs, glowering under his eyebrows as if he was the god of evil himself.

The men arrived. They were seven in number, led by Muhammad Ali who bowed his head, smiling, in greeting to Haji Agha. Then he stood up straight and said, holding his head high: "Haji Agha. The time has come for the irrigation of the land. We want you to open the water."

Haji Agha growled from his elevated position: "You know my conditions. The girl, your daughter, Muhammad Ali, or twenty thousand pieces of silver, in cash."

Muhammad Ali said: "What do you want to do with my daughter?"

"That is not your business. Perhaps I would leave her in my service, or I might sell her in the slave market."

Muhammad Ali raised his head up until it practically reached the height of a nearby palm tree: "My daughter Laila is not for sale, oh Haji Agha." Juha practically leaped out from his place to embrace Muhammad Ali as he saw holding his head high in the face of the tyrannical viper.

The face of Haji Agha was suddenly clothed in a mixture of astonishment, anger and fear. From where had this man got the courage with which he was now speaking? When he spoke, his voice came out from the depths of him like a hissing sound: "Such water as I have is for sale, you buffoon amongst men. Payment first. You will not get a single drop of water if you do not pay in advance."

Then Haji Agha turned on end, announcing by that that he had nothing further to say. But he had hardly taken a step before his ear was struck by a cry as sharp as a sword: "Hold on, Haji Agha." Haji Agha turned his head, superciliously, without turning his body. The speaker was Muhammad Ali.

"Here is the money that you want. Take it and open the water way." Then Muhammad Ali threw a heavy white bag which landed at the feet of Haji Agha and, before he had moved, the watchman of the spring had picked it up and had given it to him. Haji Agha opened the bag and astonishment clearly appeared on his face which took on the hue of several colours, one after the other, whilst thousands of light beams were reflected in it. Finally he found his voice and said: "Where did you get these?"

"It is a treasure which I found."

"Where?"

"In my garden, under the apricot tree."

"Do you think that I am mentally deranged, you foolish liar?"

"I do not lie, oh Haji Agha. I told you, I found it in my garden and I am telling the truth."

The watchman of the spring whispered in the ear of Haji Agha: "They are worth more than forty thousand!"

Haji Agha kept moving his gaze between Juha, Muhammad Ali and the bag of jewels. Finally, in a strange voice, he said, as he clutched the bag to his breast: "All right, open the water for them Abdussabur." And before Abdussabur could set off to the dam which Haji Agha had laid on the spring, in order to lift it as he had ordered him to do, so that the water could flow through the channel like the blood flows through the arteries, Haji Agha stopped him, saying in a tone of some significance: "Do not forget our appointment for tomorrow, for you to reveal the hidden secret."

Juha said, as he moved away: "Be confident, I shall not forget our appointment tomorrow, if God so wills."

* * * * * *

190

Chapter 15

As the sun gathered together the last vestiges of daylight and disappeared with them behind the mountain to the west, and night approached, casting its black cloak, studded with stars, over the village, a group of men from the village of As Sikriya have collected in the teashop, joyfully spending a pleasant evening, despite having worked throughout the day in the fields. They are recalling the events of yesterday, which ended with the delivery of Laila from the very jaws of the viper, and the lively water flowing out to the parched fields to quench their long period of thirst. And they are asking each other, in amazement, from where did Muhammad Ali obtain the jewels, which he paid to Haji Agha as a ransom for his daughter and as the price for the life-giving water?

Then one called Murjan spoke up, as he combed his white beard with his skinny finger: "Jewels do not grow under apricot trees, like potatoes and root plants, nor do they fall from the sky like rain. Somebody must have put them there where you found them, oh Muhammad Ali, is that not so?"

But Muhammad Ali did not answer, for his eyes were wandering. He was almost piercing the ceiling of the teashop with them with a curious mixture of contentment, self-questioning and bewilderment. Then, when he heard 'Abdun say: "Perhaps it was a treasure which was buried there years ago," here only, he spoke, as if he was talking to himself:

"How many times have I turned the earth, opening it up to the full depth, under this tree for decades? So why did it not appear until now? And yesterday, in particular?"

Then Safwan said: "Everything has its time, and a treasure cannot be opened until the day decreed."

Muhammad Ali burst out, excitedly: "But this is not a buried treasure. For a buried treasure is not kept in a new bag which has only been made for a few months. Some person put it there recently. But who?"

Then Murjan said, conclusively: "I know who it is. Have you not all

191

heard that the holy man, Abulayal Tahruddin, has returned, after his long absence?"

More than one voice answered: "That is true. On his birthday, the children of Sindashah awoke to find his presents filling their bags in the same way as he did with their ancestors, a hundred years ago or more. It is he who has placed the bag of jewellery under the apricot tree, oh Muhammad Ali."

Muhammad Ali shook his head wistfully, and in confusion, before he replied: "But why me, specifically, and there are no children in my house?"

"Yes, you have got Laila. Is not Laila the child of us all? On top of that he placed the jewellery in a bag and this is the normal way in which he gives his presents. Then he placed the bag under the tree which bears her name and on which Laila hangs her coloured tapes. Indeed, it is the holy man, Abulayal Tahruddin, and none other." Everybody applauded and repeated the words: "La ilaha illallah," (there is no God but God), the opening verse of the Quran, for the holy man Tahruddin.

At this moment Haji Agha appeared at the door of the teashop, and the words died on their lips and became a mere mumbling. The viper swung his gaze around the faces, in which the veins were still pulsating excitedly, whilst in his eyes could be read indignation and contempt. Then he said, as he was turning away, averting his face in disgust: "Applaud as much as you like, you stupid lot of men. It is just as if you have forgotten that this is not the last time that you are going to need water. I have something to say to you about the appointed day of the next irrigation of the land. I will not accept less than thirty thousand pieces of silver. You can take this into account as of now." And Haji Agha disappeared at the bend in the track, leaving behind him a heavy shadow disturbing their joy, as he hurried off on his way to the hut of the watchman of the spring, Al Haj Abdussabur. For tonight was the night of his appointment with him for the revealing of the important secret, the secret of the royal feasts which he presented each day to his donkey, Masoud. And Juha was no less impatient than he was for the meeting. For he had already made all the necessary preparations.

* * * * * *

All the previous days he had been setting the stage for this moment, brain-washing Haji Agha in order to prepare him, in his turn, to receive the big secret. And now, here was the snake coming from afar, as Juha sat in his place on the threshold of his hut, pounding something in a vessel and paying no attention to him until Haji Agha had approached to within a few footsteps. He then jumped to his feet and entered the hut, going towards a fire burning on one side with a strangely shaped pot on it from which steam was coming. The donkey, Masoud, however, was in the dark, far corner, stamping the ground with his feet as if there was something which was disturbing him, or which did not please him.

When Haji Agha arrived at the door of the hut the stage was fully set for his reception. For the fire was throwing strange shadows on the walls of the hall whilst the steam rising from the cooking pot was making shapes which were even more strange. And Abdussabur, with his eyes popping, was making shaky movements while standing over the pot. A view of half his back was visible to any person entering, who would see half his face covered in darkness whilst the other half looked as if it were in flames above the fire. His shrunken hands were clutching and opening out, as if they were taking hold of things which could not be seen, and throwing them into the strange cooking pot, whilst he was bringing up from deep inside himself sounds appearing to be the whispering of devils: "Shur hantur awad ya mashur abrakat annar ya sayyad annur."

Haji Agha stopped at the door, with his mouth wide open and his limbs trembling. He stumbled over his words a number of times before he said: "What are you doing here? What is this, oh Abdussabur?"

But Juha did not hear him. He just remained, repeating his incantations, with his voice rising gradually until it became more like bellowing. Then suddenly, he let out a very shrill scream which shook the walls of the hut and which almost took away what remained of the sanity of Haji Agha. He suddenly fell on his back, then turned over onto his stomach and began crawling towards the door, panting, until his head hit the leg of the appalled Haji Agha. He grabbed hold of it and began to push him outside, madly, whilst continuing his incomprehensible mutterings. When they were both outside, Juha began to try and pull himself together. He waved with both his hands, as if there was something very dangerous above both their heads, which neither of them had any power over. Finally, his words came out, breathlessly, saying: "Sir — what — brought you — at this hour? Was — not — our appointment — at midnight?"

It appeared that even Haji Agha had to search for his voice until he found it, with difficulty: "What? What's this? What are you doing with this cooking pot? By the devil, what are you doing?"

Juha said, as he pulled him towards a nearby stone which was suitable for sitting on: "Let us sit down first, until I can get my breath back. Anyway, you have seen me and seen what I am doing so there is no point in keeping anything secret."

The impatience of Haji Agha increased to such a degree that his breathing became short and sharp: "It is so, it is so, nothing is to be gaining from secrecy. Tell me — what is that on the fire?"

Juha was silent for a moment, hesitating before he said, in a voice showing confusion and distress: "Do you really want to know the answer? I promised you that I would reveal the secret only at midnight. You were only supposed to come at the appointed time upon which we had agreed. It was not within your right that you should witness what I actually do."

"Indeed, everything here is within my rights. And I will not permit you to conceal anything at all from me. Did you not say that your father, on whom may be the mercy of God, recommended to you that you should not conceal anything from he who is the benefactor of your well-being? And am I not the benefactor of your well-being? So come on. Speak up and do not conceal anything. What were you doing just now?"

"Sir, if you have no desire to be merciful towards me then at least show some mercy towards yourself. You have dealt kindly with me and I cannot reward you for this by exposing you to danger."

"What danger is this that you are speaking about?"

"It is, quite simply, that your knowledge of this secret could expose you, and me, to great danger."

"I do not care about any danger."

"One more time, permit me to warn you, that a single word, falling from your lips carelessly, could cause your death, and my death with you. Therefore, do you swear, sir, that all that you see or hear, this night, will be kept under the seal of secrecy?"

"I swear that I will not disclose a single word of what I shall hear."

"Or what you will see?"

"Or what I shall see, and now, come on speak. What were you doing, just now?"

Juha inclined his head in the direction of the hut where the donkey, Masoud, had come forward towards the door, seeking air, then he bent over, whispering in the ear of his guest: "Come, let us get further away. I don't want for a third person to hear us."

"Who is there here who could possibly hear us? There is no one, except you and me, unless, praise be to God, you are talking about that donkey?"

Juha cried out, interrupting, in a voice as sharp as the edge of a sword: "Sir, I beg of you. I have told you a thousand times, do not allow this word to be repeated by your tongue. There you go again, you glide us down to the very depths of danger, and I haven't said a word yet. What will you do when I have spoken?"

"I have not said anything except that there are only the two of us here."

"No, we are three here, sir. Three creatures capable of being seen. But the creatures who are not capable of being seen, only God himself knows how many of them there are here."

Haji Agha burst out laughing, nervously: "Magic — ha — ha."

Juha rushed to put his hand over his mouth, whispering very sharply: "Do not raise your voice like that. I have told you not to raise your voice. Do you not realise that we can be bewitched, at this very moment, and could be turned into two stones?"

Haji Agha said, whispering, in an attempt to calm him down: "Steady, steady, I will not raise my voice."

"And do not mention the name of any animal, if you want either of us to live until morning."

"I will not mention the name of any animal. And now, what is the story behind this do —, I mean this creature with the long ears to which you serve these royal banquets? Midnight has already arrived, so come on, speak up, for nobody will hear us."

"No, the unseen creatures will hear us."

"What unseen creatures are you talking about? I believe that you have got far away from the subject, oh Abdussabur. I do not believe in this tommy-rot."

"Know that the spirits of all those who have died from being killed do not go up into the heavens but remain on earth, hovering around those who have caused their deaths, and especially those who have met their death as a result of the khazuq, (being impaled on a sharp pointed stake), or the gallows or by the sword of the executioner. It is not possible for anyone to see them except those who have been endowed with special abilities, not available to the others."

"I have never seen anything like this in my life."

"Strange, very strange. I would have been certain that you, especially, would inevitably have been accustomed to seeing them. Did you not tell me that you had been in charge of the secret police of Khawarazim?"

"Yes, but what connection does that have with what we are now talking about?"

"I believe that you must have sent many criminals and persons rebellious against authority, enemies of the Khan, to the gallows, or to the khazuq. It would be natural that the spirits of such people would remain, hovering around you. They would be more like fine crystalline stars which it would be possible for experienced eyes to see, quite easily, especially around noon time. You must have seen them but you didn't know what they were. For I have seen them, often, during the day, passing around your head like a swarm of bees."

Haji Agha said, in astonishment: "Yes, yes, I see them often, but I thought that this was because of an excess of blood in the veins."

"If that had been the case then you would have seen them red, the colour of blood. But these spirits have no colour for they are more like fine glass stars."

Haji Agha cried out in agreement: "So, they are the spirits of those accursed ones. But, will they remain chasing me, for ever?"

"It is easy to get rid of them if you set aside seven nights for God, during which you recite the Quran over the spirits of all those whose death you have caused. Only then will these spirits rest and rise up to their creator. How is it that no one has told you this before now, oh Haji Agha?"

"I swear to God that I can almost see them now, hovering in front of my eyes, in spite of the fact that we are not in the daytime. Indeed, I can practically hear sounds coming from them."

"They sometimes cause sounds when they are extremely disturbed but I do hope that their condition in respect of you will not be as bad as that."

"Tomorrow we will begin the setting aside of seven nights to God. And I will attempt to remember all the names that we must read. And now, this discussion has taken us far away from our subject, so speak up, what were you doing?"

Once again Juha hesitated so Haji Agha tried to encourage him to speak: "Do not keep anything back. I have sworn that I will not speak to anyone about whatever I shall hear or see tonight and I will not break my oath. Talk, my friend, what were you doing?"

Juha leant over towards him and whispered in his ear: "I was performing sorcery, or, if you require absolute precision, I was working on the breaking of a spell, but this is a secret and must not be revealed."

"Say whatever you have to say and be confident that your secret will remain as if in a bottomless pit."

Juha bowed his head in silence for a moment, before he surprised his companion with this question: "Did you ever hear the name of the Prince Fairuz, the son of the Sultan Marziban, and his successor to the throne of the Sultanate of Khusrawan?"

Haji Agha replied, after a moment of thought: "Do you mean that one who disappeared, years ago, and up to now nobody knows whether he is amongst the living or the dead? So what is his connection with what we are talking about?"

Then Juha said, simply, indicating Masoud: "That is he himself."

Masoud was, at that moment, at the threshold of the hut digging at the ground with his hooves, greatly disturbed. He was shaking his head and snorting through his nostrils whilst curling back his upper lip from his teeth. For Juha had deliberately deprived him of his royal feast on that day, to keep him in his present state.

Haji Agha turned towards where Juha had indicated and he did not see anything other than Masoud and he turned back to look at the eyes of Juha in disbelief: "I do not understand."

Juha replied in confirmation whilst indicating Masoud yet again: "That is he himself. This is Prince Fairuz, the heir to the throne of Khusrawan."

Haji Agha burst out, in anger and derision at the same time: "What has happened to your brain, oh Al Haj Abdussabur? Which Fairuz is this that you are talking about? I do not see anything except a donkey. I do not ..."

But Juha quickly scolded him sternly: "Can you not use a more appropriate word. Say: 'that one standing on four legs', or 'this one, the possessor of the two long ears', or say, 'of the white tail, of slender shoulders'."

Haji Agha shouted out, nervously, raising his voice without reserve: "Indeed, I will not call him, other than by his name. For he is a donkey, the son of a donkey, the son of a donkey."

Juha lowered his head almost to the ground, in desperation, and he was almost sobbing: "If you cannot lower your voice, sir, then it would be better for you to remain silent and not say a word."

Haji Agha raged: "I should be silent? I should not speak a single word? And in my own house? And for what? Because of that donkey? Yes, a donkey and a thousand times a donkey — donkey."

The last word resounded like a blow from a hammer, followed by a frightening silence, broken only by the breathing of Haji Agha, which had become, as a result of his excitability, more of a rattle.

More than a full minute passed, terminated by Juha who got up and went and knelt down at the forefeet of Masoud as he nervously repeated words of apology. And Masoud found this an appropriate opportunity to remind him that he had not had any food the whole day. He raised his head high, with his nose in the air, and he let loose a loud braying which truly had a ring of protest. Juha got up on his feet, rubbed Masouds head and then led him inside. He returned, as disturbed as he had been when he went, and sat down next to Haji Agha, whispering beseechingly:

"Now, we can talk with more freedom. I humbly beg of you, sir, to allow our night to end favourably and not to mention that word again. Or, if you must mention it, then let it be in a whisper, so that he does not hear it. This is my condition, in order that I shall talk."

"I swear, to God, that I have not yet heard you say anything that was not absolute rubbish. However, I shall attempt to go along with the lying until we actually get to the door. Even though, and I tell you the truth, I do not understand anything."

"You will understand everything, right away. I believe that the suddenness of all this has confused you to such an extent that you are unable to believe that what you see before you is really an important prince and the heir to the throne of the Sultanate of Khusrawan. But he has been bewitched into the form in which you now see him. The accursed witch, Asliya, the daughter of Shahat, transformed him in order to compel him to marry her one-eyed daughter."

"I do not believe a word that you say."

"Have you never heard about persons being bewitched. Don't you know that some of the sorcerers are capable of transforming a man into an ape, or a dog, or even a frog? Did not a magician transform Qurtam, the beautiful daughter of the King of Furghana, into a spotted snake? But probably you do not know that the parrot which speaks seven languages, in the palace of the King of Sindistan, is really the brother of the king himself, who was transformed into the shape of a parrot by a sorceress?"

"I have heard things like this before but I trusted that they were nothing more than unadulterated rubbish. All this sort of thing is simply talk, without proof."

"These are facts which do not require any proof."

"One thing might satisfy me if you want to claim that sorcery can transform a prince of the Sultanate into a donkey — I mean, into this form which we see now. Come on and return this creature to its human form, now, in front of my eyes. And under these circumstances, only, I may become convinced."

"This is what I am in the course of doing now."

"What do you say?"

"I said that I shall do just that, now. You will see for yourself how the bewitchment will be removed from this being after a few moments, and he will appear before you in his original form."

Haji Agha said, challengingly: "And what are you waiting for?"

Juha replied, calmly and smiling confidently: "By good luck, tonight is the appointed date on which it is possible for me to remove the effects of the magic for a period of ten minutes. My Lord, Prince Fairuz, the son of the Sultan Marziban, will return to the form which he was in before the abominable sorceress transformed him."

Haji Agha tossed his head and said, mockingly: "Just like that. Well, what are you waiting for then?"

"Firstly, it is necessary that we should wait until the magic potion, which you saw me cooking up on the fire, has blended, and secondly, the moment of the magical transformation will only take place at midnight, exactly."

Then Juha took from his pocket a strangely shaped, black bottle, saying as he did so: "I have spent the whole of my life discovering this contra sorcery potion. When the potion is totally blended and the solids have changed to liquid, I shall pour upon it seven drops from this bottle. I will then spray the potion on our friend here, he of the four legs, and then you will see with your own eyes, his transformation into a normal human being."

Haji Agha looked intently at the watchman of the spring with two disbelieving eyes as he put the strange bottle back in his pocket. Then his gaze returned, to rest alternately on the cooking pot, which was boiling on the fire, and Masoud, standing near the door of the hut. He was clearly impatient, stamping the ground with all four of his feet, sniffing at the wind nervously and snorting through his nostrils from time to time, hoping that his owner, who had left him all day without food, would pay him some attention.

Suddenly, Juha leaped to his feet, slapping himself on the forehead in a movement which alarmed Haji Agha, saying, irritably, as he did so: "Do you know what I have done? I nearly forgot something which, if I had not remembered about it in time, then this hour would have seen the end of you and me."

Then Juha leapt to the side of Masoud and dragged him inside the hut, in spite of his opposition, after accepting kicks from his heels.

The astonished Haji Agha saw him tie the donkey with a thick rope to a stake. Then Juha returned, wiping away the sweat with the end of his long shirt. Haji Agha, at this moment, was remembering the deposit which Juha had left with him as a guarantee for his employment as watchman of the spring — five hundred pieces of silver and six hundred in total — which this trickster had forced out of him in a game of chess. Now this was a good opportunity to send him packing and get back his money and another hundred on top. Juha was not unaware of what was going on the head of Haji Agha, for everything which he thought about had now become like an open book before the eyes of Juha and his perceptive mind.

Then Juha resumed, explaining: "The moment of the magical transformation is normally accompanied by tremendous pain. When the effect of the magic is dispersed, and this person is changed back into his original form of a normal human being, you will see him with the same appearance, once again, as he had at the time when he was bewitched. That is, we shall see him brandishing his sword and it may be that the pain will drive him to the point of insanity. Or he may suddenly remember our previous conversation which made him so angry, and this makes it necessary for us to tie him to this stake."

Haji Agha, who was still thinking about the six hundred pieces of silver, then muttered: "Is that so? Is that so? We shall see."

Then Juha spoke again, quite calmly: "All that I am hoping for, from you, is that you maintain control of your nerve, for we are now on the verge of an experience which shakes the strongest of hearts. If you find yourself unable to maintain your composure, then close your eyes or look elsewhere."

Haji Agha stuck out his chest, arrogantly: "I am afraid of nothing, rest assured."

At that moment Juha wasn't listening to him. He was looking up at the sky with both eyes fixed on the moon. "I shall not begin until that cloud reaches the edge of the moon," he said to himself.

Juha took the bottle from his pocket and his face was suddenly covered by the fearful appearance which had so appalled Haji Agha when he came sneaking up, more than an hour before.

And now the mutterings of Juha came out from deep down inside him as if they were a whole corps of drums: "Shur hantur awad ya ma-shur, abrakat annar ya sayyad annur."

Then he sprang, with the bottle, to where the cooking pot was still boiling on the fire. Still continuing with his words of magic, he was followed by the eyes of Haji Agha. Juha did not require a great deal of intelligence to realise that the look of doubt had almost completely disappeared from the eyes of Haji Agha and was making way for a different look, containing a mixture of fear and curiosity. Juha then poured seven drops from the bottle, and with each drop he called out, each time higher than the previous time: "God is greatest."

Then, when he had let off his last shout, resounding like thunder, he plucked the cooking pot from off the fire and threw what was in it under the feet of Masoud, whilst crying out, as loud as he could: "In the name of God, return now, as God created you."

* * * * * *

As for what happened after that, Haji Agha would tell the story to everyone he met, swearing, by all that is holy, may he shed blood from his eyes instead of tears, that the story he was telling was the truth, the whole truth and nothing but the truth.

For Juha had already set off through the door of the hut which was open as wide as possible. He was shouting and throwing his arms about in the air, with his gown flying out behind him like the sail of a boat, until he collided with Haji Agha who was standing and watching all that was happening before him, with his mouth open and his eyes protruding. He took a frantic step backwards, as if he was surprised to find him there, in that place, and then threw him a dreadful look which almost went through him like a knife, appealing to him in a voice choked by his words: "Look well, oh Haji Agha, fix your eyes on what is behind this door in order that you may witness, for yourself, the miracle as it actually happens. As for me, permit me to turn my face elsewhere, for I do not have your courage."

At that moment a brilliant light, like a flash of lightning, came out from inside the hut, accompanied by a tremendous bang which penetrated to the very bones of Haji Agha. In the light, with his own eyes, he saw Masoud, tied to the stake in the corner opposite the door, stamping his three free legs nervously tossing his head in the air. His restlessness had already increased tenfold. Then a cloud of thick smoke surrounded him, which got bigger until it began to come out through the door. It was accompanied by an appalling shriek, high at first, like the braying of a donkey, then it began to change, gradually, to an awful wailing A minute or so passed and then the thick cloud began to disappear, little by little. But before it had totally dispersed, Haji Agha saw something which caused him to collapse on the ground, trembling.

In the corner facing the door where, just a moment ago, stood a donkey, just the same as any other donkey; tied to the same stake by the same rope on his left lower leg, there now stood a handsome, tall, broad-shouldered youth, in a clean, royal uniform, unsuitable for all except those endowed with thrones. Dozens of medals and decorations sparkled on his chest, and hanging down at his side, with the tip of it practically touching the ground, was a golden scabbard. In his right hand was a sword which he brandished in anger, with sparks flying from his eyes and with froth covering his lips and chin, and dropping on the ground. From his mouth came strange sounds, a mixture of the braying of a donkey, the bellowing of a bull and the sobbing of a child. He began to try, without success, to free his leg which was tied to the stake, whilst the incomprehensible sounds became clearer, little by little, until Haji Agha was able to distinguish what he was saying as he addressed his remarks to the watchman of the spring, Abdussabur, who was at that moment, kneeling on the ground, sweeping the ground with his beard.

"Woe be to you, you stupid servant. Have you reached such a level of impertinence as to tie me to a stake as if I was in fact, a donkey? I swear, on the head of my father, the Sultan Marziban, that I will, for certain, be the one who kills you."

* * * * * *

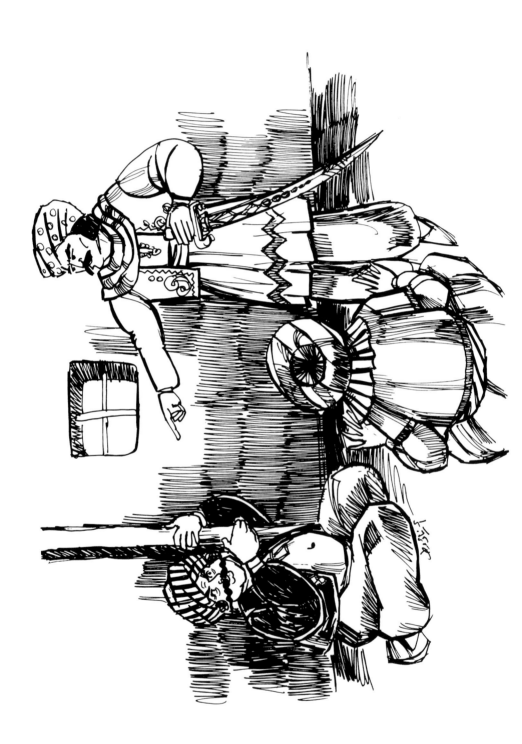

Chapter 16

Juha cried out, beseechingly, as he threw earth over his face: "Forgive me, my Lord, for I only did this for your own safety."

Skinner went into a rage — for this cavalier was none other than our friend, the Thief of Baghdad himself, swaggering in the most conceited, most magnificent, imperialistic fashion, in the dress of the Hikimdar, General Mahmar, with his decorations and sword. His voice had now begun to recover its human aspect, although the froth still obscured half of his face and was scattered around with every word which he spoke.

"Do not speak of my safety. Do you know what you did to me on the previous occasion. You allowed me to be transformed to my unimperialistic form with the sword still in my hand with the result that it was transformed with me and became part of my tail."

Juha said, whilst still kneeling down in his place: "This was the reason, my Lord. I was afraid that, whilst you were reassuming your most magnificent form, the tail might lose — I mean the sword — might lose its way and I had no alternative but to restrict your movements to the narrowest limits."

"You old nag — beast — you ought to have thought of some other method, you stupid man. And now, what are you waiting for? Why do you not release my bonds, you dog?"

Juha raised his head, repeating, pleadingly: "Give me your pledge for my safety, first, my Lord, give me your pledge for your own sake, and not for mine."

Skinner snorted with complete arrogance, as he sheathed his sword with a highhanded, imperialistic movement, lifting up his gaze to the roof of the hut: "You have my pledge."

Juha crawled forward, on his knees, and as he was untying the knots he began to prattle: "I have some good news for you, my Lord. I have finally found the magical antidote which I was searching for, and, by the will of God, it will remove this torment from you after three months, no more, when we reach Khusrawan and the palace of my Lord, my benefactor, the shadow of God on earth, the Sultan Marziban."

"And why should it not be now? I cannot bear this for three more months."

"Much time has passed, my Lord, and only a little remains. For what is inevitable must be. The antidote will not eliminate the spell totally unless you have taken it nine times, once every ten days, and on condition that, on the last time, it shall be in the very place where my Lord was bewitched on the first occasion." "Take this sword off me, and the belt also, and remove this tunic of mine and throw it on the fire."

Juha rushed to obey the order and his trembling fingers fumbled with the embroidered vest, studded with decorations as Skinner's voice could be heard, emanating contempt: "You have been working in my service for three years. And before that you were in the service of my father, His Majesty the Sultan, for seven years. Despite this you have still not learnt how you should behave in the Majestic presence. It is most likely that you are going to spend some dark days, darker even than the pods of the locust tree after we return to Khusrawan. For my father, the Sultan Marziban, is not very tolerant with those whose knowledge of the rules of conduct in his presence let them down. If God so wills, you will be a permanent guest in the dark room in the dome of the palace, where the ministers and chamberlains are whipped when their conduct gets out of hand or their mouths let fall their common language whilst in the imperial presence."

"My Lord ...."

"You do not even know how to kneel, or how to stand properly. How can a man stand in this way in the Imperial presence? Where is the look of humility? Where is the inclining of the head?"

"My Lord, my Lord..."

"Be silent. How can you permit your baser self to interrupt your master? Also, what is this rubbish with which you are feeding me since we came to this place?"

"My Lord, this is the best that I could find here."

"Shut your mouth you stupid man, and do not speak a word without my permission or when I ask you a question. Where are the fresh dates which I asked you for on the previous occasion?"

Here the eyes of Skinner fell, for the first time, on Haji Agha, who was more dead than alive and who was still kneeling, clinging to the doorstep:

"And who would this scoundrel be? And why have you permitted him to be here, in our presence?"

"He is one of the local notables, my Lord, and he was of great help in my finding the antidote which will heal and bring health, with God's permission. He is one of my Lord's faithful servants who asked for permission to appear before you."

Skinner gave Haji Agha a haughty glance, stretching out his finger towards him as if he was going to stab him, and speaking one single word, as if he was throwing a stone at him: "Name?"

Haji Agha stuttered, still on all fours and hanging on to the threshold: "Ha — ha — ma — Haji Agha."

"Ahh? I didn't hear — Hani Agha? Madi Agha?"

Juha whispered, in a voice as soft as silk: "Haji Agha — Haji Agha, my Lord."

"Ha — ha — Haji Agha, marvellous. As long as it is Haji Agha, then let him come forward. Do not be afraid of anything."

Haji Agha crawled forward until he reached the feet of Skinner, when he bent himself in the shape of an Arabic figure of eight, then straightened up a little in order to kiss, with humility, the hand which was stretched out towards him.

Skinner mumbled some words in a stately voice, expressing his pleasure: "Tremendous, tremendous, bravo!"

And he turned then to Juha: "Did you notice? This is a country man, who is uneducated, who has lived all his life in this place of exile, yet he knows how to behave in the presence of sultans and kings. Look at the bending over of his shoulders, the inclining of the head, and the look in his eyes which are never raised above the front of my sandals? You must learn from him, oh Abdussabur, in order that you may be acceptable for the post which is waiting for you in our country, Chamberlain of the Treasury and Secretary of the Sultan."

"Forgive me, my Lord, but this man did not live all his life here, in this place, out of touch with the world. Indeed, before that he held an important post in Khuwarazim and, naturally, he is aware of the rules of behavior in the presence of the upper class."

"Is that so? Then you must take a number of lessons from him in order that you may avoid visits to the dark room in the dome of the palace of my father, the Sultan. Teach him, oh Hani Agha."

"Haji Agha, my Lord."

"Haji Agha, Hani Agha or Raji Agha, they are all Aghas. I say, give him some lessons in the manners of the royal court, oh Haji Agha, and I will send you a nice reward when I reach Khusrawan. Ayee — ohh — get out of my sight, ayy-ohh-waawu-haaw ..."

The froth returned to cover the face of Skinner and his eyes protruded and his lips were pulled back from two lines of teeth whilst his voice began to change to a sharp braying. His legs began to move backwards and his back began to curve and his arms began to hang down low. Haji Agha almost went out of his mind when he also noticed that the two ears were twitching rapidly in exactly the same way as any pure bred donkey. Juha then cried out in terror: "The effect of the potion has already begun to dissipate, let us get out at once or we will be consumed by the flames."

Juha hurried away, fleeing from the door, whilst in his tracks was Haji Agha and following them was the braying of Skinner. They had hardly got ten paces away when a tremendous bang rang out and a thick cloud of smoke hid the hut from view. Gradually the noise subsided and the thick cloud of smoke dispersed as the heavy breathing slackened but the voice of Haji Agha was still trembling when he asked Juha, excitedly: "What happened? Do you think that he has been transformed, once again?"

Juha answered, in a voice no less disturbed: "I believe so. Come on, let us go and see."

Haji Agha hesitated, torn between two factors, fear and curiosity. However, fear won, for he said: "No, you have a look first."

Juha put his head round the door and turned round saying: "It is all over. There is no longer any danger there."

Again, Haji Agha hesitated before peeping with his head round the door to find everything calm and quiet as if nothing had ever happened. It was as if that awe-inspiring cavalier, surrounded by an aura of splendour and glory which does not exist except with those of blue blood, and who had been there only two minutes before, had never existed. And in the corner of the room, in the same place, was standing Masoud, troubled and perplexed, tossing his head around in hungry anger and stamping the ground with all four of his feet. In the opposite corner was the golden sword and the sleeveless jacket, decorated by medals; a genuine testimony

208

that what had happened was not simply a dream or one of the tricks of the sorcerers.

Juha went quickly to pat the head of Masoud and to lay down in front of him the covering for his meal as he spoke to him, choking on his tears, saying: "Don't be cross with me, my Lord, the effect of the temporary magic potion ended before you were able to partake of a royal meal, suitable for one in your position. However, do not feel sad, only three more months remain before the whole world will be throwing itself at your feet."

With these words Juha began to console his donkey who was becoming increasingly disturbed and more and more irritable in the tossing of his head as he expected that his owner would give him the meal for which he had long been waiting. Juha left Haji Agha in a bottomless sea of thought and ambitious desire after his fear had left him and with it all doubt in the truth of the watchman of the spring, Al Haj Abdussabur.

* * * * * *

What was going on in the head of Haji Agha was not hidden from Juha who had lit the spark of greed in the evil heart of Haji Agha and he fully realised how it would continue to grow and get worse because of his natural bent towards greed. For now, Haji Agha was not envious of Juha solely because of the great benefits which awaited him in Khusrawan on the day on which the prince Fairuz, would return to his Imperial status, after only three more months. He also saw himself as having more right, and as being more suitable than the stupid Abdussabur to accompany the prince and to win the important post, Chamberlain of the Treasury. For did not the prince himself say that but a few moments ago. It is the opportunity of a lifetime, oh Haji Agha, do not let it slip out of your hands. And do not forget that the prince has already drawn you closer to him and designated you for the task of instructing this ignorant man. Indeed, he also promised you a reward.

Haji Agha did not lose any time but immediately began to spread out his net. No sooner had Juha entered the inner room of the hut to bring the royal meal than he began to come forward with agility towards Masoud, his face masked with a look expressing a mixture of humility, loyalty and sincerity. He bent down to the right foreleg to kiss it with subservience as he said, in a whisper: "Do not be cross with me, my Lord, for being so bold as to speak to you without permission, but the behaviour of that ignorant man has irritated me. For this is not the conventional manner in the presence of sultans and kings."

At this moment Juha returned, carrying with him the food of Masoud. Haji Agha turned to him and said: "Give me the bread, the cucumbers and the apples. I shall teach you how to serve food to those who possess the imperial presence."

* * * * * *

In fact, the first lesson was very enjoyable for Juha, especially the effort made by Haji Agha and the degree to which he gave the appearance of loyalty. The contents of the two baskets were emptied inside Masoud, accompanied by an unending number of humble, elegant bows and smiles with exaggerated expressions of felicity and words of deference and praise, which not even the supplications of the slaves of the Pharaohs of the greatest influence in the old days could have approached. Then Haji Agha rushed to soak his silk handkerchief in water, to wipe out the nostrils and teeth of Masoud.

Masoud thought that this was a new type of food which Haji Agha was presenting to him and he snatched the handkerchief with his front teeth, only to find that its taste did not please him so he spat it out on the ground in refusal, in a movement which Haji Agha considered was the ultimate in haughtiness and disdain.

And so the feast ended, and with it ended the first lesson. Haji Agha turned towards Juha, who was watching everything that happened, like an dull-witted student, and announced to him, in the manner in which such announcements would be made in any sultanate court, or as the usher would announce in a civil court:

"My Lord, the Prince, has concluded his repast and the time has now come for him to rest. Come with me."

Juha followed him outside the hut until they were standing under a nearby tree. Haji Agha then said, without attempting to hide his excitement, as if he had discovered a new continent: "Did you note that the tail is now moving more flexibly?" Juha replied, showing astonishment: "In fact I did notice that, but I do not understand the reason for it."

Haji Agha cried out, very pleased with himself: "The reason, you idiot, is that he is now free of the sword."

Juha was silent, for a moment, before he said, as he shook his head, sorrowfully: "How stupid I am. How was it that I did not become aware of this simple fact?"

"And — did you not notice some thing else? He is eating now with more appetite.

Juha raised his hand in a form of protest: "As for this, I know the reason. You fed him in a manner which really gives him an appetite. How I had hoped that I might learn this exemplary method of feeding kings. I would then have saved myself from his anger all these years and I would not have worried myself, thinking about the darkened room, for a single moment."

A black idea came into the head of Haji Agha and it was as if he was a pirate ship which had suddenly sighted its victim approaching. For if Prince Fairuz had been angry with Abdussabur for three years, then how easy it would be now for him to please him. How simple it would be to enable him to see the difference between how he was treated by the common folk and those who were born to embellish the court. And just like the action of a persistent fly in the ear of an old ox, Haji Agha began to get the watchman of his spring talking and he would argue with him and inveigle him into giving information until he knew everything that there was to know about the Prince Fairuz. How, when and why did the regrettable incident of bewitchment occur? What was his relationship with the Sultan Marziban before this incident? And why did the Sultan chose him, specifically, to accompany his son on the journey between the various countries? What had happened to them since they had left Khusrawan?

If Juha had not prepared himself fully for this moment, and had not prepared the plot of his story well, closing all the gaps, he would have been drowned in the flood of questions which Haji Agha rained down upon him. However, the story was complete and, praise be to God, it was perfect without any loose ends and full of all the fine details which left no room for doubt about its veracity.

And so Juha began to talk, sometimes profusely, sometimes by a hint here and there, leaving Haji Agha to draw his own conclusions about what he forgot to say or what he did not want to say. For he talked profusely in describing the tricks of the grey-haired sorceress, Asliya, the daughter of As Shahat, and the extent of her malice, the ugliness of which was only surpassed by the face of her daughter for whom she had the ambitious desire of marriage with the Prince Fairuz. When she found herself unable to convince him she resorted to her final weapon and bewitched him into the form in which we now see him. Similarly, Juha exceeded all bounds in the description of his own life, amongst books, manuscripts and the spells of the ancients; his researches into chemistry and his efforts in order to arrive at the secret formula of the golden potion by which it was possible to turn stone into silver and brass into gold. Then, how he converted from this to sorcery, or white magic to be precise. That is, the magic which counteracts the effects of the malignant black magic, as practiced by Asliya, daughter of As Shahat, and her peers from the adversaries of God and mankind, brothers of the devil, Satan's assistants.

Haji Agha learnt from him how the Sultan Marziban had sent for him after what had happened to his son, and after he had come to hear that the only person who could alleviate the torment which his son was suffering, was the venerable and learned man, Abdussabur. Particularly after the Sultan, in a fit of anger, had killed the old sorceress, and with her the secret formula of the potion.

Haji Agha could imagine himself actually hearing the Sultan Marziban saying to the Haj Abdussabur: "Verily, I commit my son, the joy of my life, to you in a state which makes my heart bleed to see. Accompany him and stay with him until this affliction has been removed at your hands. Do not let him out of your sight for a single moment and your reward from me, on the day that he recovers, will be that you will be the Chamberlain of the Treasury of the Sultanate."

But the white magic, on which Abdussabur was carrying out his experiments, and by which he had achieved the ability to retransform certain bewitched birds and animals to the original form in which they had been created by God, was still Jacking a specific type of red saffron flower which only grows on the peaks of the mountains of Faraghana. He needed this in order to be able to succeed in the retransformation of a human being who had been bewitched into the form of an animal. Here, Haji Agha just had to use his intelligence to understand that this was the secret of the visit of Abdussabur, with his prince, to this place.

Nevertheless, he was unable to conceal his concern as he asked: "Did you find the saffron flower which you were seeking?"

"I praise God, who guided me to it at the proper time. Do you remember the day when you first met me, the day I won the bet from you playing chess?"

It was a memory which Haji Agha did not wish to recall, but now, in search of bigger game, he said, without showing displeasure: "Would a man ever forget a day like that?"

"As for me, I remember it for other reasons. It was on that day that I found the red flowers of the saffron and I picked enough of them for my needs. When I was on my own that evening I completed my potion and there was nothing left for me to do except to wait for the completion of the three years, of which only three months remain, which is more than sufficient for the return journey to Khusrawan."

"But why wait? Why can it not be done now?"

Juha replied with a ring of astonishment: "That is a very intelligent question, without doubt. You are drawing me out until I am revealing all my secrets to you. But there is no harm in that. So, you must understand, sir, that there are two reasons for that. The first is that the effect of the black magic cannot be eliminated completely, unless the potion of the white magic is used on the victim in the place where the transformation took place for the first time. This place is the bedchamber of Prince Fairuz, in his summer palace in Khusrawan. The second reason is that the magic of the sorceress, Asliya, daughter of As Shahat, was so strong that it is not possible for it to be eliminated until after three, full and complete years, even though it was possible to eclipse its effects for short periods, from time to time, during those years, as you saw just a few moments ago."

The conversation continued in this fashion. Haji Agha would ask the questions and Juha would reply, until when he had arrived at the end of his story, with all its parts completed, he said, irritably: "Yes, only three months remain and then this agonising journey will be over."

Juha released a long, sharp sigh and then added: "I shall spend a week, or two weeks, in this area, during which I shall collect more of the red saffron flower which I might need for more research, and then we will make our way to Khusrawan, and it will be the happiest day of my life, the day when my task will be completed. The happiest moment will be when I go up with the Prince to his rose bedchamber and toss my magic potion over him in order that he may return to being a normal human being."

Haji Agha then said, in completion: "And you will come down from the bedchamber to mount the chair of the Chamberlain of the Treasury. It surely is your right to say that this day will be the happiest day in your life."

"I? Who told you that I was going to take the post of the Chamberlain of the Treasury?"

"Did you not say, just a moment ago, that the Sultan Marziban had promised you this reward?"

"He promised me, yes. But who told you that I was going to accept this position even if it involved all the treasuries on earth? Indeed, no sir. I shall undertake my task because I regard it as a challenge to my knowledge, to which I have devoted the whole of my life. As for the reward, let my Lord the Sultan Marziban keep it for himself. I have no desire for it."

"I only see you as being mentally deficient, without judgement. Is there, in the whole universe, a creature who would refuse all this fame, wealth and authority?"

"Indeed, I am in full possession of my faculties and I mean every word that I say. And if there was any other person who knew the Sultan Marziban as I have known him and who had lived with his son as I have lived with him, then he would flee from this post like the clean person flees from he who has scabies."

Juha got up from his place, put his head outside the door of the hut to peep out, then he came back and said: "By good luck he is asleep now and he will not hear what I am saying. It is also my good luck that you are a noble man and, for this reason, it will not do me any harm to expose to you my innermost secrets. Know this, oh my brother, God did not create, amongst all his servants, anyone who is more malicious, stupid or more ungrateful than the arrogant youth called Fairuz, son of Marziban. For it was God, may his ability be glorified, who permitted the sorceress, Asliya, the daughter of As Shahat, to bewitch him into this form, for it is,

214

in fact, the nearest thing to his natural self and character. Did you notice him, tonight, after all that I have done on his behalf? He had hardly returned to his true form for a moment when the first thing he was thinking about was killing me. Why? Because I do not have command of the proper protocol in the presence of kings? But the biggest problem, and the most dangerous, is that his father is even more frivolous and committed to outward appearances and the rules of protocol. I, quite frankly, sir, have lived my life among books, talismans and dossiers. I am not one of the people of rulers' courts. I am not suitable to become one of the followers of the courts, I do not wish to become one of them nor am I suitable to have the position of Chamberlain of the Treasury. For I know what would happen. The next day would be my appointment with the darkened room and the day after that would be my appointment with the point of the longest khazuq in the city of Khusrawan."

Haji Agha was listening to the words of Juha and he could hardly believe his ears, his ambitious desires already filling his heart to such an extent that it caused his breathing to pant in a manner more like a rattling and his eyes were almost coming out of their sockets.

The voice of Juha rose as he said: "Do you think that I have spent twenty years of my life in the world of magic and talismans just to come to this end? And that I should abandon all my knowledge and experiments for a post such as this, whatever may be its standing and its rewards. No sir, this shall not be."

* * * * * *

In fact, Juha did not need to make a great deal of effort to convince Haji Agha that he was sincere in his refusal to accept the important post. For how many people did Haji Agha know who were foolish and stupid and were not at all suitable to be raised above ground level among the rest of the common people, because of their sick occupation with what they called 'the door of knowledge'.

For this reason he replied to the outburst of his friend with complete self-possession: "You are probably perfectly right. If you want the truth, the post of Chamberlain of the Treasury is no more suitable for you than you are for it."

And if Haji Agha had been asked, at that moment, to picture himself and Juha in a single drawing then he would have selected himself to be in the form of a magnificent rapacious leopard, setting out his trap for a gazelle which had fallen back from the herd, or as an octupus winding its arms, one after the other around an easy victim, which itself had come looking for him.

This evil thought in the mind of Haji Agha was not hidden from Juha and he allowed himself to be drawn into the net of the octupus, as he said, quite firmly, to him: "I am fully aware of this and, for this reason, I have made my decision and I will not change my mind. I shall return to the Sultan his eldest son and I shall refuse any post which he may offer to me, even though it be that of the Chief Chamberlain. I shall ask him only that he should grant me a residence, isolated in some distant spot, surrounded by trees and tranquillity, around which the sparrows and nightingales are singing, and a small pension to support me. There I shall be able to devote all my time to the great science to which I have dedicated my life."

Juha raised his eyes, hovering in the direction of the residence of Haji Agha, the residence which he had named, from the moment in which he had seen it, 'the nest of the viper'. His gaze wandered through the trees, which at that moment were receiving the early morning breeze in their elegant, dancing branches as if they were playing a tune at a festival. Then he sighed again and he repeated, as if he was talking to himself: "Yes, a house like that, in a place like that, that is all I want."

As for Haji Agha, he was the other one who was talking to himself: "It is true what the man said: 'The throat is given to those with no ears.' But if this idiot does not wish to become a chamberlain and a minister, and really, he is unsuitable for that, why should it not be me? Is it not I who was made to be a ruler and a minister?"

The imagination of Haji Agha ran away with him and he imagined himself in all the glory and magnificence of the position, with people bowing to him in the same way as he bowed to the Sultan, with the safe boxes of the treasury all at his mercy as well as the dark-eyed maidens of Khusrawan, famous for the magic of their eyes, competing with each other for his favour. He smiled to himself when he remembered that only two days ago he had been desirous of a simple country girl, Laila, the daughter of the headman, Muhammad Ali, and that for her he had been prepared to give up twenty thousand pieces of silver.

The thread of the conversation was taken up again by the two men. Haji Agha was weaving his web around the victim whilst Juha was slipping wherever Haji Agha wanted him to slip. As the sun rose and sleep refused to be banished any longer from those eyes which had stayed awake all night even up to this time of the day, Haji Agha said, sleepily: "I shall go now to get a little sleep, and I call upon you, too to rest after this great effort, but our conversation is not over yet."

Juha replied, yawning: "For certain, for certain. There is more to talk about, much more. How happy is the man when he finds that one person who is able to understand his problems. But what's this? I see that they have come back, hovering around your head today in abnormal numbers."

Haji Agha asked in a scared voice: "What are they? What are you talking about?"

"Those evil spirits which are pursuing you. Don't you see them."

After the long sleepless night, and all the great excitement, it was inevitable that the eyes of Haji Agha would see a number of small light stars, playing in front of his eyes like tiny atoms of light.

He said, as he drove them away from in front of his eye with a nervous movement: "Yes I see them. There are a lot of them, more than normal, what can I do to get them away from me?"

"There is nothing more simple than that. When you wake up, call the headman of the village to you, and ask him to restore the village mosque at your expense. And do not forget what I told you about holding seven nights of praying to God for the souls of all those persons whose deaths you have caused by sending them to the gallows or the khazuq. If you gave him a list of the names it would be better, but at least try to remember the actual number and pay to him, for the mosque and for the nights of rememberances, fifty pieces of silver for each soul."

Haji Agha replied: "It shall be so, it shall be so."

And off he went, almost reeling from his excessive tiredness. Juha saw him off, smiling and watching the man brushing himself with his hand nervously, to chase away the evil spirits from in front of his eyes.

* * * * * *

217

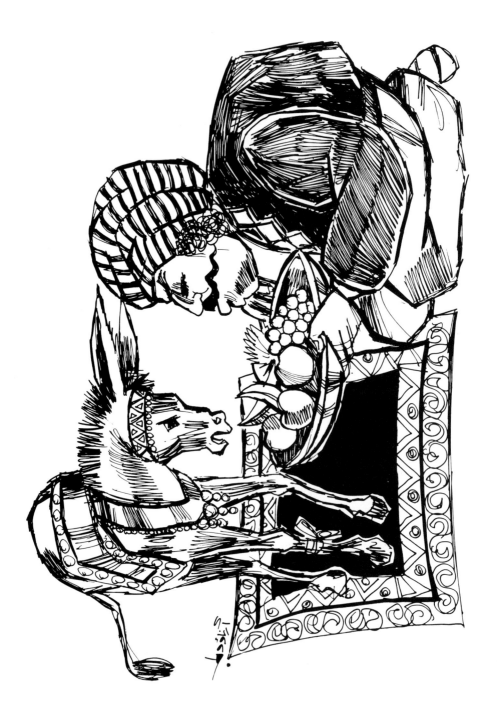

Chapter 17

The world smiled on Masoud, Juha's venerable donkey, for Haji Agha had become so convinced that what he saw there was Prince Fairuz, the son and heir to the throne of the Sultan Marziban of Khusrawan, that he interpreted every movement of his tail and every waggle of his two long ears as wishes that could not be denied. His sole care, which kept him busy during the day and sleepless at night, was that he should be close to the Prince and that he should share with Juha everything that he did for him in order that he should have a share of his favour, together with Juha, or in place of him if possible.

The first step was that he should transfer Masoud from the hut in which Juha, or Abdussabur, lived to a place more suitable for one of his elevated status. All the protests of Juha were to no avail in satisfying Haji Agha that such action was unnecessary. For the distancing of Masoud from the eye of Juha for most hours of the day was the cornerstone of the plan which Haji Agha had made in order to get close to the prince.

"It would have been possible for me to be silent about that had I not known the truth about him." This was how he spoke to Juha as he discussed the matter with him.

"He, himself, spoke to me, and showed faith in my ability, so that he even entrusted me with your instruction in the rules of courtly behaviour and promised me a nice reward, do you not remember that?"

"Indeed, I most certainly do."

"It is for this reason that I am unable to permit him to remain in this miserable hut for a single minute longer."

And so, Masoud was transferred on the same night, when the people of the village were all sleeping peacefully in their beds, to the most glorious room in the palace of Haji Agha. If it had not been for the insistence of Juha he would have moved silken coverings to the room and would have covered the floor with the finest carpets of Tabriz and the walls with mirrors. However, Juha was able to convince him that what was suitable for the prince whilst he was in his imperial form was not suitable for him as Masoud. Haji Agha did not lose any time and all his efforts were now devoted to looking after the prince and keeping Juha away from him, on any pretext, whether convincing or not. Every time Juha asked to see him he found a way of preventing him from getting anywhere near him. For the next step was to arouse the anger of the prince against Juha. One day, whilst Juha was attempting to get a look at Masoud from behind the fence, perhaps motivated by a longing to see him, or perhaps to satisfy himself about the extent to which his plan was progressing, he heard Haji Agha saying to Masoud, as he stood in front of him showing great humility: "And after that, oh my Lord, he burst out, cursing, swearing and insulting, in the foulest language. My tongue could not, nor will I permit it to pronounce the words in your hearing. Imagine, he said that there was no difference between your behaviour in your original form and the form to which you were transformed. How could he say such a thing?"

This was enough for Juha and he went off quietly. And when he came back a second time he found Haji Agha engaged in washing the head, the ears and the feet of Masound with perfume. As he did so he was chattering away, in his normal fashion, like one whispering some important secret: "What I have heard today, oh my Lord, must be told by me to you, however coarse it is. For that renegade servant, Abdussabur, said to me today, that he is not going back with you to Khusrawan, at all, and will not cause the eyes of the Sultan to rejoice by seeing his own flesh and blood and heir to his throne. Indeed, even worse than that, he has said that he will sell you to one of the caravans of the Moguls in order that they may torture you and break your back with the heavy weights which you will have to carry. But I shall not permit him to do this, oh my Lord. I shall rescue you from the talons of this traitor, though I pay for this with my life."

That night, whilst Haji Agha was engrossed in setting up his snare for the encounter between the prince and Abdussabur, our friend, Skinner, the Thief of Baghdad, slipped into Juha's hut. Juha received him with an embrace and said to him, after making sure that the door was properly closed: "I believe that the fruit has ripened and is ready to pluck."

Skinner nodded his head in amazement as he said: The truth is that I am surprised how this man took the bait so easily."

Juha stroked his long, thin beard, saying, smiling: "I made music for him on the most sensitive of strings for this type of person, the string of greed. Then I added another string, which is the string with the highest note amongst the most evil of men, the string of jealousy, and the response was as you can see."

Skinner said, pondering: "Jealousy, there is nothing which blinds the heart and vision, deafens the ears and leads man, by his own choice, to his death, more than jealousy."

And Juha completed: "Al Nu'aman, the son of Al Mundhir, had two kinds of days, one day when he was happy, and whoever appeared before him on one of those days would be in receipt of his generosity, and another day of ill-boding, during which whoever his eyes fell upon would be afflicted with much evil.

On one of his happy days, a man in poor circumstances entered into his presence, beseeching his generosity and Al Nu'aman said: "Ask for whatever you will and your request will be answered, but on the one condition that I shall give to your neighbour, double your lot."

The man thought for a moment and then said: "Then put out my left eye, my Lord."

And in this way the two friends carried on until the cock crowed, saying farewell to the night and greeting the dawn of the new day.

Skinner then said: "The time has come for me to be off. Do you have any further instructions for me?"

Juha replied: "I shall need you in two days. It will be necessary for you to go back to Sindashah."

Skinner cried out: "There is no power and no strength save in God. Every time I have thought that I had said goodbye to that city for the last time, I find myself going back there. It is just as if I was tied to it by a ship's hawser."

"No, this is the last time, and I will meet you there and we shall leave there together."

"To where?"

"To Nahawand, if God so wills, to present you to my children, and also that we may meet there, a hermit who is a strange character, in the form of a blind, deaf and dumb beggar. We must open his eyes, heal his ears and loosen his tongue."

Skinner raised his eyebrows, opening his eyes wide: "I do not understand a thing."

Said Juha: "A little bird will tell you the news, so do not be in a hurry, and await my signal."

And so Skinner departed, in the same manner as that in which he came, just as if the ground had opened up under his feet and had swallowed him up. In the flash of an eye he had disappeared, leaving Juha smiling to himself as he put the finishing touches to his scheme.

* * * * * *

On the next day, Juha went to the palace of Haji Agha, who had no sooner seen him when he rushed up to say: "My Lord the Prince, is asleep, and he has asked me not to let anyone disturb him."

Juha did not ask how the prince had asked him to do this or in what language he had spoken to him, but said to him, without any preamble: "My dear sir, I believe that you are not carrying out any of the wishes of my master, the Prince. The time for our departure for Khusrawan approaches and you have still not informed me of anything which he has requested from you, and you have not prepared me to take over my anticipated position as the Chamberlain of the Treasury and Private Secretary to my master, the Sultan."

Haji Agha said, with considerable agitation, for the moment which he was afraid of had arrived: "What, are you really thinking of moving off?"

"You know that the road to Khusrawan is long, and we have to be there after three months, no more and no less."

"But you confirmed that you were totally averse to the post which the Sultan had promised you and that you were only thinking of being left alone with your experiments, in the world of magic and magicians, and that you only wanted an isolated, remote place and a reasonable pension to provide for your needs."

"It is true, I did say this, in fact, and I am still hoping for this. But I realised, also, that man does not achieve all that he hopes for. For the Sultan Marziban, as you know, is likely to insist on the post which he promised me and, in that case, I shall have no alternative but to submit

to his wishes. For this reason, it would be a good idea for me to prepare myself in the best possible way."

Haji Agha blinked his two narrow eyes and signs of displeasure began to appear on his face: "But what are you going to do about the
pitch-black room. Are you not afraid that it is going to be your fate to
end up there?"

"That is exactly what I wanted to talk to you about. You are, as I
believe, a person of great experience, wisdom and knowledge of the
rules of conduct in the Court. So give me some of your knowledge and
I promise you that the reward which the Prince promised you will
reach you, in full, just as soon as I arrive. Indeed, I will also promise
you that I shall send you from Khusrawan, a hookah, inlaid with gold
and with two stones dancing about in the water, one of them a green
turquoise, and the other a deep red ruby, and with it a holder of the
purest silver for the charcoal."

Haji Agha could hardly believe his ears. He said to himself:
"Whatever was the stupid fool doing talking about a hookah, a turquoise and a ruby? This was like trying to quench the craving of a
man dying of thirst in the desert with two drops of water, which would
neither allay a thirst nor heal an ardent desire." For what he was avidly
desirous of and dreamt about, was the position of Chamberlain of the
Treasury in the Sultanate of Khusrawan and nothing less than this level. Indeed, his arrival at the Treasury of Khusrawan would be nothing
more than the first step towards his elevation to a more important post,
which might be that of Chief Chamberlain — and possibly? But no, he
was not going to let this stupid fool steal his opportunity from him.

The feelings of the Agha were not hidden from the perception of
Juha who had no need to look at the narrow, greedy eyes to know all
that was going on inside the mind of their owner, and when he spoke,
his words were not very far from what Juha had been expecting: "I
say, oh Haji Abdussabur, why do you not give me the Prince and let
me look after him?"

This was the moment for which Juha had been impatiently waiting
since he began his preparations in arranging his plan. Here was the repulsive cricket, of his own free will and desire, slipping into the spider's web. Nevertheless, his answer to the suggestion of Haji Agha

was a scornful laugh of disapproving rejection: "You? What is this that you are saying? Mister Haji Agha — you can only be joking."

"No, I am extremely serious, and I beg of you to do this."

"I am sorry, sir, to disappoint you, but the fact is that what you are asking for is impossible."

"Why?"

"There are more than a thousand reasons. The first, and most important of them, is that the Prince himself does not wish to have any other companion, other than myself, to accompany him on the return journey to Khusrawan."

"This is not a problem. You and I can convince the Prince, and even if we can't convince him, with him in his present state, he would not be able to ..."

"Are you trying to say that we are able to deceive him? How can you permit yourself to have such thoughts, my dear sir?"

Haji Agha retracted, saying: "It never crossed my mind that we should deceive him, but one could explain his thoughts in any way that one wished just as long as he is in this state, where he is unable to explain his opinion, clearly, in words."

But Juha objected: "Have you forgotten the movements of the tail? And the nodding of the head? And the waggling of the ears?"

"All these movements can be explained, one way or the other, just as one wishes."

Juha was silent for a moment, before he continued with his excuses: "But what will be the position when he returns to his original form and he discovers that we have behaved in a manner contrary to his wishes?"

Then Haji Agha said, quickly and strongly, confident that this time his explanation would not be rejected: "Leave that to me. For I shall know how to deal with him and gain his confidence."

But what about me? I'm afraid that the Sultan will punish me."

"First of all, you will be far away from his grasp. Secondly, we will satisfy him that the Haji Abdussabur has already died. He was drowned at sea, or he was struck down by fever."

A second time Juha looked down at the ground, silently, as if he was sorting out his affairs, and when he raised his head again his eyes met those of Haji Agha. It was clear that greed had taken over the man, heart and soul. Then Juha said, slowly, hesitantly: "There remains one more problem."

Haji Agha cried out with fluency: "Every problem has a solution — What is it?"

"What shall I benefit, having handed the Prince over to you?"

It appeared that Haji Agha had fully prepared himself for such a question and that he had perceived, from this question, a sign that the resolve of the Haji Abdussabur had begun to weaken, in so far as he had begun to enter into the details, and for this reason he was quick to answer: "What is the most important thing which you are hoping for? Are you not the person who said, just a few minutes ago, that the most that you wanted in this world was an isolated place where you could be left alone with your experiments and with your great scientific studies? Where else could you find a place that is better than the one which you are in now? Then, what do you need after that? A reasonable income to provide for your needs for the rest of your life? This spring will provide an income for you which will last to the end of time."

Juha began to stroke his beard, thinking, then suddenly he said, waving his hand as if he wished to drive the thought away from such an idea: "No, oh master, watching over the spring and distributing the water to the peasants would take me away from my studies and research."

Haji Agha cried out: "That is a simple matter, you can hire a man from the nearest city who can deputise for you in this matter and arrange everything. You will then be completely free to devote all your time to your books and your experiments."

Juha said: "That, I swear by God, is an idea. Why did it not occur to me that I could hire a watchman for the spring?"

The excitement of Haji Agha increased as he saw his target approaching: "So you see, there is no problem, there will be ample time for you to collect all that you wish from herbs and for you to find out their magical effectiveness."

"Herbs with magical properties? You say herbs with magical properties? This, I swear to God, this is the whole purpose of my efforts."

All the cells in the brain of Haji Agha went to work, for he had found the key to all the counter arguments of Al Haj Abdussabur, and he cried out vigorously: "Don't you know, you will find here a thousand types of magical herbs? You will find some kinds here which even the magicians of the Pharaohs never dreamt about. I've known about this for a long time but I did not want to tell you about it in case you should occupy your time in collecting herbs, away from looking after the spring."

Juha muttered, clearly: "So, so? But here you are, it has just fallen off your tongue."

"Yes, thousands, indeed, tens of thousands, used to visit us here. Last year, a great magician from the north African countries came to me and he told me that in these hills there are thousands of plants with magical properties, each one of which could bewitch a whole country."

Juha said, reprovingly: "All this, and you did not want to tell me? Have you not betrayed the fact that we have eaten bread and salt together?"

Haji Agha rushed along happily, pleased with the success of the key which he had found: "Look out of this window. Do you see that thin, yellow stalk, which looks like dried lucerne? It is a magical plant which opens locked hearts. And this long stalk? That is the herb of life, it lengthens the life of man by at least two hundred years. There is, on the other side of the palace garden, the gold plant. This changes various kinds of rusty metal slabs into fourteen carat gold ingots. All the plants here have their magical elements. Indeed, everything here is enchanting, magical and charmed, even the soil. In the road is magical soil, even the stones and the pebbles are magical and enchanted, and all this will be yours, oh Abdussabur. They are only waiting for the experienced hand which appreciates their value in order to pluck them. Indeed, there is a type of tree, on the top of the mountain, the bark of which is useful in changing dogs into cats and lambs into frogs. The magician Aqraban al Balawi told me that, when he passed through this place a couple of years ago."

Juha said, with great interest: "What did you say his name was?"

Aqraban al Balawi, do you know him?

Juha replied, meekly: "I cannot say that I have ever heard that name before, but I cannot say that you are wrong."

"He is a fantastic magician! Right in front of my own eyes he changed forty frogs into twenty lambs, using two frogs to create each lamb!"

Juha cried out: "How great is God, the Highest, the Most Magnificent. He was telling the truth, the one who said: 'Above every man of knowledge stands one, more erudite', but tell me, oh Haji Agha, did this magician of whom you are speaking ever carry out experiments in the transformation of human beings to donkeys or the reverse?"

Haji Agha then said: "The truth is that he did not tell me anything about this. However, he will be passing by here in a couple of months and you will be able to exchange all the latest information with him." Then Haji Agha stopped suddenly, as if he had just remembered something: "But, be careful not to say anything to him about the Prince."

Juha nodded his head, faithfully: "Of course I shan't do that. Do you think that I am out of my mind?"

And so Haji Agha continued to speak amazingly freely, assuming it would be impossible for Juha to oppose all this enticement. Talk flowed out about magic plants and magic stones and magic water and magic air and the frogs that were transformed into lambs, and possibly even into fat cows!! And in the end it was inevitable that Juha should surrender, and that he should accept giving up the bewitched Prince, or, more correctly, his donkey Masoud, in exchange for the spring, the palace and the garden. But he insisted that he should receive ten thousand pieces of silver, in cash, in addition to the spring and the garden.

Haji Agha said: "Let me be frank with you. All that I possess does not exceed seven thousand pieces of silver. And I, naturally, will need money for spending on the way to Khusrawan. And you yourself know just how much it costs for the Prince alone."

Then Juha spoke, reminding him: "Have you forgotten about the jewels which the headman, Muhammad Ali, brought to you a few days ago? You can easily sell some of them in Sindashah. I know a big merchant there, in fact he is the head of the merchants' guild, who would be able to give you a good price for them."

Finally, it was agreed that he would give Juha five thousand pieces of silver, in cash, and that he would retain the two thousand and the jewellery for the expenses of the road.

Then, suddenly, Juha came back and said: "I still believe that the Prince will not agree."

Haji Agha replied, with great patience: "I can assure you that he will not object. You don't know what good friends we have become during the last few days. I think that you might be a little jealous if I told you that he is now more inclined towards me than he was to you. He himself has indicated that to me, more than once."

Juha said, regretfully: "There is no power or strength, other than through God. Can it be that he can forget the happy days which we spent together so quickly? Truly, how harmful are the hearts of donkeys."

Haji Agha cried out as he put his hand over the mouth of Juha, as if he wished to restrict his tongue: "Quiet, are you not afraid that he will hear you?"

Juha said: "Well then, let us go to him to inform him that you, as of now, have become his companion, and let us see if he approves or not."

* * * * * *

The two of them went off to where Masoud was standing, between two silver platters, on which was everything which was delicious and good. It appeared, from the eyes of Masoud, that he was overjoyed to see his old friend. However, a stern look from Juha made Masoud look down at the ground, just as if he was shy, then he turned the whole of his attention to his new servant, as he served him apples, cucumbers and turnips, all washed with rose water and wiped off with a silk cloth.

Juha spoke to the Prince. He said that he had never thought of leaving him, even though he might be given all the treasures of the world. He hoped for nothing more in the whole of creation but that his eyes should be gladdened by seeing the joy on the face of his Lord, the Sultan Marziban, at the moment of the entrance to his presence of his son and heir to the throne, in his true form, and whole. But he was now satisfied that only a better type of person was suitable for the service of princes and kings and he was not of that type. However, his friend here, Haji Agha, was a man of government and state, and was properly trained and capable for the service of the Prince, in a manner which would please him and make him happy.

In addition, and more important, was the fact that the Haji Abdussabur was now sick and he was afraid that this might affect him on the journey, a curse which he did not wish to inflict upon the Prince. As for the magic which would remove the witchcraft, he would give the black, magic bottle, and its contents, to Haji Agha and would teach him the complicated spell which had to be chanted whilst the magic drink was being taken once every ten days, then, for the last time, in the Court of the Sultan Marziban. Then Haji Agha spoke, with a rhetoric to be envied. He told how he had become infatuated by the Prince from the moment when he first set eyes on him, tied up outside the teashop. He swore by all that was holy, and by all that was unholy too, that he would remain for ever loyal, devoted to his comfort, remaining sleepless for the pleasure of serving him, the ultimate wish of God.

Between one conversation and the other, Masoud wagged his tail, ten times to the right, and similar, or more, to the left. He shook his head, one time in astonishment, and another time enquiringly, confused by the totally unexpected change which had taken place in his life. And the movements of the tail and the shaking of the head and the waggling of the ears were all explained as being indications of his pleasure. Then the two men went back to where they had been sitting. Haji Agha went on to say, trying to look as righteous as he could: "There remains one thing which must be completed. The Chief Judge, Dabus Abdulqadus, normally lives, during the summer months, in his summer residence, Mazar Al Ward, which is not far from this place. Tomorrow, I shall send someone to bring him to draw up the necessary papers, contracts and deeds."

Juha said: "First of all I shall take this opportunity to prepare for you the magic donkey potion in a sufficient enough quantity. I will treat it completely, with all the necessary incantations and charms, so that you will have no difficulty in administering it when the time comes."

Haji Agha said: "Everything must be done within the law."

Juha replied, as he got to his feet: "That is so, naturally. Nevertheless, the Prince is in your keeping, as of now. Stay up at night with him taking good care of him. Beware, and do not let him out of your sight."

Haji Agha said: "I know how to look after him."

* * * * * *

Chapter 18

The attitude of Haji Agha had changed from that day, so much so that hardly anybody could recognise him. His look became more superior and more disdainful. His words came out from the end of his nose, elongated, as if they were connected to the stars. Then they ended, cuttingly sharp, like a blow from a sword or dagger. Even his footsteps were heavy and arrogant, as if he was on a parade for a guard of honour, whilst the movements of his hands had suddenly acquired a dignity which was not less than that shown by the statues of the Pharaohs.

For Haji Agha now considered himself, in fact, to be the Chamberlain of the Treasury in Khusrawan. Since his agreement with Juha, he had, in his imagination, gone to live in a lofty palace on the banks of the river Saihun, surrounded at night by dozens of beautiful slave girls and buried by day in piles of gold and silver, which increased continually, rather than decreased, from the revenues of the taxes which he expertly invented on the Sultan's behalf, and for his own benefit too.

Haji Agha had so assumed the role of Chamberlain of the Treasury that he could practically feel the medals and decorations weighing heavily on the breast of his embroidered robe. He could almost feel with his hand the handle of his silver sword and he could sense the banging of it on his lower leg at every step he took. He considered every extra day which he spent in the remote village of Sikriya as a lost day, stolen from his golden life as head of the Treasury in Khusrawan.

And from that day Haji Agha would not permit Juha to appear in front of Masoud. All this was happening whilst life in Sikriya was going on as normal, like every other year at this particular season. The ground had been irrigated, the buds had opened and the fragrance of the flowers filled the pathways and houses, just as in the gardens and the woods. The people forgot, for a time, the oppression of Haji Agha after he had taken the treasure of jewellery from the headman, Muhammad Ali, whilst Laila and Hassan were preparing for their marriage, indifferent to what was going on around them. It did not matter to them whether the sun rose in the east or the west just as long as everything was going well with them. People were occupied with the work of the time in the fields and did not meet together but occasionally, to chat and to exchange the latest news.

Even Al Haj Abdussabur, the eccentric watchman of the spring, wa only rarely mentioned or remembered in their conversations after his living in the hut above the gate of the spring had become something to which they were accustomed. Probably, nobody even knew that Masoud, Juha's donkey, had been transferred from his normal place in the enclosure of the hut, to the magnificent bedchamber in the palace of Haji Agha. People forgot about the royal feasts for Masoud, or if they did remember them, it was sufficient to justify them by saying that they were part of the eccentricity of the new watchman of the spring.

Suddenly, everything in Sikriya was shaken, as one item of news after another rang out from the teashop, and its reverberations were repeated in every hut. The people had hardly recovered from one item of news before they were overwhelmed by another. The first of these news items was when the immam of the mosque, Ali Al Mulla, announced after the Friday prayers that Haji Agha had donated the sum of two thousand pieces of silver for the repair and renovation of the old village mosque. The people were baffled for a long time about this donation for they had not previously regarded Haji Agha as a pious man or one who would make an approach to God and build His mosques. Naturally, not one of them knew anything about the evil spirits which resembled crystalline stars or small soap bubbles, and which hovered around the head of Haji Agha morning and evening, the raging of which increased in a particular way in the period just before noon, at the time when the heat of the sun intensifies as it passes slowly through the cloudless sky.

One possible explanation which they reached was that it was a new deception from Haji Agha in order to impose an increase in payment upon them at the time of the next irrigation period. However, some of the more intelligent ones said: "It is a request to God for forgiveness for some, as yet uncommitted, crime which he intends to carry out."

The second item of news, which came and overshadowed the first, driving it to the island of forgetfulness, was brought by Mushtaq Abdurrazak, the owner of the cloth shop. He said that Haji Agha was making preparations for leaving the place and that he had purchased from him materials which could not be useful except for a long journey. It was generally thought that the journey was for the purpose of making the pilgrimage to Mecca.

Suddenly, the third item of news dropped in amongst them just as a large stone drops into a small pond. One of the shepherds said that Haji Agha had sent three mounted messengers, each with a riderless horse, to look for the Chief Judge and to bring him as soon as they had found him. The one who brought him would receive a reward of not less than one hundred pieces of silver.

"Why the Chief Judge, especially? And what could Haji Agha possibly need with the Chief Judge?"

Those in the know said that the Chief Judge would not go from one place to another, except if he was to be a guest. And their time with Haji Agha had taught them that he never entertained anyone and that nothing was more distasteful to him in the whole of creation than guests. Or, it could be that he was required by him to draw up a contract of sale for one of the estates. The people turned to look at one another with misgivings. What did Haji Agha intend to buy? And who would be selling? The village passed around a strong rumour that Muhammad Ali, the father of Laila, would sell his garden to Haji Agha and that he would leave the village after the marriage of his daughter Laila to Hassan. There were conflicting stories as to whether they would leave with him or remain.

When Muhammad Ali, himself, gave the lie to these rumours the people were baffled but they were all agreed that there was a great scheme behind the calling for the Chief Judge, Dabus Abdulqabus and that Haji Agha was plotting something behind which lay the destruction of them all.

* * * * * *

The uneasiness of the people became stronger and it was decided that a deputation should be sent to Haji Agha himself. Perhaps they could come to know what was waiting for them, or at least they might be able to deduce what was going to happen. However, meeting Haji

Agha, since he had assumed the personality of the Chamberlain of the Treasury in Khusrawan, was more difficult than catching an eagle in flight.

Nevertheless, they were received by Abdussabur, the watchman of the spring, deputising for the Master. What he had to say to them was difficult to understand and he increased their fears and suspicions of the unknown. What he actually said was: "Each one of you will continue to irrigate his land at the appointed times. The water will never be held back from the fields and it will not be necessary for any of you to sell his possessions. Such cash as you have in your pockets will be more than sufficient, may God so will."

They answered: "But sir, oh Al Haj, our pockets are so empty that they are more like the udder of an emaciated old nanny-goat which hasn't given birth for years. Even if you collected all that there is in the village you wouldn't get more than one hundred and fifty pieces of silver."

Nevertheless, Juha reaffirmed, saying: "Let me tell you all once again. Nobody should sell anything. Keep the small amount of cash which is in your pockets, for the future will soon be here."

These words did no more than increase their confusion and pessimism. They went back to the teashop, striking one hand on the other and repeating: "Oh God, have mercy on us, we do not ask you to stop what must be but we ask that fate treats us gently."

And on the same day the messengers of Haji Agha returned from their trip searching for the Chief Judge, bringing the great news that the Chief Judge was on his way and would spend that night in the nearby village of Sanafir and that he would be there the following afternoon, if God permit.

Sikriya spent the night in great anxiety, anticipating nothing but evil.

The Chief Judge, Abdulqadus, had spent his whole life twisting the characters and meanings of his words in an unimaginable fashion so that he himself had become equally twisted, in his mind, his body and his facial expression. His bald pate was equivalent to a bleak, undulating area, with inclines and depressions, in the middle of which was a single lock of hair, dyed with henna some months ago and polished with a type of oil which made it look more like the curved horn of the rhinoceros or a withered branch of a tree. His hooked nose, the tip of which almost touched his lower lip, was like the beak of an eagle. His right eye had a permanent squint and did not look at anything except the ground, whilst his left eye was yellow, with sharp flashes coming from it which inspired fear rather than confidence. His mouth was curved and permanently twisted in an expression of disgust, whilst his beard was long and pointed, also dyed with henna. He rarely put his turban on his head. It would appear that this was due to its extraordinary size and weight, although it was possible that he might have been afraid that it would disturb the elegance of the lock of his hair which was polished with henna. The sun was just about setting when the Chief Judge, Abdulqadus, riding a grey mule, and with a billowing, black cloak trailing behind him, arrived at the outskirts of Sikriya. He seemed inside the cloak, to be like a worm curled up inside a decayed, black grape. His enormous head was leaning one way and his skinny, twisted body the other. He was almost split over the back of the mule, but to one side of it, so that there were two unequal parts.

Behind him came his clerk, Harfush, who was no less well known than his master and who had stuck with him, like a shadow, all his life. As befitted his position, he was riding a donkey which was so old that it had practically forgotten it was a donkey. He appeared on top of it as if he were a tattered, long shirt which its owner had washed, wrung out and hung in the sun to dry, with parts of him appearing through the tatters, wrinkled and twisted. On top of his head, which resembled a sweet melon, was a coloured turban, or, more correctly, it used to be a coloured turban before time, the sun and the dust had taken all its colour away.

The news of his arrival had preceded him to Haji Agha and the people saw him practically running along the open road to the entrance to Sikriya. No sooner had the mule of the judge appeared than he had seized its bridle. The mule stopped and behind it the donkey of the old clerk. Just a few footsteps away a group of seven or eight children gathered. They had been following the judge's cavalcade since he had appeared on the outskirts of the village.

The children heard Haji Agha as he insistingly invited the judge to stay with him at his palace. They heard the judge refuse, asking to be shown the way to the village teashop, where he would spend the night.

For it would not be proper for him, the scrupulously impartial judge, to accept the hospitality of any of the parties, whether he be dealing with a contract or a dispute.

The children heard this and within a few minutes the whole village knew what had gone on between the judge and Haji Agha. The people were now certain that Haji Agha was a party in the matter in question.

But what was the matter in question? And who was the other party? Haji Agha said goodbye to his guest at the door of the teashop in a very dignified manner, and went off, making the ground shake with his arrogant, new method of walking which he had adopted since he had assumed the personality of the Chamberlain of the Treasury and Secretary to the Ruler of Khusrawan.

* * * * * *

The Chief Judge stopped at the door of the teashop. His eye with the squint was regarding the doorstep as if he expected to find a silver dirham down there by his foot, whilst his yellow eye was sending out quick flashes in every direction. The owner of the teashop was clever enough to know what the looks from the yellow eye meant and he rushed off to shoo away the few customers which he had in the teashop, as if they were stragglers from a flock of sheep. Then he rushed to his store to grab piles of goat skins because the custom, in those days, was that the more elevated the position of the guest, the more covers he ought to have to sit on. A single glance from the owner of the teashop was enough for him to realise that the Chief Judge, Dabus Abdulqabus, was worth at least fifteen sheepskins, whilst his follower was only worth one old sheepskin.

When the judge was sitting crosslegged on top of his high seat, and the owner of the teashop had brought him the hookah on his left side, and the tray of tea on his right side, a look came out of his yellow eye which pierced the head of his clerk and came to rest at the back of his sunken eyes, whereupon he leaped to his feet as if he had been bitten by a snake. He went forward towards the judge, giving him his right ear whilst he covered his left ear with his hand, as if he was afraid that what he might hear with the one might penetrate through the other.

The clerk nodded the head which resembled a sweet melon, as a sign of understanding and obedience, and he slipped away at once, being followed at a distance by a group of people from the village who were burning with curiosity, until they saw him, with their own eyes, enter the palace of Haji Agha. The clerk disappeared inside for an hour, or the best part of an hour, before he returned to the teashop, to find the judge engrossed in the bubbling sounds of the water in his fifth hookah.

When his two sunken eyes met the yellow eye of the judge he extended his veined hand towards him, holding up two and a half fingers. The judge understood what he wanted to say. An agreement had been reached with Haji Agha that he would pay two hundred and fifty pieces of silver — one finger for each hundred — this sum, naturally, being by way of a present and not a bribe because the Chief Judge was an extremely impartial, honourable person. He would accept a gift, yes. Indeed his clerk entered into an agreement about the gift before he looked into any dispute, or the signing of any contract. But he did not accept bribes.

The eye with the squint moved and blinked twice. This was interpreted by the clerk to mean: "Has the payment been made in advance, or is it to be made after what we are being asked to do is completed?"

The clerk patted his pocket twice and the judge understood that the payment had been made. A whispered conversation then took place between the two men, both of whom were thinking that nobody could hear what they were saying. But neither of them realized that the candlelight was throwing their shadows on the wall before the eyes of the very intelligent owner of the teashop. He was reading the movements of their lips as they were talking and understanding all that they were saying without any difficulty.

The judge whispered: "What is the subject of the case? This is a paltry sum. No doubt it is a big deal?"

"It does not appear to be so, but the man appears to be apprehensive, as if he was afraid that he was going to miss the chance of a lifetime. He wants everything finished as quickly as possible."

The judge then said, this time not trying to lower his voice: "In accordance with the law. The important thing is that you have already made sure that it is a lawful deal."

For the first time the resemblance of a smile appeared amongst the hundreds of wrinkles on the face of the old clerk: "Indeed, it is lawful, most certainly."

Said the judge: "Then, until daybreak."

* * * * * *

This was not the first suspicious contract which the Chief Judge had drawn up, but he had not met anything, in his whole life, quite like this. A water spring, a large garden and a lofty palace, all this in ex-change for a donkey which was not worth more than twenty pieces of silver. It was quite clear that there was a hidden secret behind the deal which both parties were anxious to conceal. And here the law was quite clear. The judge could not conclude any deal where there was any doubt about its legality and in which the apparent benefits to the two parties were not equitable.

The Chief Judge must respect the law, for the contract would be registered in his record and the register must be quite clear, like the sun, pure as the souls of the angels. When Haji Agha announced, in clear, ringing tones, that he was giving up the spring, the garden and the palace, in exchange for the donkey, a murmur of dismay arose from the onlooking peasants who had gathered around the door of the teashop. They could not believe what their eyes were seeing and their ears hearing. The murmur became a wave amongst those crowded in by the door, even amongst those further away at the back, until it became like the hum of a busy beehive. It wasn't long before it had got beyond the walls and had reached the ears of every man, woman and child in the village of Sikriya.

Naturally, nobody believed it. Even those who had witnessed it themselves and had heard the words of Haji Agha, refused to believe their own eyes and ears and remained in their places, perplexed, wait-ing for the matter to clear itself and finally reveal something under-standable. Only one person showed no astonishment, and that was the judge. He understood, clearly, that he ought not to show any amaze-ment. But what was incumbent on him, now, was to find the correct wording in which this unique contract should be expressed. It should be drafted in such a way as not to detract from the spirit whilst not causing any aroma to rise from it.

The judge stared sternly from his yellow eye at the inquisitive gathering at the door of the teashop and their mumbling was suppressed in their breasts. Then he sat up straight. He adjusted his turban on the top of his bald pate and said, directing his speech to Juha in a high voice as if he was speaking from the pulpit of a mosque: "Come forward, Abdussabur Ghurbawi, the son of Qaisun." Juha went forward two steps, pulling his donkey along by the bridle. "Have you heard what Haji Agha, the son of Murtadha, the son of Kalbar, has now said?"

Juha answered in a clear voice: "Yes, I have heard."

"Do you, being of sound mind, agree to the exchange?"

Juha said: "Yes, I agree, and I am of sound mind."

Once again the judge fidgeted in his place, then he turned to his clerk who was now bent over his huge register, filling the columns at an amazing speed. When the judge was certain that he had written the two names, in full, and had confirmed that both persons were in a sound state of mind, he turned to the public, raising his voice: "Now, when both parties have confirmed their desire to conclude this deal, without compulsion and without suspicion of deception, this concludes the first part of the law. There now remains the second part. Is there anyone here who opposes this deal? If any person has any objection to this deal, then let him come forward and state his opposition."

But nobody opposed it, possibly because everyone was still surprised by it all and probably because there wasn't anyone who thought that the matter was any concern of his. The judge did nothing for a moment, then he lifted off his enormous turban and put it down carefully beside him, whilst dictating to his clerk whose pen was moving across the paper as if it had been possessed by a devil: "Write – the deal was announced publicly, and in the presence of those who benefit from the spring of water and nobody displayed the slightest objection."

The judge returned the turban on top of his bald pate and was then silent, in deep thought. For now that the contract was completed there remained that which was much more difficult, which was the recording of the matter in the register in such a manner as would not raise the slightest suspicion and cause questions to be asked. This was a task which required all the genius and intelligence of the judge. Five minutes, or more, passed and silence reigned in the teashop. It was as if it had been suddenly changed into a place of worship. Even those who were crowding the door were holding their breath. It was as if they were witnessing their breath of a miracle.

Nobody knew just what it was that the judge was thinking about during the whole of the five minutes, nor in which direction his thoughts were going, but it was apparent that they were working furiously, underneath his turban, which, little by little, was beginning to slip over his eye with the squint. In fact, it would have fallen off had he not caught it at the last moment and pushed to the back of his head, exposing once again the front of his shiny bald pate. Then he leant on his left elbow, leaning over until his head was nearly colliding with the turban of his clerk. And, when he spoke after that, it was as if his words were the announcement of a victorious commander, after a great battle. Every word was selected with great care and pronounced with an intelligence bursting with pride: "You say it is a running water spring, a garden and a house? Very good, write my boy, in the column for sold property: house, with garden and water tank attached."

In this manner did the judge resolve half of the problem in one line, for by these words he had reduced the value of the property being sold to less than one tenth of its value. There remained now the other half of the problem, to raise the price of the donkey. Here, once again, the genius of the judge exceeded itself: "Tell me, oh Al Haj Abdussabur, the son of Ghurbawi, the son of Qaisun, what is the name which you have given your donkey?"

"His name is Masoud."

"Masoud? No, no, this name is not suitable for such a handsome animal. What would you think if we gave him another name? A name which would be suitable for the exchange with a water spring, a palace and a garden."

Juha replied, submissively: "Name it what you wish."

Once again he took the turban off his bald head, to be put down, carefully, beside his friend, and he said, sighing contentedly, as if he had, only now, resolved a difficult problem: "Excellent, let his name be, from now on, 'Silver Ass'. Do you not think that this name is very suitable for him?"

Said Juha, as a little smile crept across his lips: "Let it be as you wish."

The judge raised his voice, this time directing what he was saying to his clerk: "Write, you fool — 'And that in exchange for a silver ass, the weight of which is ...' How much does it weigh, oh Abdussabur?"

"About one hundred and fifty pounds."

"No, no, I want his weight very exactly!"

"Very exactly? Then his weight, exactly, is one hundred and fifty pounds and seven ounces, nine dirhams."

The voice of the judge cracked like a whip as he shouted at his clerk: "Write, my son, write — '... in exchange for a silver ass, the weight of which is one hundred and fifty pounds, seven ounces and nine dirhams.' The handing over and the receipt has taken place in the presence of myself, the Chief Judge of the area, as laid down by Islamic law, decrees and instructions of my Lord, the Khan. And the registration of the contract and the contracting parties has been completed with my knowledge and has been signed by the vendor, the purchaser, witnesses and myself and sealed by my seal."

He said this as he signed the register and two copies of the contract, leaving the operation of the sealing to his clerk. The last few words rang out like a drum roll in the teashop and they were still reverberating as the judge replaced his turban in its place on the top of his head, settled himself down in his seat and closed his eyes, the good one and the one with the squint, as if he had surrendered himself to a deep sleep, as his clerk was handing over to both Juha and Haji Agha a copy of the contract, thereby fulfilling the legal requirements in every respect. Juha handed over to Haji Agha the bridle of Masoud.

He did not attempt to prevent a tear from his eye as he parted with his donkey for the first time after a lifetime together. He patted his head with affection before Haji Agha slipped away with him, hardly able to contain himself as he went out without giving a thought to the totally perplexed people, standing at the door.

Juha then turned towards the judge, who was practically asleep and said in his ear: "I would be grateful if you would wait, after the afternoon prayer, for I need you for an important matter."

The judge lifted his eye with the squint, questioningly, then he saw his clerk signalling to him with two fingers and understood what he meant, for he said: "You will find me here. But I hope that you will not delay me too much for I have a job to do in the neighbouring village this evening."

Juha said: "I shall not keep you long, for I too have important work this evening."

Then Juha went off, on his way to the palace of Haji Agha, followed by the glances of the people who were still in their confused state by the door. There were looks full of doubt and apprehension about the next day, for in the hearts of all of them was a question, sharp like a knife: "What evil was now waiting for them, from the new owner of the spring?"

Juha arrived at the palace of Haji Agha to find that he had already prepared himself, completely, for the journey to Khusrawan, where glory awaited him as Chamberlain of the Treasury and Secretary to the Sultan.

The baggage for the journey had been prepared for days and he was only waiting for the amazing bottle of magical liquid which Juha now brought to him, together with the incantations engraved on a patch of gazelle hide. Haji Agha snatched it from him and placed it, with trembling fingers, in the pouch of a cross-belt tied across his chest as he said: "Farewell. oh Abdussabur. The time has come to be off. I shall send you an expensive gift from Khusrawan — a golden hookah, dancing in the water of which will be two balls of turquoise and chalcedony, and with it a pair of silver tongs for the hot embers."

Juha said, as he bowed his head: "I thank you in advance for your gift, oh illustrious Master. I am confident that you will be the greatest Chamberlain of the Treasury of Khusrawan, and now permit me to assist you."

Juha went forward at once in the direction of Masoud, who was making a terrible mess in the garden, and dragged him away roughly. He went to the heaviest piece of baggage, and threw it on the donkey's back. Haji Agha screamed out, protesting excitedly, as he pulled off the sack and placed it on his own shoulder: "What is this that you are doing? Have you lost your senses, Abdussabur? How could you put a load on his back?

Juha raised his eyes in surprise: "And why not, are you going to carry all this baggage the whole way?"

Haji Agha looked hard at Juha, mockingly: "You might have handled him like that throughout the three years in which you accompanied him. The time has now come for him to be relieved of your mishandling. I shall buy a mule, or even two, to carry the baggage. As for me, I shall be on foot, because it is not appropriate that I should ride whilst the Prince walks."

"The height of good sense, Your Excellency the Minister, the height of good sense. There remains one matter I believe which must have escaped your attention. All the merchants, on the whole of the way to Khusrawan, consider the dirham which we use here, to be only half of a dirham. It is therefore better for you to change the silver dirhams which you have at the nearest point, for dirhams which will not lose their value at all."

Haji Agha asked, with some concern, for this had stirred all his natural inclinations of avarice: "Where can I do that?"

"In Sindashah, naturally, with the Shahbandar of the merchants. Ask for his trading premises, you will find everybody will be able to guide you to him. He will give you dirham for dirham and he will not diminish what you are entitled to."

"I might even be able to sell him some of the jewels?"

"Most certainly, for he is the most worthy merchant in the city. Do not trust anyone else. And now, farewell, Your Excellency the Minister."

"Farewell, I shall send you the present just as soon as I arrive."

"The important thing is that you arrive safely."

And Haji Agha went off on his way, clearing the road for Masoud, for whom the look of Juha mourned until he disappeared around the bend in the road. Then Juha returned to his hut to find. Skinner there, waiting for him.

"The time has now arrived for you to set off to play your part in Sindashah, Skinner. Do not let Haji Agha out of your sight until I catch up with you there."

"I hear and I obey, my friend."

"Always keep your eye on Masoud, I cannot afford to lose him."

"You will not lose him, oh Juha."

"Off you go then, in the safe-keeping of God."

* * * * * *

Chapter 19

Juha made his way towards the teashop preceded by a happy smile, like that of a small child who had just been given a gift which pleased him, and the people of Sikriya saw him, as he approached from afar, with a youthful step which was out of place with his white beard. From a distance there was a sound like the roar of waves on the seashore, which increased as Juha got closer to the teashop where the whole of the village, without exception, had collected in the open space opposite, and everybody was talking at the same time. Their words were clashing with each other, with an overall discord and clamour. One was commenting in astonishment and another was explaining the situation with misgivings, but everyone was in a state of consternation, with their eyes opened wide in perplexity.

Above all this came a voice in earnest: "What does it matter to us if Haji Agha has sold the spring, the palace and the garden for a donkey, or a horse for that matter? What matters is that he has left us and we are free of the nightmare of him for ever."

Then another voice rose up which was even sharper. "How do we know but that the new nightmare is not going to be even more abominable than the old?"

Then a third one cried out: "Let us hope that he remembers that we've already paid the price of the water for this season."

A fourth said: "It's more than likely that he will be even more greedy than his predecessor. The first one squeezed only our blood but this one is going to squeeze the marrow out of our bones."

"Hush, here he is, coming towards us."

All eyes were turned on the new owner as he approached, as if they were looking at a black cloud, foretelling a storm. And their eyes opened even wider as they noted that in his right hand was a cage in which was a sparrow, no different from the millions of sparrows in and around Sikriya.

Safwan whispered in the ear of Mahmoud, the son of 'Aliya: "Have you seen what the fool is carrying? A bird in a cage. How can we expect anything good from a man who imprisons a bird in a cage?"

The crowd pushed back to make room for the new master to pass through to the door of the teashop. Their looks were hanging onto him as if their fate was subject to his footsteps, attached to his very breathing. But there was something about the face of Juha and in his eye, which suggested to the people that he might just be different from his predecessor. Or, at any rate, he was not likely to be much worse than him.

"Peace be upon you and the mercy of God."

They all answered, but their answers were hesitant whilst all eyes were on the bird cage, looking at it anxiously: "And on you be peace."

Juha stopped for a moment, looking at the faces of the people. There, there was dismay, worry and fear about everything. Of the new Master, of the unknown, and even one for the other. From the sunken eyes there was not the ghost of a ray of hope, hope was non-existent, leaving the way open for permanent despair. When Juha took in the feeling of utter insignificance which enveloped the souls of these miserable people, causing them to tremble within themselves, he felt as if a sharp blade was piercing his very insides.

It appeared that most of them were getting ready to move off. Juha spoke from his heart, a spontaneous message of affection for these people, a message that did not fail to reach the hearts of those listening.

"Wait a moment, my friends. I beg of you, do not leave for I have need of you for a very important matter."

The people of Sikriya exchanged looks of astonishment, but by now they were less suspicious. Juha continued speaking, this time directing what he had to say to the owner of the teashop who was standing at the door. "Please serve everyone with tea, on my account." And before the community has completely recovered from their astonishment, Hassan suddenly appeared, coming from outside, and threw himself in to the embrace of Juha, weeping tears of joy, and mumbling incomprehensible words, whilst Juha was patting him on the back in a friendly fashion, as he said: "How are you, Hassan? How is the bride to be? When is the wedding feast going to be, with God's will?

Once again Juha turned to the people, shaking the cage in his hand, whilst his other hand was still holding Hassan: "By the way, whose is this bird?"

The people were dumbfounded by the sudden question. The spark of hope which had arisen in their breasts practically went out, there and then, whilst their mental state was saying: "How excentric can this old stranger be?"

There was a period of hesitation which was broken by Muhammad Ali, who came forward boldly to say: "This bird cannot be the property of anybody. The birds here are completely free. Nobody can claim to own any one of them."

Then Juha said, as if he was arguing with him: "What would you do if I gave it to you?"

The man replied, somewhat confused; "I don't know. It's most likely that I would set it free, at once."

Juha said, as he stepped inside the teashop: "Come with me, all of you."

* * * * * *

Inside the teashop the Judge Dabus was still sitting, crosslegged, on his throne. If it had not been for the long draws which he was taking from the hookah, his tenth, or was it his fifteenth, since he had arrived, anyone watching him would have thought that he was asleep. At his feet was the old clerk, his follower, with his head which resembled a sweet melon, buried in his chest, as if he was submitting to any fate.

The judge greeted Juha, as he entered, with a greeting to which he was entitled because he had paid the two hundred pieces of silver which he had had conveyed to him by his clerk.

And he said to Juha, when he sat down in front of him: "I am at your service. What is the subject of the claim? Or perhaps it is a marriage?"

Said Juha: "No, it is another contract of sale."

Judge Dabus was not in any way surprised, for there wasn't anything in existence which could possible surprise him.

He merely said, calmly: "Who is the .vendor, who is the purchaser? And what is the subject of the sale?"

Juha answered, saying: "I am the vendor, and the subject of the sale is a water spring, a garden and a palace. The purchaser is the whole of the people of Sikriya, without exception, all of them with equal shares."

Even this failed to astonish Judge Dabus. But the one who was surprised was the owner of the teashop, from whose hand dropped a glass of tea and he rushed madly outside to tell the people there what he had heard.

Juha raised his voice, saying: "Are all the people of the village here? Is nobody absent?"

Muhammad Ali, who was by the door, said: "Everybody is here."

The judge then said: "So, all have your seals ready. Anyone who has not got a seal must be prepared to put his thumbprint on the bill of sale."

A voice cried out from the rear, probably his was the only voice which had not died with amazement at what was going on: "What are we going to put our seals and out thumbprints to. We have not got anything to sell, nor do we have any money to buy anything."

The judge looked at Juha, enquiringly, who answered his look, saying: "I have already received the payment, in fact. It is this sparrow."

Only here did astonishment appear on the face of the judge, but it only lasted for a brief moment, after which he said, in the same calm fashion: "We shall first need a list of the names of the purchasers, with the seal or the thumbprint of the purchaser beside each name."

* * * * * *

The contract was drawn up and signed and nothing remained except the recording of the sale in the official register. The whole problem was in the price for it was not reasonable to write in the register that the running spring, the garden and the palace had all been sold for a sparrow. But the astute judge was not the one to have his hands tied by a simple problem like this. The easy solution was to give the sparrow a name and he called it, in fact, 'A Handful of Diamonds'. And the clerk wrote in the register that Abdussabur, the son of Gharbawi, the son of Qaisun, had sold the spring, the garden and the palace, as described in the attached; in the usual way, in public, and had received

248

the price, being a handful of diamonds weighing three ounces and two dirhams, in the presence of the judge and witnesses. The sale procedures were thus completed with the people still bewildered, not believing what their eyes and ears were seeing and hearing, when Judge Dabus gathered together his goods and chattels and was off. And without understanding what this man, the eccentric Al Haj Abdussabur was doing, they watched him with the same amazement, as he opened the door of the cage and released the imprisoned sparrow. Everybody's eyes followed the sparrow as he stood, hesitantly, outside the cage. Then he turned to the light coming from the door, set off, fluttering his wings, to come to rest for just a moment on the branch of a nearby tree, and went off like an arrow in the direction of the mountain until he disappeared from sight. Then the eyes returned to look at Juha, where he too, in his turn, was packing his bags.

* * * * * *

The wonders which had happened were beyond any question or enquiry. Juha said, as he was preparing to travel, raising his voice so that everybody could hear him: "Now, oh people of Sikriya, no one will be selling you water after today. For the spring of water now belongs to you all, in equal shares. Look after it in the same way that you take care of your eyes, and do not permit anyone to claim it as his own property after today. The spring is yours and the palace is for the use of every new bride and groom, in which to spend their honeymoon. And let the first couple to use it be Laila and Hassan."

Voices dampened with tears, were then raised: "You are blessed, oh Al Haj Abdussabur – May God give you long life, oh Al Haj Abdussabur."

Juha turned towards them, before setting off: "You all know me here by the name of Al Haj Abdussabur, but I now feel that the time has come for me to tell you that this is not my name. Indeed, it is a name which circumstances have forced upon me and I do not wish that you should call me by it."

More than one voice then called out: "By what name would you like us to call you then?"

Juha answered them and for the first time he was smiling, waving his hand to them all in farewell: "Think well, then chose a better name for me."

Off he went, with hundreds of eyes saying farewell to him, with affection and tears, as their bewilderment increased and questions jammed their tongues and ears. Then he disappeared around a bend in the road after he had indicated to those who were following him to go back and leave him. And they returned to join those who had remained, in considering the question: "Who do you think he could be?"

Suddenly the voice of Hassan rang out: "I know who he is! I know who he is!! How did this escape me until now?"

Everybody cried to him, asking: "Who is he? Who can he be?"

Hassan replied, running like a madman: "It's Juha — Juha — Juha himself and nobody else." And in a single moment, the truth became apparent to the people of Sikriya. Of course, no one could have done this except Juha Nasruddin.

Then Muhammad Ali, Safwan and Said, and behind them all the people of Sikriya, rushed down the road along which Juha had gone just a few minutes before, crying out: "Juha — Juha."

But the echo of the cries of the anxious people rebounded and Juha had disappeared.

* * * * * *

Juha arrived in Sindashah at the time which he had set with his friend, Skinner, before his departure some days ago. And his friend welcomed him enthusiastically: "I was confident that you would arrive on time. Haji Agha got here before you by some hours and he has not yet gone to the Shahbandar of the merchants but he is here in this resthouse, where none but the upper classes stay."

"Naturally! Is he not the Chamberlain of the Treasury of the Sultanate of Khusrawan?"

"He has not been out of my sight, for a single moment, since he left Sikriya."

"And how is Masoud?"

"He is well, but he does appear to be sad and anxious, as if he is missing his companion."

"Shhhh – he is coming out of the resthouse."

And, in fact, there was Haji Agha himself, coming out to the road, strutting along in a new outfit embroidered with gold and silver thread, all puffed up like a turkey cock with his nose in the air and with a supercilious look on his face. In his hand was a bridle with silver fittings, at the end of which was Masoud, from whom was drifting the scent of an ambergris perfume and whose back was covered with an elegant velvet fabric. But his head was hanging down to the ground as if he was carrying all the worries of the world, without heeding the changes which had suddenly occurred. His tail was between his legs as if he had forgotten how to swish it whilst there were what appeared to be tears in his sad eyes.

Juha, who was very affected, muttered: "How faithful you are! Do not despair, oh Masoud for I am coming for you."

Haji Agha went slowly down the road, followed by Juha and Skinner. They were without any fear that he might turn round and see them for it was impossible for him to recognise them whilst they were as they were, dressed as an old shepherd and his son who had come to the city to carry out some necessary task and then return to their pastures.

Skinner said to his friend: "It is most likely that he is going to the Shahbandar of the merchants."

And the Thief of Baghdad was not disappointed for it was only a few minutes before Haji Agha was standing before the Shahbandar of the merchants, greeting him: "As salam alaikum, if I am not mistaken you must be the Shahbandar of the merchants of Sindashah."

"Wa alaikum as salam, oh stranger. Please enter. What can I do for you? It would appear that you know me but I have not the honour of knowing you."

"Who is there who does not know of the most honourable of the merchants of Sindashah? He who is the highest of them in rank and the most honest in his dealings. I have heard of your fame, Sire, over there, beyond the mountains, and I came to seek you out to acquire honour."

The words of praise gave great pleasure to the Shahbandar, so that his pot-belly practically danced from the excess of his conceit.

However, what really delighted him was that he saw in the person who was speaking to him, a prey that could be easily snared.

He said, with a humility to be envied: "What you hear of a person can disappoint you when you actually see him. However, I praise God who has made my name like clear crystal. All that I hope for from God is that I may preserve this good name until I meet Him."

Then Haji Agha continued in his praises: "A good name is more important than all the wealth of the world."

The Shahbandar returned the compliment with even greater flattery: "And even more important than the good name is that a man should meet up with good people."

"You speak the truth, Sire, and I therefore praise God who has to-day given me the pleasure of this meeting."

And in this fashion the flattering courtesies continued between the two of them until Juha and his partner had practically begun to lose their patience. Finally, they got down to talking about business. Haji Agha took from his bag the dirhams which he had and which he wanted to change. The Shahbandar counted his money out before he handed it over to Haji Agha and he short changed him five dinars on the going rate in Sindashah. Naturally, this wasn't missed by Haji Agha but he did not make any objection. For, after all, what was five dinars if it was compared with the important post which was awaiting him in Khusrawan in just a few weeks.

Haji Agha put the money in his pocket as he said: "I've got some jewellery with me here, necklaces, bracelets, ear-rings and rings, if you would like to buy them."

The Shahbandar quickly put his hand over Haji Agha's mouth, cautioning him: "Shhh – have you not heard, oh stranger, that this kind of deal is forbidden in Sindashah, unless the authorities have been previously informed? But perhaps you want to spend some months with us in the prison of the Khan!"

"Yes, I have heard about it, but I believe that two intelligent men ..."

The Shahbandar interrupted him: "And two very honourable men."

Then Haji Agha said: "And more important than that, two men who know how to keep a secret."

The words were rolled out by the two men until it finally turned to laughter and then to whispers whilst the Shahbandar threw a handful of silver coins on the table just to deceive him into thinking that it was going to be easy.

Haji Agha took the bag of jewels from his belt and opened the top of it, just a little, to let the Shahbandar see them. Then he quickly hid them again between the folds of his long embroidered shirt.

And from their vantage point, behind a dense bush opposite the trading premises of the Shahbandar, Juha and his companion could see the face of the Shahbandar going red, green and then yellow, and they could almost see the whiskers of his beard, dyed with henna, trembling.

Then they heard his voice, gentle, but hoarse, sounding like the hiss of a snake: "Tell me oh stranger, from where and how, did these stones reach you?"

Haji Agha answered, lightly, without being aware of the change which had taken place in the voice and face of the Shahbandar: "Let us leave these questions, my dear sir, at one side. For what does it matter whether these jewels fell out of the sky or whether they came out of the ground. Only the police ask this sort of question."

The Shahbandar then said, trying to suppress his anger: "Let me look at them again."

Haji Agha took the bag of jewellery out from the folds of his long shirt and opened it, once more, under the eyes of the Shahbandar who put out both hands together to take the bag, but Haji Agha hung on to it and said: "They are yours, if you pay me thirty thousand pieces of silver."

Here, the Shahbandar was unable to bear it any longer for his words came out like the lowing of a slaughtered ox breathing its last, as he tried to grab the bag: "Pay you? And thirty thousand pieces of silver? The price of my own jewellery which was stolen from me?"

The hands of Haji Agha were holding on fast, for he had already realised that the Shahbandar was trying to cheat him, and the two of them were standing, each one facing the other across the table, with all four hands locked on the bag. Two of them were pulling towards the inside of the premises whilst the other two were pulling the bag to the

253

outside. From all four eyes sparks were flying, in defiance and with hatred and anger, but at the same time both of them were careful that their actions should not draw attention to themselves, or that by raising their voices they might attract the attention of the guards.

Haji Agha said, in a confidential voice: "Let it go, it will be better for you."

The Shahbandar replied through his teeth, raging: "It's my jewellery, you thief."

And with all this going on, even though the two of them were struggling with all their strength and effort, each one attempting to tear the bag from the claws of the other, anyone who might see them, from amongst the passers-by would not doubt, for a single moment, that the pair of them were two friends having a friendly conversation.

The fight continued, with the likely outcome going to and fro, with all four hands clutching at the bag, not letting go. And when the two of them were exhausted, they stopped for a short truce, during which they exchanged insults, oaths and curses, which the pen of the writer is unable to repeat. The merchant spat in the face of Haji Agha, who then butted him on the nose, and the Shahbandar bent down in an attempt to bite the hand of Haji Agha. Then they both went back to butting each other until, once again, they both stopped, panting, whilst their eyes were still giving out sparks.

Suddenly, the Shahbandar jumped up in a surprise movement and snatched the bag with all his strength. The snatch was so strong that he not only snatched the bag but he snatched Haji Agha with it. He was pulled, behind the bag, over the table and the three of them, the Shahbandar, the bag and Haji Agha werecolliding and struggling together, with the four hands clutching the bag just as if they were inseparable parts of the bag. The struggle went on with the feet, the legs, the heads and the teeth, and the beards of the two men became entwined as the two turbans fell off whilst they pushed each other with their bellies. Nevertheless, they still appeared to the onlooker, as if they were both looking, together, for something that had fallen behind the table.

* * * * * *

Juha winked at his friend: "Now it's our turn."

Juha let out a secret whistle from his lips and no sooner did the ears of Masoud pick it up than he raised his head, attentively, as if his release had come after a torturous journey. For he knew that whistle well and whatever might be said about his stupidity he could distinguish it amongst a thousand noises and sources of discord.

Juha sounded his whistle, once again, this time showing his face to the searching eyes of Masoud. No words will ever be able to describe the joy of Masoud. Nor was there any bridle in existence which was capable of preventing Masoud from flying to his owner, even though the bridle be tied to the belt of Haji Agha. For he began to buck madly from all four of his legs, with his tail in the air, and braying loudly which drowned the clamour inside the shop. At that moment Haji Agha was battling under the table, attempting to tear the bag from the hands of the Shahbandar, which were locked on it. He felt the strong pull on the bridle and he said to himself that the prince was helping him to get away. And, in fact, this was exactly what happened. For the bucking of Masoud did help Haji Agha and in a flash he was flying through the air. He fell on his back in the road outside the premises, with his hands holding onto the bag of jewellery, whilst the Shahbandar raised his voice, screaming as loud as he could as he saw his jewellery slip out of his hands to fall on top of Haji Agha: "Thief, thief."

Once again Juha showed his face to Masoud who was struck by a fit of madness and he leapt with such force that the bridle parted and he was off, jumping in the direction of Juha and Skinner who quickly ran away with Masoud behind them.

* * * * * *

Haji Agha suddenly became aware that the rein and the bridle had parted, and that Masoud, or Prince Fairuz, was getting away. He had to choose, now, between the bag of jewellery and the Prince. There was no alternative, naturally, other than to rid himself of the talons and fangs of the Shahbandar, and to leave with him the bag and its contents, in order to catch up with the Prince before he was lost. But he was unable to do this. For, at that moment there were more than twenty guards who were flinging themselves upon him and grabbing his collar whilst the Shahbander was getting to his feet from the ground and roaring like a bull: "Don't let him go, the thief, don't let him go."

Haji Agha cried out, with his eyes on the road where Masoud had disappeared: "Let me go. Leave me, you fools. Don't you know who I am? I am the Chamberlain of the Treasury of the Sultanate of Khusrawan. I will flatten you all, you dogs."

The voice of the Shahbandar continued: "The thief, the vagabond, don't let him go. The Hikimdar himself knows that these are my jewels and he'll have no mercy on him."

But Haji Agha never heard him. For by now he was completely insane as he saw the chamberlainship of the treasury getting away from him, slipping out of his fingers and he began to scream as he waved his hands in the air: "I shall take revenge on you all, you rogues. I shall transform all of you to apes and frogs."

And in a fit of madness he took the black bottle which Juha had given to him before his journey and began to sprinkle the contents on the faces of the guards as they laid into him with blows and kicks, saying: Abrakad Abrabeshin Katin Abrakad Abrabeshin Katin."

But his magic spells were lost amongst the yells of the guards: "Grab him. Beat him. Tie him up."

He was still screaming his incomprehensible words, even when they bound his hands and his feet, brought a pole to which they tied him and carried him through the streets in the same way as hunters carry their kills on the return journey from the hunt. He continued to scream, madly: "I am the Chamberlain of the Treasury. Abrakad Abrabeshin Katin. His Majesty the Sultan will hang you all," as the people poked fun at him and ridiculed him, cursing and not believing anything except that he was mad.

* * * * * *

Juha said to his friend: "Leave Masoud to me, so that I can hide him in a safe place, but you go off to the house of the widow, the owner of the jewellery, and go with her to the court. It is most likely that there will be no need to mention what happened."

The Hikimdar did not believe a single word of what Haji Agha said. How could any intelligent person believe that these jewels, which the Hikimdar himself knew well, had suddenly been transferred to the garden of a man called Muhammad Ali in the village of Sikriya, for him to find them under an apricot tree. Nor did the judge accept the story of the bewitched prince. And when Haji Agha insisted that his story was correct, this was considered by the judge to be contempt of court, warranting a heavier punishment. The sentence of life imprisonment was pronounced, to be served in the vaults prison. Before the judge could order the handing over of the jewellery to the Shahbandar, the widow cried out, demanding justice and security. She told her story and produced documents proving her ownership and the jewellery was handed over to her.

* * * * * *

Days later, Juha was on his donkey, Masoud, accompanied by Skinner, entering the gate of Nahawand. There, at the door of the old, abandoned mosque, was the blind, deaf and dumb beggar, sitting in his place, without movement, holding his hand out, as if he were a statue.

Juha stopped in front of him: "Peace be upon you, oh venerable, holy man. The task has been completed successfully and the spring has been returned to the people of Sikriya. As for Haji Agha, he will spend what remains of his life in the vaults of Sindashah Fort."

And two tears rolled down the cheek of the old, holy man.

The End

The Translator

Jack Briggs has spent most of his working life in the Middle East, where he has acquired an extensive knowledge and understanding of the Arab language and culture.

He was born in London in 1929, but grew up in Lancashire. He served with the Palestine Police from 1941 to 1948, then moved to the Gulf in 1949, and became Commandant of Dubai Police in 1965. This important post lasted ten years, during which Jack obtained his BA in Classical and Modern Arabic as an external student of London University. Employed for many years in a civilian capacity by the Dubai Police, he has now retired and lives in the UK, but is still kept busy with Arabic translations.

The Author

The late Mustapha Kamal was born in Egypt in 1924. While still at Cairo University, he became involved in journalism and began contributing to *Young Egypt* magazine, where he became Foreign Affairs Editor after graduation. Following a successful journalistic career in Egypt and Bahrain, he moved to Dubai in 1980, where he became Senior Editor and Head of the Department of Strategic Studies at *Al Bayan* newspaper.

Mustapha was also a well-respected translator, poet, novelist and writer of political essays. The two titles for which he is best known are 'A Diary of a Journey', published in 1974, and 'The Way to Geneva', in 1975, which tackles the Palestine problem. He died in 1999.

Acknowledgements

It remains for me to express my thanks to Mustapha Kamal for not only allowing me to translate his work but for actually encouraging me to do so; to Motivate Publishing for agreeing to publish the book; to Julia Roles of Motivate for her assistance with the final editing; to my wife, Cath, whose tolerance knows no bounds; and finally to

without whose sponsorship this book would not have been possible.

Royalties from the sale of this
book have been donated by the translator
to the Al Noor Training Centre
for Handicapped Children
Dubai, UAE.

The Arabian Heritage Series

*If you have enjoyed this book, you might like to
know about some of the other Motivate titles.*

COUNTRY GUIDES

Enchanting Oman
Bahrain - Island Heritage
Shirley Kay

Kuwait - A New
Beginning
Gail Seery

Saudi Arabia - Profile of a
Kingdom

UAE GUIDES

Dubai - Gateway to the Gulf

Abu Dhabi - Garden City
of the Gulf
*edited by Peter Hellyer
and Ian Fairservice*

Sharjah - Heritage
and Progress
Portrait of Ras Al Khaimah
Land of the Emirates
Shirley Kay

Fujairah - An Arabian Jewel
Peter Hellyer

Al Ain - Oasis City
*Peter Hellyer
and Rosalind Buckton*

**NATURAL HISTORY AND
CULTURE**

Birds of the Southern Gulf
*Dave Robinson
and Adrian Chapman*

Falconry and Birds of Prey
in the Gulf
*Dr David Remple
and Christian Gross*

The Living Seas
*Frances Dipper
and Tony Woodward*

The Living Desert
Marycke Jongbloed

Wings Over the Gulf
Seafarers of the Gulf
Shirley Kay

Sketchbook Arabia
Margaret Henderson

Seashells of Eastern Arabia
S Peter Dance

Snorkelling and
Diving in Oman
*Rod Salm
and Robert Baldwin*

Beachcombers Guide
to the Gulf
Tony Woodward

GUIDES

Off-Road in the Emirates
*Volumes 1 & 2,
Dariush Zandi*

Off-Road in Oman
*Heiner Klein
and Rebecca Brickson*

Off-Road in the Hejaz
*Patrick Pierard
and Patrick Legros*

The Off-Roader's Manual
Jehanbaz Ali Khan

The Green Guide
to the Emirates
Marycke Jongbloed

PREMIER HARDBACKS

A Day Above the Emirates
A Day Above Oman
John Nowell

Forts of Oman
Walter Dinteman

The UAE - Formative Years
Ramesh Shukla

Dubai - A Pictorial Tour
Abu Dhabi - A Pictorial Tour
Yemen - A Pictorial Tour

UAE - Visions of Change
Dubai - Life and Times
Abu Dhabi - Life and Times
Noor Ali Rashid

THE THESIGER LIBRARY

Crossing the Sands
Desert, Marsh and Mountain
The Thesiger Collection
Arabian Sands
The Marsh Arabs
Visions of a Nomad
Wilfred Thesiger

ARABIAN ALBUMS

Dubai
Abu Dhabi
Sharjah and the North East
Shaikdoms
Travels to Oman
*Written and photographed by
Ronald Codrai*

*Further titles are available.
For a copy of the
Motivate books catalogue,
call 971 4 824060 or
fax 971 4 824436.*

MOTIVATE
PUBLISHING